High School Prodigies Have It Easy Even in Another World!

4

©Sacraneco

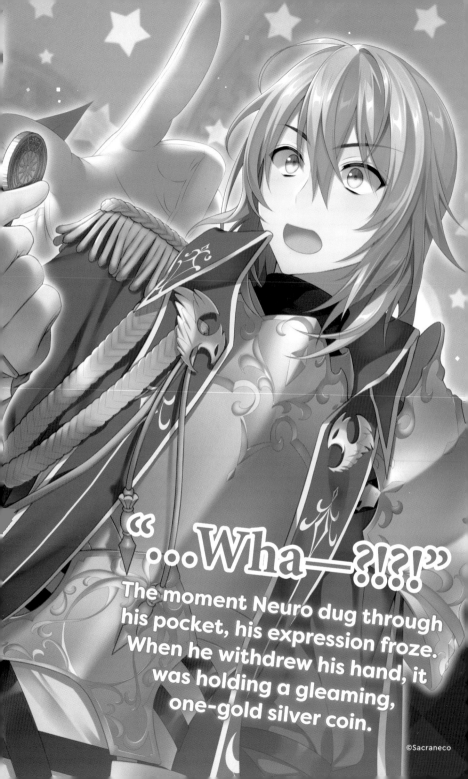

"...Wha—?!?!"
The moment Neuro dug through his pocket, his expression froze. When he withdrew his hand, it was holding a gleaming, one-gold silver coin.

©Sacraneco

"Adding **cat noises** really **isn't necessary...**"

"When I'm using a **knife**, I should hold my other hand in a **cat's paw**...like I'm doing **meow?**"

©Sacraneco

Shouting. Cannon fire.
Screams of the dying.
It was the sound of combat.
Roo dragged her wounded,
bleeding body across the ship
to escape the flames.

©Sacraneco

CONTENTS

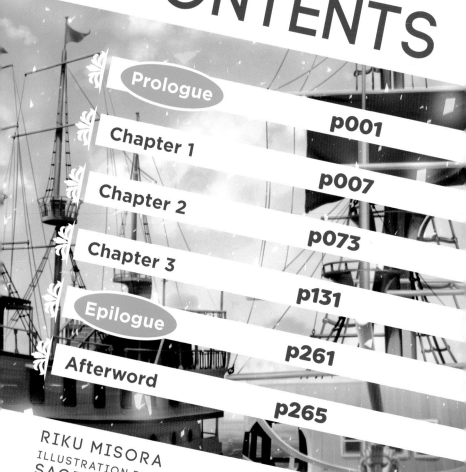

RIKU MISORA
ILLUSTRATION BY
SACRANECO

High School Prodigies
Have It Easy Even in
Another World!

High School Prodigies Have It Easy Even in Another World!

4

Riku Misora

Illustration by SACRANECO

YEN ON

NEW YORK

High School Prodigies Have It Easy Even in Another World! 4

Riku Misora

TRANSLATION BY NATHANIEL HIROSHI THRASHER
COVER ART BY SACRANECO

CHOUJIN KOUKOUSEI TACHI WA ISEKAI DEMO YOYU DE IKINUKU YOUDESU! vol. 4
Copyright © 2016 Riku Misora
Illustrations copyright © 2016 Sacraneco
First published in Japan in 2016 by SB Creative, Tokyo.
English translation rights arranged with SB Creative, Tokyo through Tuttle-Mori Agency, Inc., Tokyo

English translation © 2021 by Yen Press, LLC

Yen On
150 West 30th Street, 19th Floor
New York, NY 10001

Visit us at yenpress.com
facebook.com/yenpress ★ twitter.com/yenpress
yenpress.tumblr.com ★ instagram.com/yenpress

First Yen On Edition: May 2021

Yen On is an imprint of Yen Press, LLC.
The Yen On name and logo are trademarks of Yen Press, LLC.

Library of Congress Cataloging-in-Publication Data
Names: Misora, Riku, author. | Sacraneco, illustrator. | Thrasher, Nathaniel Hiroshi, translator.
Title: High school prodigies have it easy even in another world! / Riku Misora ;
illustration by Sacraneco ; translation by Nathaniel Hiroshi Thrasher.
Other titles: Chōjin-Kokoseitachi wa Isekai demo Yoyu de Ikinuku Yōdesu! English
Identifiers: LCCN 2020016894 | ISBN 9781975309725 (v. 1 ; trade paperback) |
ISBN 9781975309749 (v. 2 ; trade paperback) | ISBN 9781975309763 (v. 3 ; trade paperback)
| ISBN 9781975309787 (v. 4 ; trade paperback)
Subjects: CYAC: Fantasy. | Gifted persons—Fiction. | Imaginary places—Fiction | Magic—Fiction.
Classification: LCC PZ7.M6843377 Hi 2020 | DDC [Fic]—dc23
LC record available at https://lccn.loc.gov/2020016894

ISBNs: 978-1-9753-0978-7 (paperback)
978-1-9753-0979-4 (ebook)

1 3 5 7 9 10 8 6 4 2

LSC-C

Printed in the United States of America

❧ Enduring Embers ❧

Darkness.

A darkness so deep you couldn't see how far down it went.

Tsukasa Mikogami stood on the edge of that ebony abyss and peered in.

Why?

Not even he himself knew.

He couldn't move.

It was like his whole body had turned to stone.

He didn't know what to make of it.

Then, suddenly, it happened.

An arm extended up from the void.

The limb was flaming and burned to a crisp.

It grabbed Tsukasa by the throat.

Then it squeezed.

When Tsukasa glared downward, trying to see who it was—

Such hubris—and from a common imposter. We cannot save anyone.

—he saw a corpse wreathed in flames.

Did it belong to the man who'd made that ominous prophecy to him, Oslo el Gustav? …No.

The cadaver, with its bloodshot eyes full of malice, was Tsukasa's father, Mitsuhide Mikogami.

With his hand still clasped around Tsukasa's neck, Mitsuhide pulled his arm back and began dragging Tsukasa forward.

Tsukasa was powerless to fight back.

He didn't resist as the limb dragged him over the edge and into the darkness.

When it did, Tsukasa realized something.

His father wasn't the only one reaching out to grab him as he tumbled down toward the bottom of the pit.

Tsukasa's mother was there, too, as was Oslo el Gustav, the terrorist who'd once pointed a Beretta at him, and everyone else he'd ever had to sacrifice. They all dug their nails into his flesh—

"Ah…!"

Then…Tsukasa Mikogami leaped up from his bed.

He looked around with ragged breath.

There was no abyss—he was in his office in Dulleskoff, the capital of what had formerly been the Buchwald domain.

Upon seeing that, Tsukasa finally realized he'd merely had his usual nightmare.

"That same dream again…?"

He pushed his bangs off his sweat-covered brow.

It was a recurring vision of his, one that he'd been having since long before he was whisked off to that other world.

However, it had been particularly bad over the past few days.

And Tsukasa knew the reason for that full well.

…It was those final words Oslo el Gustav had uttered moments before his death.

The Fastidious Duke hadn't spoken them out of hatred or malice.

His grim prophecy had been given with an expression of pity.

…Of course, the words themselves had been nonsense.

The thought of bending a knee to Freyjagard's empire, of submitting to the man who would allow such a despicable nation to exist, was unthinkable.

Tsukasa was entirely sure of that.

And yet…even so, he couldn't get Gustav's words out of his head.

The reason for that was, without a doubt…

Because he hit the nail on the head about what I genuinely am…

Out of the seven people collectively known as the High School Prodigies, Tsukasa was the bunch's sole impostor.

One of them was a merchant whose ability to make out a hundred voices simultaneously allowed him to manage tens of thousands of people and whose keen intuition let him predict how the world would ebb and flow.

Another was an inventor possessed of an intellect that had advanced humanity by centuries.

There was even an illusionist among their ranks whose tricks befuddled other magicians the world over.

The other six all possessed unique talents that enabled them to achieve incredible feats.

They all were, without a doubt, geniuses.

Tsukasa alone was different, however.

All he did was orchestrate politics, utilizing tactics anyone could've used to arrive at the same results.

Before an election, politicians made campaign pledges to their people, promising to govern with a fair and even hand.

Tsukasa was merely rigorous about making good on any such oaths he issued.

As long as they didn't give in to selfishness, in theory, that was something anyone could do.

I'm no Prodigy.

And that was why…he couldn't save everyone.

That was why he failed the way he did.

Each time Tsukasa stood on the edge of that dark, bottomless abyss, a thought sprang unbidden to his mind.

If he was really a "political virtuoso," then shouldn't he have found another option, one far superior to the ones he'd actually devised?

Gustav… Was he the same way…?

Naturally, Tsukasa had studied up on his foe. During his research, though, he came to learn something wholly unexpected.

It was about the relationship between Blumheart, the Blue Brigade's founder, and Gustav, the Blue Brigade's sworn enemy.

Not only had they attended the Knight Academy at the same time, but the two of them had actually been exceedingly close friends. And that wasn't all. There was also the matter of the tragedy that had befallen Jeanne Leblanc.

Back when Blumheart had stood up against the nobles' tyranny, Gustav had been one of his allies in the fight.

It was hard to believe, but Gustav's signature on the letter of protest Blumheart had presented to the aristocracy proved it. Once Gustav earned his dukedom after the war against Yamato, however, his relationship with Blumheart underwent a rapid shift.

Gustav began treating Blumheart with animosity. That was when Gustav drove the other man out to the sticks and started his fanatical worship of the emperor.

One had to ponder the reason for such an unexpected change of character. Unfortunately, the man himself was dead, so it was impossible to know for sure, but in all likelihood...

"In time, you, too, will learn that this world exists for one man alone. Not an impostor—a *genius, chosen by the heavens to rule!*"

...he'd seen something during the war.

Whatever it'd been, it was enough that Gustav threw away a lifetime of fighting back against the world and the evils of man.

In all likelihood, the thing he glimpsed was some quality of Emperor Lindworm von Freyjagard.

"A genius chosen by the heavens to rule, huh..." As Tsukasa murmured the words, he looked out the window toward the mountain range faintly visible to the far south.

That was where the Gustav domain lay, and beyond it, the Emperor domain.

As Tsukasa gazed off into the distance, there was some trepidation in his eyes. More than any hesitancy, however, the little heterochromatic orbs burned with resolve.

What will we learn there? And what will we witness?

CHAPTER 1

⚜ High School Prodigies and the Imperial Grandmaster ⚜

After a plane crash of an unknown cause, seven high school students found themselves stranded in a foreign world that they'd never so much as heard of before.

Once they arrived there, they discovered that it was home to a cruel, feudalistic society like that of Earth's Middle Ages.

After being saved by this new land's locals, the septet of teenagers decided to repay that kindness by taking down the Freyjagard Empire, the nation that had established that inhumane system.

It was a bold decision, to be sure.

However, what could seven mere children hope to accomplish? Their goal should have been impossible to achieve.

Surprisingly, the high schoolers took that obvious conclusion and threw it right out the window.

Back on Earth, a planet several centuries more advanced than this one, the group was known as the High School Prodigies. They led the fields of politics, business, science, medicine, swordplay, journalism, and entertainment.

Now they had turned the full force of their talents on this alien world.

The septet started out by defeating an evil lord, gaining the people's trust, and seizing control of the domain's government.

Subsequently, in just three short months, a series of consecutive military victories over the empire allowed them to unify all four of the empire's northern domains.

At long last, the world became home to its first-ever democratic nation: the Republic of Elm. The Prodigies' resounding successes sent a wave of excitement through the fledgling nation's populace.

"Equality for all."

With a new value system set in place by the High School Prodigies, the era in which circumstances of birth determined one's lot in life had come to an end. Now, one's work was properly rewarded, regardless of whether they'd been born into aristocracy or not.

The people celebrated the new system's advent for days on end, happiness practically emanating from their bodies.

As the lively festivities went on, a letter arrived for the Republic of Elm's governing body, the Seven Luminaries.

The sender was one Neuro ul Levias.

He was one of the four Imperial Grandmasters and, while the emperor was off on his campaign, the empire's acting governor.

In short, it was from the Freyjagard Empire's de facto leader.

And as for its contents...

"You're telling me that the empire proposed a cease-fire?!"

A shout echoed out within the Seven Luminaries' office in Dulleskoff City Hall.

The wide-eyed speaker was Winona, who came to Dulleskoff with the newly healed Ulgar in tow to deliver a *certain item* to Tsukasa.

Elch replied with a nod. "Yep. The offer came from the Imperial Grandmaster himself."

"Wait, wasn't the emperor s'posed to be the one in charge over there?"

Ulgar's question was answered by Lyrule, a blond girl who was staying in Dulleskoff like Elch. "The emperor is off conquering the New World, so apparently this grandmaster is the one who's in charge of all the empire's affairs right now."

"Basically, he's our foe's current leader," Elch added.

"Well, hot damn. So they got the enemy's top brass to come crying to them and begging for mercy?!"

Elch nodded. "I don't think the letter was quite as pathetic as you're making it sound, but just looking at the facts, then yeah."

"Couldn't it be a trap designed to lure Tsukasa and the others down there?" Winona asked.

"They considered that possibility, but...," Lyrule replied.

"Even if it's dangerous, this cease-fire negotiation is essential," Tsukasa had said.

If they could successfully negotiate peace with the empire under favorable terms, they could avoid vast amounts of needless bloodshed.

That was meaningful enough to be worth the seven of them taking on a little risk.

As such, Tsukasa had accepted the empire's invitation. The Seven Prodigies had boarded a Ringo Oohoshi–designed bus the previous evening and departed for Fortress City Astarte, the city that guarded the Emperor domain's northern border.

After hearing all that from Elch and Lyrule, the two who'd been entrusted with watching over the republic in the Prodigies' absence, Winona smiled with an astonished sigh. "Whew... Just three months, and they already managed to drag out the empire's top brass, huh. We sure stumbled across some amazing kids."

"Ga-ha-ha, you can say that again!" Ulgar laughed.

Elch and Lyrule nodded in agreement as well.

Even Elch, who'd doubted the seven teens when they'd first showed up in the village, had nothing but respect for the incredible group now. He could hardly believe what reliable allies his people had been blessed with.

Part of him had to wonder if perhaps the Prodigies were really the heroes sent from the heavens to change the world as in the story his mother had once recounted.

However…

"But if their talks go well…they might end up going back to wherever they came from."

Ulgar tilted his head at Elch's mutterings. "Hmm? Why's that?"

Winona, who was standing beside the older man, explained. "Isn't it obvious? Those kids are from another world, remember? Once the war's over, and they've built a nation with equality for all, there won't be any reason for them to stick around and keep meddling in our affairs. Makes sense that they'd hunker down and get serious about looking for a way home, right?"

"Ah, so that's what you meant." Ulgar nodded—then gave voice to his immediate doubts. "But this new country's sorta been built on their backs, hasn't it? Is it gonna be able to survive their absence? The empire's makin' nice about cease-fires and whatnot now, but who knows when they're gonna turn around and hit us with all they got…"

As Elch glanced through the economics textbook he'd gotten Bearabbit to retrieve from his database and translate into Altan for him, he gave his grandfather a determined reply. "If that happens… then as people of this world—of this nation—we'll just have to show the emperor what we're made of."

"…Oh?"

"That's why Tsukasa said what he did on his broadcast, why he asked if we were prepared to take responsibility for preserving our freedom and equality. These are our lives we're talking about here. Relying on Tsukasa and the others isn't a permanent solution."

Things might go well, or everything could come crashing down. Either way, it was Elch and everyone else's responsibility to bear as the citizens of their world.

Elch gave his answer in a tone flush with resolve. After leaving his small village, he'd seen the Gustav domain's grim state of affairs with his own two eyes. Calling it appalling would have been an understatement.

We can't let something like that ever happen again, and to do that, we need to make sure we don't depend on any single ruler.

Each member of the new nation needed to put all they could muster into safeguarding freedom and dignity.

That was the only way that democracy, the system that enabled the concept of liberty, could exist.

Tsukasa and the others had given them the environment and skills necessary to make that happen.

Everything past that was up to them.

"Ga-ha-ha! Look at that; my grandson's making big ol' speeches of his own now!" Upon hearing Elch's resolute words, Ulgar let out a hearty chortle and clapped Elch on the back.

"Ow!"

"Your mom and I might not be able to help much when it comes to reading and writing, but if things come to blows, those wimpy imperials don't stand a chance against us. They won't even know what hit 'em!"

Ulgar's grandson had always been cleverer than most, but he'd lacked guts. Now, though, Elch was using his smarts to help out not just their small village but an entire nation.

It filled Ulgar with joy, watching Elch grow up like that. And Elch's mother, Winona, felt the same way.

I look away for half a minute, and he's got the face of a right proper man. Winona smiled at her son, who was looking more and more like the man she'd once loved by the day. She hadn't failed to notice the change in her other child, either.

As soon as they mentioned the possibility of Tsukasa and the others going back to their original world, Lyrule had begun dejectedly staring at the floor. Undoubtedly, she was concerned for her friends traveling into enemy territory, but there was more to it than that.

A single glance was enough for Winona to figure that much out. She'd learned quite a lot in her thirty-plus years.

And over here, Lyrule's got the face of a true woman, too… Heh.

After leaving the tiny world that was their little village, both of Winona's kids were growing up fast. She smiled, squinting as though it was too bright to see, then turned her thoughts to the people who had sparked these welcome changes.

…Come back safe, everyone.

Winona looked up at the dragon flying through the air outside the window and prayed for their safe return.

Meanwhile, the Bearabbit AI-manned electric bus carrying the Seven High School Prodigies, Bearabbit, and their two guards made its way into Astarte.

"Wh-whoa!"

"What is that?! A…box? A moving box?! But it doesn't have a horse or anything!"

"Hey, there're kids inside! Who do ya suppose they are?"

When the self-propelled metal container rolled into town, it naturally caused quite a stir among the residents. However, the seven teenagers from another world were more or less used to such reactions.

Ignoring the inquisitive gazes being directed their way, they instead muttered their own little remarks of amazement as they looked out over the townscape gradually rolling past them.

"W-wow…"

"Man, they've got it good down here. It's like night and day compared to the other domains."

The roads were all paved with alabaster stone, and the buildings beside them were tall and aesthetically pleasing. Furthermore, all the people they passed were dressed elegantly, emphasizing how high the living standards were here.

As if that wasn't enough—

"Keine, m'lady, look! Elephants!"

"Oh my. And lions, even."

"They probably brought 'em over from the New World. I took my daughter to see the exhibition when they held it in Dormundt."

It was just as one of the two guards, the Order of the Seven Luminaries' *byuma* commander, Zest du Bernard, said. Astarte was holding an exhibition of rare and exotic animals in its central plaza.

Astarte's shopping center also boasted a theater, a concert hall, a casino, and various other recreational facilities.

The town's well-developed infrastructure was home to every luxury a resident could ask for. Commoners and nobles alike walked the streets with content expressions.

The Freyjagard Empire was a major nation, so it was only natural for the settlements near its capital to be so opulent. However…

Masato Sanada's gaze narrowed. "…Looks like animals aren't the only thing they brought over."

He was looking at the dark shadow cast by Freyjagard's glorious prosperity. It was a group of brown-skinned people wearing tattered rags. They had been brought over from the New World as slaves, just like Masato's own employee, Roo.

The Prodigies saw captives being exploited all over the city as the imperial citizens wore fineries and sated their every indulgence.

And there was no small number of servile people, either.

"There were certainly *some* slaves back in Findolph and Archride, but nothing like this," Tsukasa remarked.

"I heard that, in the Emperor domain, even commoners are provided with slaves to use as they please... This is my first time outside the Gustav domain. I never quite believed it, but now that I've seen it with my own eyes, I suppose I don't have much choice."

Their other guard, the female redheaded knight Jeanne Leblanc, was right. Here, even the commoners delegated everything to slaves and spent their days in comfort and leisure.

By pushing all their duties onto this worker caste, the imperial citizens were able to live free of want.

In the Emperor domain, that was simply the standard state of affairs.

"Survival of the fittest is their national policy, and this close to the capital, it definitely shows." As Shinobu voiced her sympathy in a hushed tone, she snapped photos of the Astarte scenery.

The sight of people using others as livestock made for a horribly twisted little paradise.

In one of her pictures, a *byuma* child no older than Roo was being savagely lashed at a construction site.

"_____"

"Tsukasa, don't let it get to you. We don't wanna be picking fights this deep in enemy territory."

"...I know."

Tsukasa shot down Masato's warning. He understood full well already. Those slaves weren't their responsibility at the moment. The people of Elm were.

Giving in to emotion and making a move here would accomplish little more than endangering the captive workers' lives.

Right now, the Prodigies were on the verge of finally solidifying their democracy. They couldn't afford to start wars over personal sentimentality.

There was more to it than that, however.

"We won't be the ones to save them. Rescuing people here and there on idle whims won't actually do this world any good. After all, sooner or later, we're going to leave this place behind."

And so...

"Our true goal should be to foster ideals that won't allow such horrors in the first place—and to engender the strength in this world's people to be willing to rise up and save the downtrodden. Even if it means sacrificing their own peace."

Accomplishing such a thing was by no means a simple task, though.

By Tsukasa's calculations, it would take thirty years at the very least.

That was how long it took for a new generation to mature and take over.

In other words, their task was to build a sturdy enough foundation for the Republic of Elm that it could survive in that interim, *no matter what the world threw at it*. As Tsukasa saw, it was their responsibility to get Elm up to that baseline.

"To do that, we need to emerge victorious. To buy...a period of peace for this world, no matter how temporary it might be."

As the words left Tsukasa's mouth, the bus rolled to a stop.

Standing before the seven of them was a majestic blue-and-white building that looked almost like a temple—Astarte City Hall.

That was where that messed-up nation's current ruler was waiting for them.

It was the empire that had produced the likes of Findolph and Gustav, and the man inside was closer to its heart than most.

Would they be able to broker peace? Or would they end up fighting to the bitter end?

Either way, the results of their talk would have a massive impact on the Republic of Elm's future—not to mention their own.

Tsukasa stepped off the bus, took a deep breath, then turned back toward the others. "Let's go. It all hinges on this."

After leaving Bearabbit behind to watch the bus, the High School Prodigies, along with Zest and Jeanne, headed into city hall.

Naturally, the staff inside had already been informed they were coming. They welcomed the Prodigies with the utmost decorum and then took them to the dining hall set up for the negotiation.

After showing the group to their seats, a middle-aged noble addressed the Prodigies. "Please wait here for a moment while I call the grandmaster."

"Of course," Tsukasa replied.

The noble gave a practiced bow and turned to leave.

As they watch him go, Tsukasa and the others pulled out their chairs to sit down.

However, they were soon interrupted by the dining hall's doors slamming open.

"Heya! Sorry for keeping you waiting, my good angels!" The man's greeting loudly echoed as he strode into the room. His hair was blue, and it was almost odd how good-looking his face was. He appeared reasonably young, but his dignified outfit made it clear that he was no ordinary aristocrat.

A sudden premonition struck Tsukasa.

Could it be...?

Then, not a moment later, the middle-aged noble who'd led the Prodigies there verified it. "L-Lord Grandmaster...?! Wh-what are you doing here already?!"

Indeed—the young, handsome man was the very one who'd requested the presence of Tsukasa and the others.

"I-I'm terribly sorry for my lack of timeliness. I was just about to go call for you, but..."

"Yeah, my bad. I just got bored of waiting, y'know? Oh, and you can leave now. Ta-ta!"

"P-please wait just a moment...! I'll summon your guards at once, so—"

"No, no, don't bother. We're trying to end a war here, not start one."

The grandmaster, somewhat annoyed, waved the attending noble away.

Then he approached the Prodigies and flashed them a genuine smile. "Anyhow, thank you for coming all this way! Apologies for asking you to meet me down here, even though the talk was my idea to begin with. I'm in charge of keeping an eye on the Emperor domain while His Grace is off conquering, so it'd be a problem if I just up and left it. Ha-ha-ha."

Despite the apology, the man didn't seem ashamed in the slightest. He reached out and offered each of the seven teenagers a handshake.

Aoi, Ringo, and Akatsuki seemed flustered, but they all accepted the grandmaster's proffered gesture regardless. However, Keine, Shinobu, and Masato were a little more composed, mirroring Neuro's relaxed tone and telling him not to worry about it.

When the man reached the last member of their group, he finally announced himself.

"It's a pleasure meeting you all. I'm Imperial Grandmaster Neuro ul Levias."

Tsukasa introduced himself in kind as he returned Neuro's hand-shake. "...I'm Tsukasa Mikogami, entrusted by God Akatsuki in matters of state. The pleasure is ours."

"I must say, though, this is quite a surprise. I wasn't expecting you angels to have warm blood like ours."

"We've taken human form on this world for the time being."

As Tsukasa replied, Neuro continued overenthusiastically shaking his hand up and down.

The bit about the Prodigies being divine beings was something they'd decided to go with when they first started calling themselves the Seven Luminaries.

Neuro narrowed his gaze. "Then...if I stabbed you, would you die?"

A faint smile played at his lips.

Zest and Jeanne, who were waiting by the wall, immediately tensed up.

Surprisingly, Tsukasa didn't seem perturbed in the slightest. In fact, he replied with a provocative grin of his own. "Who knows. Care to try?"

He knew from the look in Neuro's eyes and the tone of his voice that the grandmaster wasn't actually serious.

"...Oh, I think I'll pass. Wouldn't want to be uncivilized."

Just as Tsukasa had predicted, Neuro released his hand and stepped back.

"More importantly...," Neuro said, sweeping his gaze over the visiting group again, "I've heard all sorts of exciting things about you people. Healing your body after being cut in half, making mountains vanish... Those are some impressive miracles you've got! Could I be so bold as to ask you to show me one?! I must say, I've been looking forward to this ever since I first sent that letter!"

...*He looks like a child who just got his hands on a new toy.*

Neuro's spirited demeanor came as a shock to Tsukasa.

For the acting ruler of an empire, his expression hardly seemed that of a man about to participate in an essential international negotiation.

There was certainly a chance he was feigning buffoonery to get them to lower their defenses, but still...

Real or fake, there's no good reason for us to play along.

For one, all of Akatsuki's miracles were just magic tricks.

In short, he needed to set up tricks and contrivances in order to make them work. He couldn't just summon them at the drop of a hat.

Tsukasa quickly shut Neuro's request down. "I apologize, but we came here today to discuss a cease-fire, so—"

Or rather, he tried to.

"Very well."

However, it was none other than Akatsuki himself who spoke up. He stepped toward Neuro.

"Akatsuki..."

Tsukasa gave him a look. *Are you sure?*

If Akatsuki messed up here, it would call his divinity into question and potentially prove problematic for their negotiations.

Akatsuki responded to Tsukasa's concern by whispering, "Don't worry; I got this," and taking a deep breath.

When he spoke to Neuro next, it was the feigned voice and indomitable expression he used in all his performances. "Bwa-ha-ha! Now, allow me to introduce myself once more! I am Akatsuki, the god of the Seven Luminaries!"

"Oh wow! A real god?!"

"Verily. Heh... You're amazed, aren't you? Shocked and awed?"

"Oh, absolutely! I never expected God to be quite so cute!"

"D-don't call me cute!"

Upon having his psychological sore spot prodded, Akatsuki unthinkingly let his true colors show.

Then he felt Tsukasa's icy gaze bear down on his back.

Tsukasa's silent "I told you so" was quite plain.

Akatsuki broke out into a cold sweat, but he rallied and got back on track after clearing his throat. "...Neuro, was it? Well, if it's a miracle you want, then it's a miracle you'll get. Consider this a great honor... Now, do you have a coin on you?"

"Oh, I don't know," Neuro replied. He fumbled around in his pockets with a fretful expression. "I don't tend to carry a purse... Ah!" Suddenly, his eyes gleamed. Deep in his pocket, he'd found a single one-gold silver coin. "How's this, God?"

"That'll do fine. Hand it over."

"?"

What was Akatsuki going to do with it?

Neuro tilted his head to the side as he placed the coin atop Akatsuki's petite palm.

Akatsuki squeezed it tight...then quickly opened his hand back up.

"Hwuh?!"

The coin that should have been sitting atop his palm was gone.

In the blink of an eye, it had vanished without a trace.

Neuro was clearly shaken. "Wh-whaaaat?! But the coin?! I could have sworn I just handed it to you...!"

"Bwa-ha-ha-ha! I see you're quite flummoxed, Grandmaster! But instead of just standing there dumbfounded, why not check your own pocket?!"

"...Wha—?!?!"

The moment Neuro did as instructed, his expression froze.

Masato and the others leaned forward in curious anticipation.

When Neuro gingerly withdrew his hand from his pocket, he saw that he was holding a gleaming, one-gold silver coin. "Impossible..."

"Nice one, Prince," Masato remarked.

"My oh my. It never fails to impress, no matter how many times I see it," agreed Keine.

"Bwa-ha-ha! Why so surprised?! If you're confused, well, don't be! It's simple—all I had to do was turn time back a little! Such a feat is child's play for my divine hands! Now, never call me cute again unless you want to get reverted into a baby!"

Neuro's jovial countenance from before was gone, replaced with a look of abject astonishment. After coming up with a plausible-sounding bluff, Akatsuki stepped back behind Tsukasa.

As Akatsuki passed Tsukasa by, he shot him a proud look as though to say, "How'd you like that?"

Tsukasa replied with an apologetic shrug.

Akatsuki was a consummate professional, and it was clear that Tsukasa's concern had been misplaced. Having predicted that he'd be called upon to show off his miracles, Akatsuki had undoubtedly set up some sort of trick back when Neuro first offered them all handshakes.

All in all, it was a brilliant piece of work.

Neuro was visibly impressed, and he piled on his praises. "Wow, that was really something else, pulling that off without using any magic! I guess that's divine power for you! I wasn't sure what to believe before, but you just blew all my doubts out of the water!"

That statement was enough to confirm Tsukasa's suspicions about Neuro's true motive. He'd been checking to see if Akatsuki's miracles were some sort of magic.

As I hear it, Blue Grandmaster Neuro ul Levias is a skilled mage himself...

When Neuro initially heard the rumors about Akatsuki's powers, his first suspicion had probably been that Akatsuki was a swindler passing magic off as divine acts. That was why he wanted to see a miracle in person, so he could check for himself.

However, his prediction had been off the mark. A miracle had taken place right before him without a whiff of magic to be sensed.

In other words, the time was ripe.

"Grandmaster Neuro, now that we've fulfilled your request, would you mind if we got this discussion started?"

Neuro wasn't letting it show on his face, but learning that Akatsuki's deeds weren't spells must have saddled him with a fair bit of psychological pressure. There was no good reason to give him a moment to get his thoughts in order. Acting decisively, Tsukasa had urged Neuro to start the meeting.

"Of course, of course. I'm sorry; I got a little carried away from seeing something so marvelous. Ah, how embarrassing. Ha-ha-ha." With a deceptive smile, Neuro circled around to the other side of the table. Once he was across from the Prodigies, he took a seat and encouraged them to do the same. "Feel free to sit down wherever, by the way."

His grin seemed nigh indomitable. If he was shaken the way Tsukasa was hoping he'd be, it didn't show.

I suppose it makes sense... After all, the man's governing an entire nation right now.

It looked like it would take more than a single act of sleight of hand to shake Neuro.

This time, Tsukasa was the one whose prediction had been off the mark.

That said...

I never really counted on him screwing up anyway.

Tsukasa's philosophy was to anticipate every possibility and develop strategies for dealing with all of them.

As such, Neuro's mental fortitude fell well within acceptable parameters.

"Commander, I want you to take Jeanne and wait in the hallway."

"You sure about that?"

Tsukasa gave Zest's question a nod.

Even without them, they'd still have their strongest fighter with them, Prodigy Swordmaster Aoi Ichijou. Furthermore…

"Grandmaster Neuro had his soldiers stand down, so it would be rude to meet him with an armed escort."

"Yes sir."

Zest and Jeanne followed Tsukasa's order and left.

After watching them go, Tsukasa and the others took their places at the table.

Then Tsukasa focused his gaze on Neuro and got the ball rolling.

"Now, shall we begin?"

"Yes, let's. This conference will determine the future of both our empire and your republic."

And thus, their head-to-head showdown with the Freyjagard Empire began.

All right…

Now that he was finally face-to-face with the Freyjagard Empire's representative, Tsukasa took a moment to go over the tasks they needed to accomplish on their trip.

Broadly speaking, the Prodigies had three goals.

First, they needed to get the empire to acknowledge their republic as not a band of rebellious upstarts but as a legitimate nation.

Second, clear borders between the empire and the republic needed to be established.

Third, the empire had to agree to a nonaggression pact.

Those were their bare-minimum requirements. If they couldn't achieve at least that much, the entire meeting would be pointless.

Nothing but those three items mattered. In other words, the discussion's topic was going to be how the Prodigies were going to get what they wanted.

What would they have to give up, and what would they force the other side to cede?

Neuro was the first to speak. "Well, I'm the one who called this gathering, so I guess I'll kick things off."

Tsukasa nodded in approval.

To begin with, he wanted to see where his opponent stood.

"The Freyjagard Empire has no desire to see any more bloodshed. If at all possible, we'd like to reach an amicable reconciliation with you...and given that you agreed to come here today, can I guess you feel the same way?"

Tsukasa bobbed his head in acknowledgment. "Of course. We've yet to suffer any fatalities on our side, but we Seven Luminaries preach equality for *all*. We grieve for the Freyjagard Empire's deaths, and we came here today in hopes that we could prevent any more blood on either side from being spilled."

"Truly, what a wonderful doctrine. Let's work together to make this cease-fire a reality, then."

"I agree wholeheartedly."

Neuro smiled happily, but immediately thereafter, he lowered his tone and fired off a verbal arrow. "...By all rights, though, none of our men had to die at all. And they wouldn't have if you hadn't riled the people up."

The first round had begun.

Hearing Neuro's timbre change caused Tsukasa to ratchet up his guard.

Neuro went on. "Everyone who lost their lives in those battles had

©Sacraneco

every right to live to see today. If you hadn't started the war by agitating the people with your talk of liberty for everyone, then those dead would still be here. But you killed them. You wanted to force your ideology onto others so badly you were willing to sacrifice fathers. You were willing to offer up sons. You were willing to destroy families."

""…!""

Neuro purposefully chose his words to evoke images of those tragedies as he laid the war's blame at the Republic of Elm's feet.

Ringo and Akatsuki went pale.

There was a certain level of truth to Neuro's words, one that they couldn't deny.

Even as he blamed the Prodigies for starting the war, though, Neuro continued. "Well…I say all that, but even I recognize that the fault doesn't lie solely with you. Gustav, in particular, took things too far. In a way, it was almost inevitable that a group like yours would eventually rise up. What I'm saying is: While it was definitely you all who started the war, the Freyjagard Empire has its share of the blame for not reigning in the nobles whose abuses inspired your action. In acknowledging that…we hope we can call it a draw and broker for peace."

"A draw?"

"That's right. We could spend all day assigning blame, but that wouldn't get us anywhere, would it? The opposite of justice is another brand of justice, after all. Neither of us would end up backing down, and all we'd have for our efforts is a whole lot of wasted breath. So I say: Why not find a compromise? For example, try this on for size—you people admit fault for starting the war and agree to pay the empire three million gold in reparations. In exchange, we'll admit culpability for not dealing with the misgovernment and cede the rights to all the land you took from us in the war. How does that sound?"

"…!"

Masato, who had a firm handle on how much this world's currency was worth, gasped.

Three million gold was a hefty sum, but for all four of the empire's northern domains, it seemed far too cheap to be real.

Did the grandmaster truly feel shameful over what his side had done?

There was no way.

If he were really that admirable, he wouldn't have let the Gustav domain get so foul in the first place.

Neuro undoubtedly had some trick up his sleeve. Masato had no idea what that might be, though. Stuff like that was outside his area of expertise.

However, the same wasn't true of Tsukasa. For him, this kind of bureaucratic maneuvering was his bread and butter. That was why he knew exactly what Neuro's plan was.

There was only one answer the Prodigy politician could give. And so he gave it, his voice sharp and clear.

"We refuse."

""""Huh…?"""""

Neuro wasn't the only one surprised at Tsukasa's response—Ringo and the other Prodigies were shocked as well.

As they'd seen it, three million gold was more than a reasonable price for being able to secure all three of their conditions in one fell swoop.

Despite that, Tsukasa's answer remained firm. "I'm sorry; did you not hear me? I said we refuse."

"…How odd. I thought you just made it clear that you wanted to work together to help end the fighting. Was all of that just a lie?"

"Not at all. I meant every word I said."

"What, would you have us make more concessions, then?"

"That's not it, Grandmaster. You see, your very premise is flawed."

"Hmm?"

Neuro tilted his head to the side, and Tsukasa outlined his reasoning with utmost certainty.

"In this case, the opposite of justice *isn't* another brand of justice. Justice exists solely on our side, and your side is that of evil."

"Wh...?"

To no one's astonishment, Neuro was visibly taken aback at the thoughtless, unilateral declaration.

Even so, Tsukasa continued undeterred. "That war was a necessary step to rescue the powerless from a corrupt, depraved empire. The actions we took were good and proper, and I can say with utmost certainty that the justice we represent is pure and unambiguous. As such, it's completely unreasonable for you to ask that we take even a tiny amount of responsibility for that war. When I said we wanted to help you, I meant that we were willing to listen to your apology and help you convey its sentiment to our angry citizens. That cooperation in and of itself is a substantial concession, and it's the only one we're prepared to make."

"You're saying you don't feel a shred of guilt for the hundreds of people you killed?"

"None whatsoever. All of that was collateral damage, the fault for which lies solely with the Freyjagard Empire."

"And what about all the nobles who had to flee to the Emperor domain? Could you say the same thing to them after you started the conflict that robbed them of their families and homes?"

"Without a moment's hesitation." Tsukasa's expression didn't waver in the least, and he gave his reply as though it was the most natural thing in the world.

However, all of that was a bluff.

In truth, Tsukasa Mikogami was plagued by constant doubts.

Was there truly no better option? Was there not some way to reduce the number of casualties?

And because Masato knew all that—

...*Ah. So that's what this is about.*

—he finally realized.

At last, he understood what Tsukasa was trying to protect...and what Neuro was gunning for.

The terms he's offering seem great, but secretly, they're garbage.

If all you did was look at the three-million-gold price tag, it appeared like a steal.

By accepting that proposal, however, Elm would be acknowledging something. It would be tantamount to admitting that the republic had been established via unjust means. That would be a hefty weight to bear. Once they accepted responsibility for starting the war, it would haunt the new nation for the rest of its days.

In fact, there was a good chance that the seeds of democracy that the Prodigies had gone to such lengths to plant would be forever stained.

That was why Tsukasa couldn't back down.

Plus, there was a reason why not accepting responsibility for the war hadn't been one of the three goals—it was merely a core tenet of diplomacy and a basic premise of the art. Even if your side was clearly at fault, you had to use whatever illogical justifications you could come up with to force the blame onto your opponent. Although the enemy's hands were clean, you had to assert that they were soiled. Your side may have unilaterally massacred theirs, but you always had to insist that you were the victim. Politics was a world where the only things that determined the victor were the claims each side made. Logic had no place in such a realm.

At the diplomacy table, honesty and impartiality were nothing but useless vices.

Only an utter fool would admit their own fault.

That initial upset hardly spelled the end for Tsukasa's first maneuver. "Please don't misunderstand me, though. I was sincere when I stated that we wanted to reconcile with the empire. So allow me to say this: We Seven Luminaries, and by extension, the Republic of Elm, are prepared to make certain concessions regarding the fact that the Freyjagard Empire caused this war."

Once again, Tsukasa reiterated his desire for peace. Furthermore, he insisted that he was prepared to make sacrifices to achieve it.

The implication, then, was that if the negotiations fell through despite all the effort he was putting in, the Freyjagard Empire would be entirely to blame.

This is some bone-chilling shit.

Masato gave a pained smile. People called him a devil, but even the dirtiest deals ever made in the world of business paled before the utter amorality that was political discourse.

Still, this Neuro guy's no pushover.

By trying to get the Republic of Elm to admit fault for the conflict, Neuro had been trying to damage not just the young democratic nation but the concept of democracy itself. He must have realized how this new style of governing was poised to infect every nook and cranny of his world.

Not only was Neuro perceptive, he fully comprehended the gravity of the situation he was in.

Faced with that, Masato had to admit that the grandmaster was a formidable foe.

We're gonna have to pull out all the stops for this guy.

Meanwhile, Neuro seemed to have come to the same realization about the white-haired boy before him.

"Ah, I see. If I pick this fight, we'll both end up rolling in the muck." He let out an exasperated sigh. Then he gave Tsukasa a small, knowing smile and posed a question. "All right then, let's hear it. What do you want from us? What would be enough to demonstrate our remorse? Gold? Land? Or perhaps…just peace?"

Not even sparing a moment to consider, Tsukasa responded, "All of that."

"What?"

"The Republic of Elm has the following three demands for the Freyjagard Empire. First, you will pay the citizens of Elm reparations for the oppression they faced under your rule. The Empire must also recognize the legitimacy of the Republic of Elm's territory and sovereignty in perpetuity. Finally, your nation must enter into a treaty of nonaggression with the Republic of Elm. Nothing less."

"_____"

Even the other Prodigies found themselves taken aback at Tsukasa's aggressive demands. Naturally, Tsukasa himself was well aware of how outrageous he was being. He was asking for as much as possible, the greatest imaginable fruits of victory.

As such, he was under no illusions that the other side would accept the terms as is. Neuro would undoubtedly demand numerous compromises in return, and Tsukasa had decided well in advance how much leeway he was prepared to relinquish in any given category.

However, there's no reason for me to tell him what I'm willing to compromise on from the get-go.

After all, negotiations were nothing more than vehicles for two parties to try to get what they wanted at the other's expense. The only thing that mattered was what you walked away from the discussion with.

If you spent your efforts on trying to resolve negotiations quickly, you were liable to end up making concession after concession and ultimately not get nearly as much as you could have.

It was a common trap for the peace-loving Japanese to fall into, but Tsukasa wasn't about to have any of that.

He wouldn't show so much as a shred of mercy, nor would he expect any from his opponent.

Normally, people looked out for others and hoped that others would look out for them in turn. That naive way of thinking had no place at the negotiation table, however. Diplomacy was like a shoot-out where words served in the place of bullets.

In short…

It all starts here.

This was where the true battle began.

Tsukasa was going to need to carefully read his opponent and play his carrots and sticks accordingly.

It was time for Prodigy politician Tsukasa Mikogami to show what he was made of.

Or rather, it should have been.

After a prolonged silence, Neuro said something completely unthinkable.

"Sounds good. The empire unconditionally accepts all three of your demands."

"_____"

Tsukasa was careful not to let it show, but the fact that Neuro had agreed to his outrageous demands without the slightest show of resistance had him utterly baffled.

What game is he playing?

Earlier, Neuro's quote of three million gold for the four northern territories had seemed like a ludicrously low price. The reason for this was because the offer had been a clever ploy to poison the Republic of Elm.

That had at least made sense. This latest surprise was of a whole different order.

There was absolutely nothing Neuro stood to gain by accepting Tsukasa's terms without asking for anything back. Not anything Tsukasa could think of, at least.

As far as he could tell, Neuro was essentially offering a unilateral surrender. Such a situation seemed impossible, though. The deal was too good to be true. There must have been some sort of catch.

Tsukasa wasn't the only one with alarm bells going off.

Masato, who was sitting beside him, piped up in a casual tone. "Hey, whoa, slow down a sec. You're just a stand-in for the actual emperor, right? Are you really authorized to accept our terms, just like that? Seems kinda dicey for a guy in your spot, no?"

Given that Tsukasa was the one making demands, it was difficult for him to ask those kinds of follow-up questions. Understanding as much, Masato had chosen to break the silence and give voice to the doubts that Tsukasa couldn't. It was a masterful piece of support work.

Neuro replied with a light chuckle. "Ah-ha-ha. Sure, why not? Emperor Lindworm left me with the Great Seal of State, after all. So long as he's off on his campaign, I have absolute authority. For now, my will is the will of the empire. Doesn't seem dicey at all. Besides, I think I've gotten us a pretty good deal. After all…

"…*it's a small price to pay for a nation with nuclear missiles.*"

""""———!!!!"""""

A shock shot through the High School Prodigies like lightning.
Did he just say…?
He did.
"Nuclear missiles," Tsukasa muttered.

It was a piece of vocabulary nobody on this more primitive planet should have known.

"Heh-heh. Now that sure got a rise out of you."

"How does someone from this world know of such things…?!"

Neuro gave Tsukasa's blunt question a shrug. "Oh, well, that's simple enough. Truthfully, the answer's kind of boring. *You see, I'm like you all—I'm not from this world, either.*"

"Oh my…!"

"You've gotta be kidding me."

None of the Prodigies had expected that particular development and several who'd been planning on staying quiet through the conference couldn't help but let out exclamations of surprise.

"W-wait, hold on a minute! Y-you mean, you came here from Earth, too?!"

However, Neuro replied to Akatsuki's question by shaking his head. "No, sorry. I can't say I've ever heard of this 'Earth.' My world's probably a different one from yours. There, nukes and other technology like it were supplanted by magic long ago. I'd never actually seen one until you all bombed Uranus. And wow, those clouds really do look like mushrooms, don't they? That was a big surprise for me. Oh, and speaking of surprises—Akatsuki, that magic trick you showed me was delightful! Even though I knew it was just sleight of hand, I couldn't for the life of me figure out what you'd done or how you'd done it! It's no wonder you've been able to fool everyone for so long."

"Ah-er-wha-thanks?"

"_____"

After watching Neuro and Akatsuki's exchange, Tsukasa's expression grew sterner.

One had to wonder if the grandmaster was being truthful.

He claimed that he wasn't from this world, nor from Earth, but some other, third planet.

Between Neuro's knowledge of atomic weapons and the fact that the seven high schoolers' presence proved that more than one developed world already existed, it was certainly plausible.

If it was true, though…then it was terrible news.

That their miracles were nothing but magic tricks was the Seven Luminaries' Achilles' heel. Now that someone from the empire knew that, Tsukasa and the others were in big trouble.

Amused, Neuro laughed when he saw Tsukasa tense up. "…Heh-heh, no need to look so grim. I'm certainly not planning on blowing your cover and telling everyone that you're just average Joes. The people of Elm probably wouldn't even believe it, coming from an Imperial Grandmaster, and besides, why would I? After all…I'm on your side here."

"You are?"

"Most definitely. And I'm a good friend to have. After all, I can help you out. It's the main reason I sent for an audience with you."

Neuro sat up straight and broke the news.

"Let me get to the point. I have the power to return you all to your original world."

"………!"

"Wh-whaaaaaaaaat?!?!"

"Is that true? Is it?"

None of the Prodigies could stay quiet after hearing *that*.

They all rose to their feet and started bombarding Neuro with questions from across the table.

Seeing their gazes fixed on him, Neuro nodded. "Absolutely. I guess the proof is in the pudding, though, so it'd be faster just to show you."

With that, Neuro slid his teacup to the center of the table.

Tsukasa and the others all looked down at it.

At a glance, it looked like an ordinary cup of black tea, but...

"What's this supposed to be?"

"Tsukasa, could I trouble you for a strand of your hair?"

"Okay..."

Tsukasa agreed, then plucked out a piece from his bangs and handed it over.

"Thanks. Wow, it really is white to the root."

"What do you plan on doing with it?"

"Oh, you'll find out soon enough."

With that, Neuro did something utterly inscrutable. After taking the proffered hair, he dropped it into the teacup.

Initially, Tsukasa was confused. A moment later, though, Neuro tapped the edge of the cup—and then it happened.

"Huh? Wh-what's going on...?!"

All of a sudden, the tea's surface flashed, engulfing the entire room in light.

What *was* going on?

The seven high schoolers were utterly befuddled.

Once the glow died down, they could see again, though their confusion vanished without a trace. For what they saw in the cup was...

"Wait, whoa, that's..."

"It's Tokyo... That's the Tokyo skyline! Look, there's the Skytree!"

That's right. It was the displaced septet's homeland, a truly nostalgic sight for all of them. Unfortunately, the image projected onto the tea's surface only lasted a moment. It soon wavered, then vanished, leaving behind nothing but the liquid's dark-brown hue.

While it'd only been for a moment, all the Prodigies were certain of what they'd glimpsed. The world they needed to return to had been right there in front of them.

"Grandmaster Neuro, was that...?"

"Based on your expressions, I guess it hooked up to your planet all right."

"Was that...magic?"

"Yep... My original world, well, let's just say that certain events left it inhospitable. In order to find new homes, my kind developed a type of spell that creates gates in space-time. That's what I used to come here. Just now, I combined that magic with information fundamental to Tsukasa to find the planet you were born on and create a temporary link to it. Now, that was just a quick, spur-of-the-moment thing, so all that passed through it was light. Transporting material across space is a much more involved endeavor. But with a little time and preparation, even that becomes possible. In other words, with this sort of spell—"

"We can go home to Japan?!" exclaimed Akatsuki.

Neuro nodded. "Precisely."

After that answer and having seen that Neuro's powers were the real deal, Akatsuki completely abandoned his deific act and leaped up and down with joy. "Y-yeeeeeeeeeeeah!!!!"

Who could've blamed him? After being cast adrift with seemingly no way back to the life he'd once known, he'd been offered an apparent, definite lifeline of safe return.

Akatsuki wasn't alone in his exultation, either. Everyone else rejoiced at their sudden stroke of exceptional fortune.

Everyone except Tsukasa, that was. He had his doubts. Was that tantalizing proposition really all it seemed?

"Grandmaster Neuro, you're saying you can use your magic to send us back to our world. Is that right?"

"That it is."

"And what would you ask of us in return?"

"In return? Oh, perish the thought. I found a group of lost children; the only decent thing to do is help get them home."

"…What a wonderful sentiment and what an appealing offer. Why, it's so tempting…it makes me feel like I'm striking a deal with the Devil."

"Ha-ha-ha. You're a cautious one, aren't you?"

"It's my job to be cautious. Let me say this, Grandmaster Neuro—we're deeply grateful for your proposition. However, would you mind indulging this stubborn, suspicious ingrate and clearing up my last niggling doubt? …Are you really rendering such aid solely out of the goodness of your heart?" As Tsukasa posed his question, he stared straight at Neuro so as not to miss the tiniest flicker of emotion in the man's eyes.

Neuro answered—

"Of course! …Well, okay, fine. It'd be a fib to say it was an entirely benevolent gesture. Yeesh, that intuition of yours is something else."

—with praise and the truth.

"To be perfectly honest, you people are becoming something of a thorn in my side."

"How so?"

"I came to this world to live a rich life free of want or hardship. It doesn't take much to tell that you're all going to cause trouble for me—and my new home, the Freyjagard Empire. You already have, no? Come now, you can't pretend you don't realize you just snatched up a full fifth of the empire's land. So when I say I want to get you home as soon as possible, I mean every word of it. It'll be a headache and a half if you're still around the next time we want to go to war."

Ringo, detecting the ominous implication behind Neuro's words, blurted out, "Y-you mean…!"

Once everyone turned to look at her, though, she clamped her lips tight shut. "Mmmmm…"

"Don't worry. I'll say it for you."

Tsukasa could tell what Ringo was trying to say. He'd noticed the same foreboding portent in Neuro's statement.

He picked up where she left off. "Are you saying that you plan to attack Elm the moment we're gone?"

Neuro gave him a faint smile. "I'll neither confirm nor deny that. I'm under no obligation to share the empire's classified plans with you, after all." Having dodged the question, the grandmaster stated, "... And besides, what does it matter to you? You aren't actually gods or angels, and you have no intention of setting down roots here. As I see it, you're trying to leave as soon as you can. Am I wrong?"

As Neuro put it, they didn't even have the right to ask that question.

The only ones qualified to talk about this world's future were its native inhabitants. Even if the empire was to break the nonaggression pact and attack Elm after Tsukasa and the others left, the people who abandoned this planet and left it behind would be in no position to criticize them.

It was a perfectly valid argument.

The Seven Prodigies had a home they had responsibilities toward—but it wasn't this one. No, their world was the one on the other side of that teacup. That was where they lived, and that was where their duty lay. And because of that, Tsukasa reached his decision.

"Thank you for answering my rude question, Grandmaster. You're absolutely right; we do have obligations back in our world, and we have every desire to return there without a moment's delay."

"Right? Then I can get started on the preparations right this—"

"*However.*"

"..........!"

"We've made promises to the populace here, and we intend to keep them. Leaving will have to wait, at least until the Republic of

Elm has its footing firm and a system is in place to ensure that democracy will flourish. Only then will we have fulfilled our commitments."

That would take a year. Six months, at a bare minimum.

After explaining that, Tsukasa repeated his request once more. "But if you still feel the same way afterward... If you're still amenable to help us, even after we've built up a nation that may well become your enemy, would it be all right if we relied on your goodwill then?"

They couldn't depart now, not until Elm was mighty enough to stand up to the empire even once after they'd gone. When faced with a concrete method of returning home, that was the answer Tsukasa gave.

Neuro let out an exasperated sigh. "...Ugh, what an obnoxiously bullheaded sense of duty you have. What if I were to refuse, hmm? What would you do then?"

It was a reasonable response. From his perspective, Tsukasa's request was egotistical and selfish in the extreme.

After all, he was trying to help Neuro's enemies yet still take advantage of his goodwill.

However...

"No, no, it's fine; I get it. I know just how entrenched you've gotten in that little nation of yours. Go on then, do your good deeds. When you're finished, just give me a holler. I'll get the gate ready for you in the meantime." Neuro's expression was sour, but he accepted Tsukasa's request all the same.

"We thank you for your generosity." Tsukasa stood and gave Neuro a respectful bow. Then he looked over at his teammates. "And there you have it. Once we've solidified the Republic of Elm's position in this world, we'll be returning to Earth thanks to his help."

Tears began rolling down Akatsuki's face, and he turned and wrapped Masato in a big embrace. "We did it, Masato! We're going home! Waaah!"

"Ha-ha. What, you're so happy you're crying? Guess I can't blame you."

"I—I…need to tell…Bearabbit…!" Ringo stuttered.

"Who would have imagined we would find a way back so quickly? Hmm-hmm. How very fortunate," Keine remarked.

"Yeah, it feels like we're in a manga that just got axed," Shinobu replied.

Trying to find a transportation method back to Japan had felt like they were chasing after clouds, but now they had a clear endgame in sight. The Prodigies were overcome with joy.

Neuro smiled. "I'm glad to see you're all in such high spirits. All right, now that the boring meeting's over with, let's get some dinner in here! I promise you, the Emperor domain's cuisine will blow anything you had up in the boonies out of the water." He then rose, ostensibly to order his subordinates to bring in food.

The peace talks with the Freyjagard Empire had been full of shocks and surprises, but now they were finished.

The startling truth Neuro had sprung on them partway through had thrown the Prodigies off guard, but just looking at the results, the negotiations had ended in an overwhelming victory for them.

Without giving up a single thing, the Republic of Elm had obtained land, sovereignty, and reparations.

Plus, Tsukasa and the others got something they hadn't even been planning for—a way back to Earth.

The seven high schoolers were utterly thrilled. All their minds were filled with thoughts of their homeland and what they would do first when they got back to it.

As everyone relaxed, Tsukasa called out one final time to stop Neuro before he left. "Oh, Grandmaster, one last question."

"Hmm?"

*　　*　　*

"Does the phrase *evil dragon* mean anything to you?"

Upon hearing that final inquiry, Neuro replied—

"...Should it? Sorry, I don't have any idea what you're talking about."

—with a *complete and utter lie.*

As the words left his mouth, he gave a sinister smile, as though mocking the very world he stood in.

After dinner, Neuro and the Prodigies hammered out the specifics of the bilateral agreements they made in the meeting. This included the exact location of the border between their countries, the wording of their pact, and creating an exchange-student program to help solidify the treaty's longevity. Each article was written out, looked over, and then signed by both parties. That done, the nonaggression pact was official, and the Republic of Elm and the Freyjagard Empire formally became allies.

Neuro offered rooms to his new friends so they could stay the night in Astarte, but Tsukasa politely turned him down. The Republic of Elm was still just finding its legs, so he didn't want to stay away for too long. Neuro understood, and that night, he saw them off as they left the city.

Now they were back on the bus.

"...And thus, I assumed the mantle of God to rescue the impoverished populace. The enemy took sword in hand, clad themselves in armor, and sent tens of millions of men to try to slay us, but they were like ants before our might. Thanks to my brilliant leadership, we crushed them all! We pulverized them! And yet, even so, we held back! Why, you ask? Well, that should go without saying. If we'd gone all out, we'd probably have broken their world!"

"…Akatsuki, what're you going on about?" Shinobu asked.

"What do you mean? I'm practicing for our press conference, duh. I mean, we're obviously gonna have one once we get back. Heck, I figured you'd be the one running it, Shinobu. I gotta figure out what I want to say in my speech when we tell them about all the awesome stuff we did!"

"I feel like there was a lot of exaggeration going on there."

"C'mon, it's good entertainment. Nothing the masses love like a thrill."

"Also, didn't you plagiarize that line about breaking the world from Tsukes?"

"It's fine; I asked permission!"

"Seriously?"

"Oh, and speaking of entertainment, block off an hour for me immediately after the press conference. I'm gonna do my first post-return magic show and blow the audience's socks off!"

For so long, returning to Earth had felt like a far-off pipe dream. The Prodigies hadn't even known if it was going to be possible. Now that it was right there in front of them, however, Akatsuki was revved up and ready to go.

In his excitement, the young magician had utterly forgotten that he was supposed to be acting as a deity and was spouting off one taboo phrase after another.

Fortunately, Tsukasa had anticipated his utter lack of self-control. When they boarded the bus, he sent Jeanne and Zest off into the walled-off room in the back. It had been soundproofed so Tsukasa and the others could hold private conversations, so that was one problem nipped in the bud.

As it turned out, Akatsuki wasn't the only one who was excited, either.

"That sounds like a beary good time indeed! If you need any help

getting ready, I'd be happy to lend a paw! Ringo, you're pawbably going to want to write your speech down on index cards. Whenever you get in front of a crowd, your mind always goes as white as a polar bear."

"I-I'm…good… You should just…give the speech…for me, Bearabbit…"

"That'd bruin everything! The people back home are probably worried sick about you, so you have to go tail them that you're doing okay."

"O-oh… Okay, I'll try…"

It wasn't clear when he found time to make them, but the moment Tsukasa and the others got back to the bus, Bearabbit had greeted them by setting off a hundred party poppers. He, too, was pretty amped up about the news, a fact that was evidenced most clearly by how much more reckless his driving was than it had been on the way down. If Ringo was considering the notion of public speaking, she must have been excited as well.

Shinobu Sarutobi gave them a pained smile. "Ha-ha, I think you two are getting a little ahead of yourselves. There's still no guarantee we can actually make it home, y'know."

"Huh? What do you mean?"

Shinobu responded to Akatsuki's question by turning to Masato. "…What about you, Massy? You think we can trust the grandmaster?"

"As if." Masato snorted. "I've met car salesmen who were more trustworthy than that guy."

"Right?" Shinobu concurred. "That guy was fishier than a weekly gossip mag."

Even Keine agreed with the dismal impression of Neuro. "My faith in him runs about as deep as it does for unlicensed dietary supplements."

Akatsuki and Aoi looked at the three in bewilderment.

"Huh? What? You guys, what're you talking about?"

"You three… You think the grandmaster untrustworthy?"

"B-but until we got on the bus, you guys looked just as enthused about going home as we were!"

"That's 'cause doubting him wasn't part of our role." With that, Masato glanced over at Tsukasa, who hadn't said a word since they'd boarded the vehicle. "Tsukasa's one thing, but if Neuro saw the rest of us lookin' suspicious, too, it'd make his next moves harder to read. Plus, he's more likely to let his guard down if it looks like we're dancing on his strings."

"S-so when you were getting all pumped up, that was all just an act?!"

"The surprise wasn't."

Shinobu and Keine nodded in agreement. The three of them had played along during the negotiation, but that didn't mean they trusted a word that came out of Neuro's mouth.

"Prince, man, you're way too trusting," Masato remarked. "You gotta get your act together before someone suckers you into buying sketchy-ass pills that claim they'll make you grow taller or something."

"Uh, I—I-have-no-idea-what-you're-talking-about-no-sir-not-me."

"Oh geez, did you really?"

Then Shinobu cut in to ask, "Anyhoo, Tsukes, what about you? Was the grandmaster lying?" Shinobu knew that Tsukasa had been carefully observing Neuro during the whole meeting. That was why she'd asked.

However, Tsukasa shook his head from side to side. "No. When Neuro revealed that he was from another world, and when he said that he found us bothersome and wanted to get us back to Earth as soon as possible…those were his true feelings. Based on his gestures, eye movements, breathing, and several other external factors, I find it hard to imagine any of that was a lie. If we asked him to, I'm reasonably sure he would send us to Earth."

"S-see! I told you the grandmaster was a solid guy! Masato, I'm disappointed in you, doubting an upstanding gentleman like that. Whatever happened to the innocence you had as a child? When was the last time you smiled, like, really smiled? Here, how about I show you a magic trick. That'll make you smile."

"Shut up, Prince," snapped Masato.

"However…at the same time, I can't bring myself to accept his proposal as is," amended Tsukasa.

"Y-you too, Tsukasa?" Akatsuki asked falteringly.

"Something caught your attention, did it?" Masato inquired.

Tsukasa nodded. "Most of what he told us came from the heart. At the very end, though, he lied."

The "evil dragon" was a memetic concept, one that had been mentioned by both Winona and whatever mysterious entity had tried contacting the Prodigies through Lyrule. And Neuro was hiding something about it.

"Neuro's the acting head of the largest nation on the continent, so it wouldn't be strange for him to have heard the legend of the Seven Heroes. But why would he mislead us about that? It's only important to us because of its parallels to our current situation, but it should just be a centuries-old fairy tale as far as he's concerned. What reason would he have for intentionally trying to conceal it? It doesn't make any sense, at least not to me," Tsukasa explained.

"M-maybe he was just hungry and wanted to get dinner started?" Now that he'd finally found a shred of hope, Akatsuki was loath to relinquish it. He was holding on to it for dear life. Denial of having heard of the evil dragon wasn't the only curious thing about Neuro, however.

"And there was another thing that bothered me, too. I imagine Merchant, Shinobu, and Keine noticed this as well, but…how did he know we couldn't return to Earth on our own?" Tsukasa asked.

"………?"

Akatsuki tilted his head to the side in confusion, so Masato elaborated. "Prince, imagine you made it to this world on your own, and then some guy with crazy tech who clearly isn't from around here showed up. Your first assumption wouldn't be that they got dragged onto this planet by some strange power, right? You'd probably think they came on their own like you and that they could get back to their original world just fine."

"Oh…"

"But that guy knew right from the get-go that offering us a way home was something we'd value. Why do you think that is? That's something he cleverly left out of his little explanation."

"Now…that you mention it…that *is* weird…," Ringo remarked.

"Th-then why didn't you just ask him yourself back then?" Akatsuki countered.

This time, Tsukasa was the one who replied. "Because we weren't nearly prepared enough to do so."

Tsukasa remembered the words he'd heard from Lyrule back at Castle Findolph. They'd been staticky and hard to make out, but the audible parts sounded like they went as such:

"This world…is being engulfed…in a massive, evil dragon's maw…
"I beg of you, O Seven Heroes, you must save this world."

If Tsukasa took the words at face value and combined with them the Seven Heroes story Winona had told them, he could guess at a number of rules that this planet operated under.

Rule 1: There existed some sort of threat to the world referred to as the evil dragon.

Rule 2: There existed some sort of entity that opposed the evil dragon.

Rule 3: There existed a group known as the Seven Heroes affiliated with the opposer and was called in from somewhere beyond.

"Now, there probably aren't very many people who know of these parameters. The original Seven Luminaries religion had some connection to them, but it collapsed hundreds of years ago, and all that's left of it are oral accounts passed down as legends. In other words, anyone who knows the rules probably falls into one of two buckets."

There was the entity from Rule 2 that summoned the Seven Heroes.

And there was the evil dragon from Rule 1—or whatever being that term referred to.

It had to be one or the other.

"The latter would be particularly bad. Hypothetically, if it turned out that Neuro himself was the evil dragon...then we might very well be playing with fire."

Unfortunately, even Tsukasa could only guess at the true nature of this evil dragon. It wasn't clear in what way it was devouring the world, either. With scant information to go on, there was little the Prodigies could be sure of.

However, depending on where Neuro's allegiances lay, pressing him for answers there and trying to get to the heart of the matter could well have proven exceedingly dangerous. The grandmaster's intentional hiding of information about the evil dragon made that all the more accurate. Neuro had undoubtedly dodged the question because revealing any information would have put him in a disadvantageous position. There was no telling what might have happened then.

That was why Tsukasa had avoided pressing the issue. More accurately, that was why doing so had been the prodigious politician's only option.

"There's just too many things we don't know, both about the world as a whole and about Neuro ul Levias in particular. The only thing we can do in situations like that is flee. But that can't go on. We need to learn more—not just to assess whether accepting Neuro's help getting home is a good idea, but to fulfill our obligations to Elm and ensure that it doesn't fall before equality can take root in this world. We need to find out what the exact rules are."

Lacking such knowledge, the Prodigies wouldn't know what kind of power they needed to muster, nor what the best course of action would be.

To make a plan, they needed information.

"So with that in mind, I have your new instructions going forward."

But right as Tsukasa was about to start addressing the group, he was interrupted.

It all happened in an instant.

A thunderous roar cracked the air, and an impact struck the bus head-on.

"Eeeek!"

"Wh—?!"

The bus rocked from the back-to-back explosions.

Bearabbit responded quickly and slammed on the brakes, and Jeanne and Zest charged out of their soundproof room with weapons in hand.

"Shinobu! Are you all right?!" Jeanne exclaimed.

"Yeah, I'm awesome. Tsukes, was that…?"

"Whoever it was, it doesn't look like they come in peace," replied the young prime minister.

"Forces bearing arms detected on the surrounding hills! And their flags…they're flying the Freyjagard standard!"

At Bearabbit's declaration, everyone looked out the windows toward the gently sloping hills to their sides. The dark of night kept them from seeing any particulars, but they could definitely make out some sort of group gathered atop the ridge. From what they could tell, there were several hundred people in all.

Balls of fire arced from the hilltops, hurtling through the air and crashing into the bus. This hostile force was bombarding them with magic.

"Could it be some sort of patrol that hasn't heard about the peace deal yet?" Jeanne wondered.

Zest's expression hardened as he replied, "No, that's too big a group just to be a patrol. Plus, there's no way they'd have that many mages unless this was planned. If I had to guess, I'd say they're—"

Tsukasa had come to the same conclusion. He was already quite certain, as it happened. However…

"In any case, we need to formally announce ourselves. Bearabbit, turn on the parabolic sound system and pass me a mic," requested Tsukasa.

"Fur sure!"

Bearabbit grabbed a small wireless microphone and tossed it to the white-haired young man using his spiderlike manipulator arms.

Tsukasa caught it, then addressed the assailants. "Attention, imperial troops. This vehicle is under the control of the Seven Luminaries, representatives of the Republic of Elm. Yesterday, we of the Republic of Elm signed a nonaggression pact with the Freyjagard Empire. Our nations are now allied. You are in gross violation of our treaty. Cease this hostility at once."

Tsukasa's voice cut through the bombardment and echoed clearly through the hills. His words seemed to bring the unwarranted attacks to a halt.

Had the misunderstanding been cleared up? For a moment, it seemed almost possible.

Then the bus's parabolic sound system picked up the high-pitched voice of a man who seemed to be the enemy force's commanding officer.

"Those Four Grandmaster swindlers may have fooled the emperor and taken control of the capital, but they have no authority over us! The will of the empire is the will of those who carry royal blood in their veins! And besides, our nation operates on the survival of the fittest! The emperor would never deign to make peace with you peasant lowlifes, much less under such degrading terms!

"That treaty is based on nothing more than that Blue Grandmaster fool's delusions of grandeur, and it won't stop us of House Weltenbruger, true loyalists of the emperor, from carrying out justice as we see fit!"

Right as the man finished speaking, Bearabbit got a lock on his position and brought him into focus on the bus's cameras. An image of a short, old man popped up on the vehicle's interior monitors.

His face was wrinkled, his back was hunched, and his eyes were large. Between that and his high, shrill voice, he gave the impression of a monkey. As he shouted to proclaim his righteousness, he gesticulated like a stage actor.

All in all, it made him look almost intoxicated.

Tsukasa looked him in the eyes through the camera. "…Grandmaster Neuro was entrusted with the Great Seal of State by Emperor Lindworm directly. Doesn't going against his wishes constitute an act of treason?"

"Not in the slightest! We swore allegiance to the empire itself, and we are its will manifest! The cowardly Blue Grandmaster failed to teach you your lesson, so it falls on me, Lucius von Weltenbruger, to teach you how we do things here in Freyjagard! Shwarzrichtenritter, my Obsidian Knight Order, trample the enemies of Freyjagard beneath your feet!"

*   *   *

""""RAAAAAAAAAAAAAAAAAAAAAAAAH!!!!""""

When Lucius finished his speech, an aide blew into a bugle.

Its call riled up the soldiers, and they charged down the hills as one toward the bus below them. A force of three hundred men was now bearing down on the Prodigies. By this world's standards, it was a reasonably impressive military force.

"A-ahhhh! We're under attaaaaack!" Akatsuki cried.

The weight of the soldiers' footsteps was enough to shake the ground, causing the bus to wobble from side to side.

Inside, Masato cocked his head. "He just said House Weltenbruger, right? I feel like I've heard that name before."

Shinobu, well-informed as she was, gave him a quick rundown. "Maybe you saw it on some sort of trade documents? Lucius von Weltenbruger is an archduke. He's the previous emperor's nephew, the leader of a group of aristocrats called the Bluebloods, and the most powerful noble in the empire."

"Ah, that's what it was. I guess that means this aggression is their dumbass way of lashing out at the Four Grandmasters for stealing the emperor's affection."

As Shinobu and Masato calmly laid out the situation, neither of them seemed concerned in the slightest.

Upon seeing that, Akatsuki raised his voice in disbelief. "Uh, guys?! Why don't you look more worried?! We're under attack, in case you hadn't noticed! Ts-Ts-Tsukasa, what do we do?!"

"Settle down, Akatsuki. Magic like that doesn't stand a chance against this bus's armor and reinforced glass. Right, Bearabbit?"

"Yup. We'll be completely safe fur as long as we stay inside."

Bearabbit was right. The vehicle was under constant fire, yet none of the strikes had so much as dented it yet.

Its reinforced glass had clouded up a little, but even that hadn't cracked or warped. When the soldiers tried charging it on horseback, their results were just as poor.

"Aaaaagh! My aaaaaarm!"

"Wh-what's this box *made* of?!"

"How'd it take that much fire without a scratch?!"

When the approaching enemy soldiers rammed their lances into the bus at full speed, all they accomplished was shattering every bone in their arms from the shoulder down. They screamed.

The infantry tried hitting it with their swords as hard as they could, but the recoil reverberated through their bones and caused them to faint in agony.

In moments, their righteous vigor and enthusiasm evaporated.

At a loss for what to do, the forces of the Shwarzrichtenritter stared at the strange vehicle in befuddlement.

"The bus has onbeard machine guns. Should I give them what fur?"

Tsukasa shut Bearabbit's proposal down. "That won't be necessary. We still have the treaty of commerce and a few other points to hammer out with the empire, and causing casualties immediately after we signed a nonaggression pact would give them unnecessary ammunition to work with. I'd much rather use this incident as ammunition against them instead. For now, we should flee without meeting their attacks head-on. Bearabbit, fire warning shots at the soldiers straight ahead of us. We're going to break their ranks, then charge through. If anyone's still dumb enough to get in our way afterward, though, then go ahead and run them down. We don't want to look *too* accommodating, or we'll come across as weak."

"Pawger that!"

Bearabbit did as instructed and began warming up the bus's external machine guns.

As he carefully fired in between the soldiers standing around them, he also laid on the horn and filled the air with an earsplitting honk.

The soldiers were under attack by more bullets than should have been possible to fire at once, and their eardrums were bursting at some alien sound. Terrified of the unknown threat, they scattered like cockroaches.

Bearabbit, taking advantage of that opening, revved the engines and got ready to charge their line.

However...

"What a cowardly sight. Grown men, screaming and fleeing like little children. You people are an embarrassment to the Shwarzricht-enritter's good name."

Directly in front of them, one soldier had yet to flee.

He was a middle-aged *byuma*, nearly ten feet tall and clad in a kimono.

His face was covered in powder foundation with an imposing crimson design that was the spitting image of a Kabuki actor's *kuma-dori* stage makeup.

It was undoubtedly odd attire for a foot soldier to be wearing. The curious *byuma* showed no signs of trying to flee from the bus barreling toward him, instead merely drawing the sword resting at his hip in one fluid motion.

"_____!"

At that moment, a shiver ran down High School Prodigy Aoi Ichijou's back—

"EVERYONE, TO THE WINDOOOOWS!!!!"

—and the vehicle they were riding in split in two.

The samurai, whose outfit looked like it came straight out of the Kabuki play *Renjishi*, had sliced the bus vertically down the middle in one swing.

Each half of the bisected thing whizzed by him on opposite sides.

Thanks to Aoi's sudden cry and their own quick decision-making, none of the bus's passengers fell victim to the slash. As soon as the out-of-control vehicle flipped over, though, they'd all end up getting violently ejected.

And the automobile was still going just as fast as ever.

Even if the fall itself didn't kill the passengers, they'd be stuck surrounded by enemies. That would likely end just as poorly.

Bearabbit was the first to act. *"Bear with meeee!!!!"*

Because he was a machine, it only took him an instant to figure out the optimal course of action.

Specifically, he shot a series of anchor cables from his manipulator arms toward each half of the vehicle.

Then, once the anchors were hooked into the bus's frame, he was able to pull the split thing back together forcibly.

Now they didn't have to worry about anyone getting dumped out.

However, that didn't change the fact that the transport had been chopped in two.

It was electric-powered and didn't run on fuel, so thankfully, it hadn't exploded, but the shock from the brute-force reassembly sent the right front wheel flying off, driveshaft and all. Having lost its support, the front-right corner of the bus made contact with the ground. Dirt went flying up as they curved to the right, then crashed straight into the bare cliff face to their side. Now they were at a complete stop.

After getting up from being knocked around by the forceful

reassembly and the sudden crash, Masato smiled wryly. "Oh man, you've gotta be kidding me... It looks like they've got a real piece of work on their side."

"Is everyone all right?!" Aoi asked.

"Yeah, somehow. But..." As Shinobu stood, she looked out the window.

"Shishi did it, the madman!"

"I tell you, those samurai are something else! He cut up that tough box like it was cheese! Fighting against 'em is hell, but it's great having one on our side!"

"All right, now's our chance! Surround them! Don't let any of them escape!"

The imperials had rallied and were heading right for the Prodigies.

"Ahhhhh!" Akatsuki cried. "They're all coming for us!"

At the moment, the bus was *only just barely* being held together by Bearabbit's cables.

It was not without its openings, however. If their enemies surrounded them and pried it open, they'd be able to make their way inside. They didn't even have to go that far—all the Shwarzrichtenritter forces had to do was toss a bomb in, and it'd be game over.

"Okay, this has gone past the point where we can afford to worry about future negotiations. Bearabbit, can you fix the bus?" asked Tsukasa.

"It's pawsible, but it'll take about thirty minutes to—"

"No, it won't," Ringo Oohoshi cut in. She could tell just how urgent the situation was.

Not caring that she was in front of people, Ringo stripped down to her tank top, got out her tools, and gave Tsukasa a confident "I'll have it running in ten...!"

It was clear what the rest of them needed to do.

"Got it. Then we'll go and buy you time. Merchant, Shinobu,

Jeanne, Commander. We're heading outside to return fire. Don't let a single person anywhere near the bus," Tsukasa instructed.

"We're not gonna use it for cover?" Shinobu asked.

"I want to spread out their focus while Ringo's working. Our ride out of here taking even more damage would defeat the whole point," replied the white-haired young man.

"Ah, makes sense. In that case, aye, aye! Sha-sha!"

Masato smirked. "Man, those cease-fire talks went so well, and yet here we are shooting one another again. Not that I mind."

Once the four received their orders, they all pulled out the machine guns from under their seats and got to work loading in their ammo belts.

"Bearabbit, are the bus's defense systems still online?" inquired Tsukasa.

"*The only grizzly damage is to the circuits, so all it'll take is a simple bypass to reboot them.*"

"Then you're our backup. Prioritize giving us cover when we run out of ammo."

"*Pawger that!*"

"And, Aoi, as for you—," Tsukasa began.

"My task is to stop that man, I take it?" finished the swordfighter.

"…I suspect you're the only one who can."

Aoi reached down and ran her fingers over the katana hanging from her waist. Her beloved Hoozukimaru had shattered during the battle with Gustav, but Ringo had made her a replica. Aoi nodded with conviction.

"Very well…!"

"In that case, I'll stand by and resupply anyone who runs out of bullets," Keine offered.

"Perfect." Tsukasa nodded.

"U-um, Tsukasa…wh-what should I do?" Akatsuki stuttered.

"Akatsuki...you can cheer us on."

"A-all right, I can do that! You picked the right man for the job! Go, team! Go, team!"

Tsukasa found himself invigorated by Akatsuki's encouragement. Well, not really, but in any case, he took it as a signal to dash out of the bus with a machine gun in hand. As Aoi headed up their vanguard and hurtled like a gust of wind toward the dangerous man who cut their bus in half, the rest of them fanned out to protect the bus. After pointing their machine guns at the oncoming soldiers, they pulled their triggers and mowed them down in unison.

In terms of raw numbers, it was three hundred versus six. Such a disadvantage was monumental enough to make a person's head spin. The reality of the situation was skewed the opposite way, however. The battle around the bus was overwhelmingly in the Prodigies' favor.

After all, each fighter on the Prodigies' side was equipped with a machine gun that would've been cutting edge even back on Earth.

Thanks to their rapid-fire capabilities and penetrative power, each armament took down ten enemy soldiers in the space of a single second. This skirmish was being held on open ground with no cover to speak of, which only made things easier for those with the automatic weapons.

With nowhere to hide, the imperial warriors toppled like dominoes before the veritable storm of bullets.

"Aaaaagh!"

"Wh-what the hell's up with those guns?!"

"The bullets just keep on coming!"

The soldiers cowered in fear at the sight.

Lucius, the monkey-like geezer, standing at the back of their ranks, shouted at them in his shrill voice. "You call yourselves the Shwarzrichtenritter, losing your nerve against wretches like that?! If the enemy has firearms, all we have to do is send in our own gunmen and shoot them down!"

However, that was a wrong move.

For one, there was a stark difference in effective range between this world's matchlock weapons and Ringo's specially made machine guns.

The imperial troops' only option was to figure out a way to avoid the deluge of lead raining down on them until they got in firing range themselves, and that just simply wasn't feasible. All they were doing was casting themselves into the abyss. It was no different than committing suicide.

No matter how many people they threw into the meat grinder, Lucius's people couldn't so much as start to close the gap.

At that point, even Lucius realized that throwing good shooters after bad was an exercise in futility. He then tried bombarding the Prodigies from afar with his mages...but that ended unsuccessfully as well.

The Shwarzrichtenritter's mage unit was typically made up of Imperial First-Class Mages. However, because of how valuable of a military asset they were, most of them had been recruited to provide support over in the New World. At the moment, all that Lucius had were unproven Second-Class Mages who'd been temporarily conscripted straight out of the academy.

There weren't very many of them to begin with, and the fireballs they were loosing didn't even begin to compare with Gustav's in terms of speed and power. Tsukasa and the others weren't encumbered by armor, so they could dodge them all without breaking a sweat.

Nothing was hitting.

The Prodigies' line wasn't breaking.

After things persisted in that way for a little while...

"W-we need to pull back, Lord Lucius! At this rate, we're the ones who'll be wiped out!"

"Lord Lucius, give the order to retreat! We need to retreat!!"

Eventually, the soldiers began shouting their complaints. Seeing the sorry state their enemies were in filled Tsukasa and the others with confidence.

They only needed another minute. Surely the Prodigies could hold out for that long.

Unfortunately, their hopes were dashed yet again by *the exact same man.*

""""Wh—?!""""

All of a sudden, a loud, heavy smashing sound echoed through the night and drowned out the gunfire.

Everyone turned in the direction of the noise, toward the bus behind them, to see what had happened.

"Gah…! Rgh!"

"Aoi…?!"

There, they saw Aoi's body half-buried under the now-sunken mess of crushed frame and warped glass at the bus's rear.

"Your skills are true. And there is little fault to be found in your training. It truly is a shame, though. The blade you wield ill suits you."

The one who smashed her into it…was the same Kabuki samurai who bisected the bus. His murmur indeed did sound apologetic.

"Huh?"

Then, the next moment, he closed the hundred-foot gap between himself and one of the bus's defenders in an instant and appeared directly before the redheaded knight Jeanne.

"I have heard tale of your good deeds. But alas, what I do, I do for the people of Yamato. Now die."

"JEANNE!"

"_____"

Shinobu screamed, but she was too late.

The white-faced samurai's katana glowed faintly like a firefly as he brought it down to bear on Jeanne.

It was so sudden that all Jeanne could do was freeze up.

Much to everyone's surprise, however, the *byuma* man's blade never reached her.

"Hraaaaaaaah!!!!"

At the last moment, Zest du Bernard shoved her aside to protect her. Aoi's defeat had left everyone else stunned, but Zest's wealth of combat experience had allowed him to react to the samurai's attack in time.

He brought up the massive slab of iron that was his trusty sword to block the white-faced samurai's assault, but—

"Rgh... Gah!"

—even though he guarded against the blow, the samurai's blade sliced through weapon and wielder alike.

"C-Commander Bernard!"

Zest's knees buckled, and his hefty frame toppled over.

However—

"Hrrrrgh!!!!"

—he used the last dregs of his strength to grab onto the samurai's right leg.

"Mr. Tsukasa, now!"

"_____"

Tsukasa, who was the second to act after Zest, charged the samurai and brought his special weapon to bear—a stun baton.

The moment he started running, he threw his machine gun aside. Firing it on full auto would have been liable to hit Zest in the crossfire, and more importantly, trying to shoot a man powerful enough to beat Aoi with ease, even with a machine gun, would likely have been an exercise in futility.

However, Tasers and their like didn't exist in this world.

In other words, the enemy would respond to the attack as if it were a mere strike with any plain, blunt weapon.

And with any luck, that knowledge gap would let him emerge victoriously!

"Unph."

The samurai blocked the attack with his katana, exactly as Tsukasa had hoped. No sooner had he done so than electricity ran up its blade and coursed through his entire body.

Thanks to the gap in their civilizations, Tsukasa was able to pull off his surprise attack successfully. Then, taking full advantage of the opening, he used his other hand to draw his government pistol from his suit—

"...!"

—and fire off seven melee-range rounds at the samurai's unprotected chest.

There was no way the powerful foe could dodge them. The bullets were going to bury themselves in his chest and end his life.

Or at least, they were supposed to.

"A cudgel clad in lightning? How peculiar. Some manner of cursed weapon?"

Unfortunately, the samurai was unharmed.

Despite being flooded with electricity, he had still been able to move just fine. By gripping his katana with only his left hand and pulling up the iron sheath hanging from his waist, he had blocked every one of Tsukasa's shots.

"That shock should have easily been enough to knock you out."

"I am a samurai. My mind is perfectly clear—your paralysis spell cannot bind me."

The man's inhuman feat left Tsukasa at a loss for words.

To make matters worse, while the electricity might not have worked on the samurai, it had been plenty effective on Zest. His last threads of consciousness snapped, and his hand dropped from the *byuma*'s leg.

Now the mighty assailant was utterly unfettered.

"And for your slight, your life is forfeited."

His slash rent the air as though being sucked toward Tsukasa's neck.

"Awoooooooooooooooooooooooooooooooooooo…"

"!"

The moment before it landed, though, a lupine cry echoed through the night air, and the samurai stopped in his tracks.

The white-faced man wasn't the only one who froze upon hearing the sudden call.

"That howl just now, it can't be…!"

Once the samurai had broken the Prodigies' defensive line, the Shwarzrichtenritter had been about to charge them, but they seized up as well. The alarm was plain in their eyes.

They knew that howl. They'd heard it before.

It was the sound of an enemy who'd slain countless of their brethren back when the empire had invaded Yamato.

Everyone looked up toward the top of the cliff the bus had crashed into.

Upon that outcrop was a pair of figures with their backs to the full moon.

One was an imposing white wolf and the other, mounted atop the beast's back, was an animal-eared girl wearing a kimono. Her hair was the same argent color as the wolf's.

©Sacraneco

"Shura…"

"It's Shura, the White Wolf General…!"

"So Shishi's daughter…still lives…!"

The soldiers went pale.

As the kimono-clad young woman gazed down at the Shwarz-richtenritter army from on high, she drew her incredible blade—a *nodachi* greatsword over six feet long—from its sheath and planted the scabbard in the ground.

Then the wolf threw itself off the cliff with the girl still astride and charged straight toward the group of soldiers trying to surround the bus.

"Sh-she's coming our way!"

"H-hold your ground! She's alone. We can take her!"

"Get herrrrrr!"

The warriors grouped up and held their spears at the ready.

However, the wolf had predicted as much.

The moment before it rammed into the spears, it took a mighty leap into the air.

After clearing the polearms and soldiers' heads with ease, the large beast landed right in the middle of the enemy formation.

""""GAAAAAAAAAAAAH!!!!""""

The moment it did, the girl spun her *nodachi* in a circle, striking down a dozen men through their armor.

That sight was more than enough to drive terror into the Shwarz-richtenritter fighters' hearts. They descended into an unorganized mob, and the young woman and wolf broke through the line with ease. In the blink of an eye, they closed in on the samurai facing off against Tsukasa, and the girl swung her blood-soaked weapon.

The white-faced swordfighter responded in kind, and the two silver streaks met with a thunderous roar.

"Shura… I see you still refuse to understand how your actions imperil the people of Yamato."

"Bite your tongue. I'm not here to hear you talk."

Neither party yielded an inch, and they began exchanging blows.

The girl and the wolf used their *nodachi* and claws to attack in waves. The samurai's sword work didn't seem particularly swift, but his complete lack of wasted movements allowed him to parry the entire onslaught.

Sparks flew as the two sides vied for supremacy.

In the middle of all that, the girl shot Tsukasa a quick glance with her crimson eyes. "You owe me a debt for this."

"!"

That moment, the bus's rear lights flashed on, and Bearabbit's voice came booming over the speakers. *"Everyone! The rebears are finished!"*

Tsukasa responded immediately. "Everyone, retreat! We're getting on!"

After giving the order, Tsukasa helped Jeanne retrieve Zest and boarded the bus along with them. Then, as the wolf-mounted girl held the samurai off, the three-wheeled vehicle took off, fleeing the battlefield at top speed.

Thanks to the mysterious young woman's help, Tsukasa and the others successfully escaped their attackers. However, none of them looked relieved in the slightest. All were dead silent as they waited for Keine to finish treating Zest back in the soundproof room.

About half an hour later, the stifling quiet was broken by the sound of Keine exiting the sectioned-off portion of the vehicle.

Jeanne immediately rushed up to the doctor, practically clinging to her as she asked for any news. "Dr. Keine! Is Commander Bernard going to be all right?!"

Keine gave Jeanne her best bedside-manner smile. "Not to worry, he pulled through. He'll need bed rest for the time being, but he should wake up in about two days."

"Th-thank goodness..."

Jeanne crumpled to the floor.

At long last, they all breathed sighs of relief.

Now that the tension had dissipated, their pent-up anger finally had time to surface.

"What were those guys' problems?!" Akatsuki cried. "I thought the war was finally over, and then...all *that*. Tsukasa, you gotta file a complaint with the grandmaster!"

"Oh, don't worry. He'll be hearing from me about this."

Tsukasa had no intention of letting the empire get off scot-free.

The biggest shock lay elsewhere, however.

"...Still, Aoi, I've never known you to be bested in a one-on-one duel. Honestly, I was surprised."

"........." Aoi slumped her shoulders apologetically.

She'd been tossed around pretty roughly during her fight with the white-faced samurai, but fortunately, there was a reason people called her a Prodigy swordmaster.

It was only thanks to her astounding skill that she'd been able to keep her injuries to a minimum. She was covered in scrapes and bruises, but nothing more serious.

"Ah, about that." As Keine got to work disinfecting Aoi's wounds, she asked the other girl a question. "Aoi, dear, why were you holding back?"

"...!"

Aoi was visibly startled.

"Huh?"

"What're you talking about?"

"I spent quite a lot of time traversing battlefields with Aoi before we came to this world, so I noticed it right away. Aoi was intentionally restraining her own movements," Keine replied.

"Aoi, is that true?" Tsukasa inquired.

"I..."

Aoi didn't answer. Given her reaction, though, it would seem that Keine's observation had hit the mark.

If that was the case, though, then the other Prodigies needed to know why.

"If you're sick, you need to tell us. It's a rude way to put it, but you're the best weapon in our arsenal. As such, I put a lot of trust in you when I come up with battle plans. You being out of form endangers us all. This is why it's important to share information like that with the group."

As Tsukasa lectured, Aoi hung her head. "...A thousand apologies." She expressed her regrets to the group and, in doing so, acknowledged that she hadn't been fighting at her best. "However, there is nothing wrong with my body, that there isn't... Perhaps it would be faster simply to show you."

After asking everyone to back up a little, Aoi held her katana at the ready. The bus had basically just been stapled back together, so it was incredibly wobbly, but even so, Aoi stood tall and steady.

Then, after slowly raising her katana—

"Hyah!"

—she swung it down with a vigorous shout.

That's when the weapon she was holding snapped at the base, and its blade fell lifelessly to the floor.

Akatsuki gawked at it in shock. "Th-the sword broke just from you swinging it..."

"Ringo made that one for you to replace the one that broke in the battle against Gustav, as I recall," Tsukasa remarked.

"Man, it snapped way too easily. Did it have cracks in it or something?" Masato wondered.

However, Bearabbit immediately shot the businessman's doubts down. "Th-that's impawsible! That there was a pawfect-koality, one-to-one replica of Hoozukimaru's design! Ringo made sure to scan it fur imperfections before giving it over, and all its durability tests came back green! I'm tailing you; there's no way Ringo could have screwed up!"

"He's right, that he is," Aoi agreed. "Ringo, m'lady, the weapon you crafted for me was well forged. It was free of cracks and fissures, and in terms of sheer cutting power, it surpassed even my Hoozukimaru. Unfortunately, that alone was insufficient, that it was."

"Huh...?"

"Craftsmanship alone is not enough for a katana to withstand my techniques. A weapon must have a soul, as a cursed sword or bewitched blade does, to be able to keep up with me."

"Ah, now that you mention it...," interjected Shinobu, "you said something like that back during an interview you gave me. You told me that Hoozukimaru was an ensorcelled katana imbued with a vengeance that a young swordsmith forged in the flames of his family's cremation after they all got killed by robbers."

"Precisely. Zeal or hatred, it matters not—any blade tempered by fierce emotion will not easily break, for it knows it has a duty it must fulfill. But without an edge such as that...no sword can withstand my techniques, that it cannot."

As they just witnessed, a lacking weapon couldn't even endure a single swing.

To avoid breaking the replica, Aoi had been forced to rein in her power.

"...However, Ringo took time out of her hectic schedule to craft it for me, so I could never bring myself to tell her that it was insufficient for me to fight properly with. But in doing so, I've caused you all a great deal of trouble, that I have. My sincerest apologies..." As Aoi explained the situation, she bowed her head low to all present.

Ringo, in an unusual display, spoke up. "Please don't...apologize...! It's my fault...for not...making it better..."

"No, the guilt lies with me. The war seemed to be waning, and I allowed myself to grow careless. None of this would have happened had it not been for my negligence."

"B-but...!"

"All right, that's enough."

"Ts-Tsukasa, m'lord?"

It looked like the two of them were about to start fighting over who was to blame, so Tsukasa stepped in to stop them.

"We're all in the same boat here. There's no need to argue about whose fault it was. It's a waste of time. If you feel guilty, then reflect on it on your own time. None of us would ask anything more of you. Right?" Tsukasa turned to the group.

"Of course," Masato declared. The others nodded in agreement. "Instead of focusing on useless stuff like who to condemn, we gotta figure out how to deal with the bigger problem—the fact that our best weapon, Aoi, can't fight properly."

"Exactly, Merchant... Ringo, would you be able to make a sword stronger than the one that just broke?" requested Tsukasa.

The genius inventor weakly shook her head side to side. "Um... S-sorry..."

"I suspected as much. If you could, you would have just done so in the first place."

"Besides, Aoi's talkin' about occult stuff. That's, like, the exact opposite of Ringo's area of expertise," Shinobu added. "...Looks like we're gonna have to source our new spooky sword locally."

"The man I fought and the girl who came to help us... Both of their swords were impressively sharp, that they were. Whoever forged them might well be able to make a blade that could withstand my power, but…"

When Aoi mentioned the girl, Akatsuki let out a low murmur. "That reminds me, I hope she's okay… We kinda left her on her own back there."

"She'll be fine," Aoi replied. "The man I faced was skilled, but the girl was a master, at least his peer. Even if victory eluded her, she could have fled with ease."

Tsukasa concurred. "That's right. She told me that we owed her a debt now, which leads me to believe that the only reason she showed up in the first place was to rescue us. Once we got out safely, I imagine she simply withdrew."

"O-oh, okay. Well, I hope you're right," said Akatsuki.

"Still, I do wonder who that young lady was," Aoi admitted.

"If you're fine with hunches, I've got a pretty good one," Shinobu replied. "She's probably a samurai from the Yamato Empire."

The Yamato Empire was a country that had existed on that continent up until a few years ago, and the name still popped up every now and again.

Unlike the Freyjagard Empire, whose culture resembled Middle Age Europe's, the Yamato Empire bore a closer resemblance to ancient Japan. The katanas and *nodachi* they used were just like the Japanese weapons of the same names, and the soldiers who wielded them were called samurais and ninjas.

Tsukasa knew the basics about that country, too.

Between the girl's outfit, her weapon's shape, and the imperial soldiers' reactions, Shinobu's guess was likely accurate.

However, that meant…

"The white-faced samurai, too, perhaps." Tsukasa thought back to what the soldiers had said. They called the Kabuki-style samurai

Shishi and the girl, Shishi's daughter. "There's also a chance that those two…were parent and child."

"Now that you mention it, they did both have pale-colored hair, and they had those same wolflike eyes," Shinobu agreed.

"But if they're related, why were they fighting?" Akatsuki asked.

"I don't know," Tsukasa replied. "I don't have enough information to reasonably speculate. However…"

For the Prodigies, the biggest problem wasn't why those two were fighting, but rather, it was why survivors from an empire that had fallen years ago were choosing to show their faces in front of them, the Republic of Elm's representatives. What was their reason? What was their plan?

When the Republic of Elm was born, the balance of power in this world started shifting…

Tsukasa turned his thoughts to the future, then let out a whisper.

"The debt we incurred today may cost us more than we know."

Before long, Tsukasa's prediction would end up coming true.

The Yamato Empire.

A few years ago, it had been wiped out by the Freyjagard Empire. However, its ghost still lurked in the continent's shadows, and when that specter came out into the sun, the Republic of Elm would find itself divided.

CHAPTER 2

⚜ Women's Resolve ⚜

Fortress City Dulleskoff, capital of both the former Buchwald domain and now of the Republic of Elm, was surrounded by a pair of pentagonal walls.

Within those barricades, two figures walked hand in hand through its high-end residential area.

One was a young *byuma* girl, and the other was a brown-skinned woman.

The Republic of Elm had a standing military called the Order of the Seven Luminaires, and both of the women were well acquainted with its commander, Zest du Bernard. The girl was his daughter, Airi, and the woman was a former slave Zest had bought, Coco.

"Coco, guess what?! In today's race, I was the fastest one in my whole class!"

"Oh my, really?"

"Yeah! I even beat all the boys!"

"That's very impressive. You take after Master Bernard well."

"Do you think Papa will be happy to hear it?"

"I'm certain of it, dear."

Seeing Airi in high spirits, Coco smiled at her. She wasn't just putting it on to placate her boss's daughter, either. Her smile came from the heart.

The fact of the matter was that Coco loved Airi the same way she did her own daughter. And that was all due to Zest's good character.

Coco had been initially taken from the New World and brought over to Freyjagard as a slave, but now she had a nice Freyjagardian husband and a family of her own. That had only been possible because Zest paid for her honorary Freyjagardian citizenship, and those didn't come cheap.

Although the naturalization itself had become unnecessary when Findolph passed hands from Freyjagard to Elm, Coco would never forget the kindness Zest had shown her.

As such, Coco had vowed to watch over Airi and protect her with all her might until she grew up. No matter what happened, Coco always made sure to do her best to uphold that oath. Perhaps it was that determination that caused her to notice something strange.

"………"

She and Airi were the only two people on that hilly road, yet she sensed someone else's presence all the same.

Someone was lurking in the shadows, watching them. Coco could feel it like a weight on her back. She'd sensed it the day before, too, after she went and picked Airi up from preschool.

They were being followed.

"………"

"Coco? Is something wrong?"

"No, no… It's nothing. Come along now; let's hurry on back. We have to tell your father about your wonderful accomplishment. I'm sure hearing about it will help him get better in no time."

Coco forced herself to grin, then pulled Airi along by the hand. As she did, she felt for the dagger she kept concealed within her garment.

"Haa…"

A castle stood in the center of Dulleskoff behind its protective walls. Once, it had served as Dulleskoff City Hall, but now it housed Elm's Department of the Interior. Lyrule's brilliant blond hair bobbed as she walked atop the hallway's deep-blue carpets and sighed.

Her heart was overflowing with gloom, and there was no end to it in sight. It was because of Tsukasa and Ringo's exchange that one day.

She saw them, hand in hand.

Now, they probably weren't lovers. Lyrule had been around the pair for a few months. Undoubtedly, she would've noticed if they were dating. After witnessing that scene, though, there was one thing Lyrule was sure of: Ringo's feelings.

She had glimpsed Ringo's face when she took Tsukasa's hands, asked him to rely on her, and decided never to leave him on his own.

That one glance had told Lyrule everything. After all, she herself harbored the exact same emotion. Ringo Oohoshi loved Tsukasa Mikogami. She probably had for a long time.

It was probable that Ringo had loved Tsukasa for far longer than Lyrule had.

I…

Whenever Lyrule thought about that fact, her heart ached. She didn't know what to do with these feelings she had. Ever since that day, she and Ringo had been on strained terms.

When they passed each other in the hallway, they would avert their gazes and quietly exchange generic pleasantries. Ringo had probably realized how Lyrule felt, too.

…It hurts.

Lyrule had never known that loving someone could hurt so badly.

What...what should I do...?

She had no idea.

Despite her confusion, the young woman was certain of one thing. Elch had been right—at some point, Tsukasa and the others were going to leave this world behind.

Compounding things, Lyrule had heard the shocking news that the Imperial Grandmaster was allegedly from another planet, just like her friends were, and he knew a way to send them back home. That meant that the Prodigies' departure was probably going to come sooner rather than later.

Lyrule and Tsukasa were from different worlds. That alone was an unfathomable gap. Eventually, their shared path would split. And if that was the case, then could Lyrule really justify getting in Ringo's way? In the end, the inventor was the one who would get to stay by Tsukasa's side. Wasn't continuing to pursue anything with Tsukasa selfish of Lyrule? No matter how much she thought about it, no answer seemed forthcoming.

"Haa..." Instead, all that poured out of her were pained sighs. If Lyrule didn't let them out, she felt like the gloom was going to swallow her whole.

Lyrule continued brooding until she reached her destination. It was the interim secretary of the interior's office. That's where Tsukasa worked.

A short while ago, Tsukasa had called for Lyrule over the portable terminal she'd been given. She didn't know what he needed her for, but in all honestly, she didn't really want to see him at the moment.

However, Lyrule's personality wasn't one that would let her shirk her duties for personal reasons, so she dragged her heavy heart and body to his office anyway. After another depressed exhale, the young blond woman steeled herself and knocked on the door.

"Tsukasa, are you there? It's me, Lyrule."

"Hello! I'll come open it, so please just wait a moment."

When she did, a soprano voice she'd never heard before responded from the other side. The door opened, and Lyrule was greeted by an unfamiliar *byuma* boy sporting glasses and a golden fox tail and ears.

Who's this…?

Lyrule was bewildered. She hadn't expected to be greeted by some strange boy two or three years her junior.

For the boy's part, he froze and gawked at her for a moment, perhaps dumbstruck by her beauty. However, he quickly remembered his role and gave her a broad, friendly smile.

"I apologize for the wait. Please, come right on in."

He opened the door wide and stepped out of Lyrule's way. Inside, she saw the person who summoned her, Tsukasa, as well as Winona.

"Hey there, Lyrule!"

"Lyrule. Sorry for calling you here so abruptly."

"O-oh, don't worry about it. I was free anyway…" came Lyrule's timid response as she meekly entered.

Upon seeing her uneasy gaze and gait, Tsukasa quickly figured out what was giving her pause. "Ah, him? He's an exchange student from the Freyjagard Empire. A part of the nonaggression pact we signed included a study-abroad program designed to deepen the friendship between our two nations. He and a few other students came to Elm to learn about our ways and technology."

"My name is Nio Harvey, and I arrived in the Republic of Elm yesterday. Since then, I've had the great honor of shadowing Mr. Tsukasa and learning about your country's unique political system."

Tsukasa watched Nio give Lyrule a courteous greeting, and he smiled wryly. "He's too kind. We only just founded our republic, and I've been so up to my neck in work that I've just been using him as my secretary. I'm such a poor excuse for a mentor that I haven't found the time to give him a single lesson yet."

©Sacraneco

"Oh, not at all! Just being by your side is far more educational than any of my classes back in the empire, Mr. Tsukasa!"

When Winona heard that, she giggled from atop the guest sofa. "Ah-ha-ha. Found yourself quite the cute little disciple there, didn'cha? …Still, though, isn't equality sort of a dirty word back home for ya?"

Nio smiled evasively. "Well, you might say that. We aren't too fond of democracy itself, but even without equality for all parts, we still have a lot to learn from you regarding health care policy and efficient governing. For example, Mr. Tsukasa, your attitude about being prepared for any situation that might arise is an invaluable example to learn from for any leader."

"I just do what's necessary to carry out my responsibilities, that's all," Tsukasa replied. Then he looked over to Lyrule and Winona and moved on to the main topic. "Now, we can leave the exchange students' formal introductions for another time. The reason I called you two here today was that I have a small request I wanted to make."

"A request?"

"For Lyrule and me?"

Tsukasa nodded, then explained, "You heard the news, I imagine? We were attacked on our way back from the cease-fire meeting by a group acting on behalf of the notable Weltenbruger family. Our commander, Zest du Bernard, is currently at his house recuperating from his injuries."

"Y-yes, I did," Lyrule said.

"What about it?" Winona inquired.

"Well, it would seem that a suspicious person began following him at almost exactly the same time he began his bedrest," said Tsukasa.

"What sort of suspicious person?" Lyrule asked, almost afraid to hear the answer.

"I wonder if the empire's tryin' to stir up another mess," Winona spat with disdain.

"The border is under strict guard, so the possibility of that is slim. I suspect they're from inside Elm, and they're probably affiliated with the former nobles. Bernard went from an Imperial Silver Knight to the commander of the Order of the Seven Luminaries, and that didn't make him any friends among the empire's supporters."

"Yeah, that's plenty reason enough to want to mess 'im up," observed Winona.

Tsukasa nodded. "Bernard realized that himself, so he sent his maid, Coco, and his daughter back to his parents' home in Dormundt just to be safe. It was a good decision, but his wife passed away some time ago, so now there isn't anyone left to take care of him here. That's a problem, especially because Keine gave him strict instructions to stay in bed." He turned his focus to Winona and Lyrule. "I was hoping I could ask you two to serve as his nurses for the time being."

That was why he'd called them there that day.

Lyrule nodded her assent without so much as hesitating. She'd heard from Keine just how bad Zest's injuries were, and she could imagine how difficult it would be for him to so much as prepare a meal in that state. "Of course. Things have settled down for Keine, so she won't need my help for a bit."

"I don't have much that needs doin', either, but…I'm not too good with fiddly stuff like nursing, y'know?" Winona stated.

"Oh, I'm well aware," Tsukasa quipped.

"You pickin' a fight with me, kiddo?"

"Ah, forgive me. I shouldn't have said that out loud."

"Y'ain't even takin' it back?!"

Winona was utterly indignant, but Lyrule knew exactly where Tsukasa was coming from.

Right after the Prodigies' plane had crashed, when none of them were well enough to move, Winona was the one in charge of taking care of the boys (with one exception). Her methods weren't negligent per se, but she lacked any sort of moderation. She had a bad habit of winding bandages so tight that they cracked bones, and Lyrule often had to come in afterward and rebind them.

Winona insisted that tighter was naturally better, but any reasonable person would realize that such a thing stopped being the case once you started causing hypostasis.

Lyrule couldn't blame Tsukasa for holding a grudge about that.

Disregarding Winona's protest, Tsukasa continued. "Winona, the job I had in mind for you was less nursing and more acting as Bernard and Lyrule's bodyguard. Whoever this stalker is, they might try something. We'll have soldiers standing watch as well, but considering that this person might be affiliated with the former nobles, we need to account for the connections and money they'll have access to. They could easily plant their own men in among the guards."

Tsukasa had full faith in Winona, both in terms of her integrity and her fighting prowess.

"With Aoi unable to fight at her best right now, you're the best woman for the job. As powerful as Lyrule's magic is, she's not suited for turning it on others."

"Ah, I getcha... Well, I wasn't planning on stickin' around here too long, but...yeah, sure. Leave it to me. And if there really is some creep slinking around, I'll be sure to nab 'em for ya."

"I'm glad to hear it."

After thanking Winona, he turned to Lyrule and offered the same sentiment.

"And thank you, too, Lyrule."

Unfortunately, the moment the young woman saw Tsukasa's red and blue eyes head-on, all the gloom from before came rushing back to her at once—

"O-oh, it's nothing… Helping people out when they're in trouble is what we Elm Village people do."

—and she reflexively averted her gaze.

After being entrusted with protecting and nursing Zest, Lyrule and Winona headed to Dulleskoff's high-end residential district later that day.

The house was a two-story building with a blue roof, and it was a good deal too large for just three people—a father, a child, and a live-in maid—to live in.

Lyrule stopped before the front door.

"Mr. Bernard, it's Lyrule. Pardon the intrusion." After two knocks, she took the key Tsukasa gave her, unlocked the door, and went inside. Then she headed to the room where Zest was resting and knocked once more.

"Mr. Bernard, I'm coming in." After announcing her presence, Lyrule entered.

There, Zest was waiting for her atop his king-size bed. "Sorry for having you come all this way, Lyrule. I told Mr. Tsukasa I could manage on my own, but…"

"Oh no, Mr. Bernard, that won't do at all. If you don't follow Dr. Keine's instructions, you'll slow down your recovery."

"Fair 'nuff. By the way…who's the lovely *byuma* lady?"

"Nice ta meetcha! The name's Winona. I guess you could say I'm one of the original members of this big movement y'all are running. Word is there's a creep about, so I came along to protect you and Lyrule."

"Ah, you must be Elch's mother. He told me about your work back at Findolph's castle, making fools of those Bronze Knights with a sickle and whatnot. I tell you, women from hunting villages are some-thin' else."

"Oh, you. That's no way to praise a lady. I mean, just look at this smooth, silky tail just beggin' to be complemented."

Winona wagged her well-maintained tail back and forth, to which Zest replied, "Bein' smooth was never one of my strong points," with a placative smile.

"Still, these are some nice digs you've got. You might not be a Silver Knight anymore, but you sure live like one," Winona observed.

"Nah, this is just a rental. I ain't exactly the smallest guy around, so I always end up havin' to stay in giant-ass houses like this one."

Although Zest wasn't on the same level as the white-faced samurai named Shishi, he was pretty large in his own right. In any ordinary house, he'd end up banging his head on every doorframe.

As a result, he always ended up living in places much too big for three people.

"Honestly, I'd be happier just staying in the barracks, but that ain't exactly a place to raise a kid. My maid's always grumbling about how much work these places are to clean, though," Zest admitted.

"Why not just remarry? You used to be Dormundt's captain of the guard, no? Surely there's plenty of ladies who'd've been happy to have ya," remarked Winona.

"You sure you're one to talk?"

"Oh no, a good woman like me stays faithful to her husband even after he passes."

"Ha-ha… Well, I'm a guy, so I guess that don't apply to me, but… I'd feel bad, makin' someone put up with a geezer with a kid. Between that and me not knowin' how my daughter would take it, I can't bring myself to take the plunge. The old mayor kept trying to set me up with people, but I always turned him down."

"All that for your daughter, huh?"

"'Course. She's my whole life."

"There's such a thing as too doting, y'know… Not that I don't get how you feel."

"Winona…"

Suddenly, Winona loudly clapped her hands together and changed the subject.

"Anyhow! Can't stand around yammering all day. C'mon, Lyrule, let's get to work cleaning the giant-ass house."

"Ah, right."

Winona made to exit the bedroom, and Lyrule followed.

As they left, Zest gave them a bow. "Sorry for the trouble, and thanks for the help."

Once she made it into the hallway, Lyrule sped up so she could catch Winona. "Winona, I can take care of the cleaning by myself. Why not give Mr. Bernard some company?"

"Really? This big ol' house? All on your own?"

Lyrule nodded and withdrew her magic wand from her pocket. "Not alone, exactly. I'll have the spirits help out."

"Ah, that's right, I heard you learned how to use magic."

"…I'm afraid I won't be any assistance in a fight, but I'm an expert when it comes to chores."

"Well, ain't that something. I'll have to take you up on that later."

"Hmm? Later?"

"Yup. After I'm done with *my* job."

As Lyrule cocked her head in confusion, Winona grabbed one of the swords hanging from the corridor wall.

"Wh-what do you need that for?"

"I can smell 'em."

"You can what?"

"There's the three of us, sure, but there's a fourth smell wafting through this place. It's the scent of a human who's somewhere they shouldn't be."

When Lyrule looked at Winona's face, she could see her expression had a focused hunter's tension. Winona's olfactory sense was as sharp as it had ever been, and she was confident there was a foreign entity lurking in the house. Both she and Lyrule had a pretty good idea of who that must be.

"Oh no, could it be…that suspicious person Tsukasa was talking about?"

"You wait here."

With weapon in hand, Winona began tracking the scent.

"W-wait for me!" Once again, Lyrule rushed after her. "I can at least back you up."

"All right. I'm counting on you, then."

Winona looked back. When she saw Lyrule clenching her wand with a white-knuckle grip and a tense expression, she gave her a gentle smile…then stopped in her tracks.

"Here."

The domicile had so many rooms that Zest had taken to stuffing some of them full of unneeded goods, and before long, they'd basically become storehouses. The space before them was one such chamber.

Lyrule gulped.

Winona reached for the doorknob. "We're going in. Get ready."

Then she threw the door open and charged in with her sword brandished.

The moment she did—

"*Myaaaaarwl!!!!*"

—the cat who'd been napping atop the mountain of crates inside leaped up and snarled at her.

"........."

"A-a cat...?"

It looked like someone had forgotten to close the storehouse's window. That must have been how the cat got in. Seeing that, Lyrule relaxed.

"O-oh, well, that's okay. Look, Winona. A cat snuck in; that's all."

However, Winona was different. Her expression was just as tense as before.

"Nah, there's a big ol' rat in here, too. Right...*here!*"

She plunged her sword into the wardrobe right beside the cat. Or rather, she tried to. Her goal had been to skewer both its door and the person lurking inside in a single strike.

And yet...

"...!"

All of a sudden, the armoire exploded from within. When its doors swung open, one of them hit her sword and knocked its thrust away. Thankfully, Winona had foreseen as much. When the door struck the sword in her left hand, it went flying off with next to no resistance. She had already let go of it. Winona's true strike was the one she was making with the self-defense knife in her right hand.

No sooner had her sword been tossed away than she shoved her other weapon into the armoire. Unfortunately, when she did, she didn't feel the soft give of flesh like she'd expected. Something hard had met Winona's attack.

A naked sword glinted in the darkness. That was what had stopped her knife.

Not bad!

The blade was digging into the knife's hilt, preventing it from going any farther.

Winona was impressed. Whoever this burglar was, they managed to stave off her chain of blows narrowly.

It was a vain struggle, though.

The moment they chose to hide in that wardrobe with no way to escape, it had become their coffin. Winona pushed the knife forward with all her strength—

"P-please waaaaaiiiiit!"

—and when she did, she and Lyrule heard a decidedly out-of-place feminine shriek.

Wait, was that...?!

Recognizing the voice, Lyrule rushed into the room and turned her gaze toward the wardrobe.

"J-Jeanne?!"

Inside was their new ally that Shinobu had poached from the Blue Brigade. The former Imperial Silver Knight Jeanne Leblanc.

The identity of the assailant left Lyrule speechless.

When Winona realized that, she let up on her knife just a little and shot her a question. "What, you know her?"

"Ah yes. She's a member of the Order of the Seven Luminaries, like Mr. Bernard."

"So you're saying the suspicious person was one of his knights all along?"

Jeanne frantically shook her head to deny it. "S-suspicious person?! Me? No, no, this is all a misunderstanding! I—I can explain!"

"A misunderstanding, huh? Don't think you're talking your way outta this one, missy." Winona pressed back down on her knife.

However, Lyrule quickly put a hand on the older woman's shoulder. "Winona, would you let me talk to her for a moment?"

"…Fine."

Winona, still on her guard, lowered her knife and took a step back. Lyrule stepped forward as though trading places with her, then spoke to Jeanne. "Jeanne, um…what exactly are you doing, lurking in a place like this?"

Jeanne stepped out from the wardrobe and began explaining the situation. Why had she been sneaking around Zest's house? Oddly enough…it was the exact same reason Lyrule and Winona were there.

"From your conversation just now, it sounds like you already know, but I heard that, ever since he got injured, Commander Bernard's had a suspicious figure following him. The commander only got hurt because he was protecting me, so I thought that, this time, I should be the one to guard him…"

"So you're saying you came here to protect him from them, just like us?"

"Exactly." Jeanne nodded.

Lyrule had heard from Shinobu just how strong Jeanne's moral character was. It was hard to imagine that she was working with the nobles. In all likelihood, she was telling the truth.

That was enough to satisfy Lyrule. "What, so it was a false alarm?" Winona sighed. "Still, you shouldn't go sneaking into a person's house all suspicious-like."

"I-I'm terribly sorry." Jeanne bowed apologetically. "But even now, with the republic established, the commander still has many enemies from when the empire was in control. With his injuries rendering him immobile, I couldn't overlook the possibility that they would take that opportunity to claim his life. Up until yesterday, I was merely watching over his family in secret to make sure no such villains could attack them, but given the news about this suspicious stalker, it would seem I was lax in my guard. That's why I decided to hide somewhere that would allow me to rush to protect Commander Bernard at a moment's notice, impropriety be damned."

"Ah, so that's why."

Zest had been wounded while protecting Jeanne, so the honorable young woman was prepared to throw her pride to the wind to make sure nothing happened to him. That sense of diligence and obligation was entirely in character for her.

And yet…

…*Hmm?*

There was something about Jeanne's explanation that seemed off to Lyrule.

"It's odd, though… I've been vigilantly watching over the commander and his family, but I've yet to so much as spot this stalker. Whoever the fiend is, they're quite skilled. They might even be a professional assassin," Jeanne admitted.

"………"

A moment later, Lyrule figured out what seemed strange about this whole situation.

Winona, who'd been listening in from behind Lyrule, seemed to come to the same realization. "Y'know, I feel like I just cracked this whole darn case, and the answer is really, really stupid."

"…What a coincidence. So do I," Lyrule said.

"Hmm? What are you two talking about?"

The two of them looked accusatorily at Jeanne, and she stared back at them blankly.

Winona spoke. "So from what you just said, you've been following the man's family around since before you heard about the suspicious person, yeah?"

"That's right. I was afraid that one of Commander Bernard's enemies might try to take them hostage."

"And a short while later, the maid sensed someone suspicious following her and talked to the commander about it."

"Exactly. That was what proved to me that he was in real danger. However, I'm embarrassed to admit that I didn't detect this person in the slightest... It would seem that I still have a ways to go."

"No, no, no. That ain't it at all."

"Huh?"

"You followin'? The maid felt *you* watching her and turned around. But she couldn't see you 'cause you were hiding in the shadows. She knew someone was watching her, but she didn't know who, so she got scared and told Zest about it. In other words..."

With that, Winona thrust her index finger at Jeanne and revealed the decisive truth.

"...You were the culprit all along."

Jeanne's eyes went wide. After hearing Winona's chronological breakdown, she finally realized how the situation had looked from Coco's perspective.

"Oh...oh noooooooo!" Jeanne yelped, her cheeks so red it looked as though they'd caught on fire. "Wh-wh-what an utter fool I've been, t-to cause such problems for everyone! How can I ever apologize?!"

Her own culpability hadn't even crossed her mind. Realizing that she'd inadvertently been terrorizing Zest's family sent Jeanne into a panic. She looked to be on the verge of tears.

The situation was ridiculous enough to laugh at, but Jeanne's expression was heartbreaking all the same.

I feel kind of bad for her...

Jeanne did everything with the best of intentions, but her actions backfired spectacularly.

Given the circumstances, it would be downright heartless to drag her off to Tsukasa and Zest and brand her as the perpetrator.

"Oh, it's not that bad," Lyrule said, comforting her. "Nobody's in any danger, and that's what matters. It's for the best that it was all just a misunderstanding. Isn't that right, Winona?"

"True 'nuff," Winona agreed. "If you were that worried about Zest and his family, why not just talk to him about it? That would've prevented this whole mess."

It was a perfectly legitimate concern. Lyrule, agreeing with Winona, turned her gaze toward Jeanne. For some reason, though, Jeanne started fidgeting.

"Well, you see... I, um..."

Her face flushed red again, but this time, it wasn't from panic and self-condemnation. She seemed embarrassed and oddly tantalized.

Lyrule couldn't understand why, but...

"Ah-ha-ha. What, you're head over heels for the guy?" Winona inquired with a broad grin.

"Come on, Winona, you're being ridiculous," Lyrule admonished. "Just think about how different their ages are. Why, he's old enough to be her father."

Plus, Zest had a child of his own. The more Lyrule thought about it, the sillier it seemed. Besides, it was rude to make wild assumptions like that about people anyway.

"Right, Jeanne?" Lyrule asked, hoping the red-haired woman would validate her refutation of Winona's proposal.

"I..."

Instead of agreeing with Lyrule, Jeanne merely hung her head, face utterly scarlet.

Wh-whaaaaaat?!

Somehow, Winona's bold claim had been right.

Jeanne's reaction made that more than apparent. However...

"...W-wait, it's true?"

"I-it's strange, right? Falling for a man old enough to be my father and one who already *is* a father..."

"Huh?! N-no, I wouldn't say...it's strange..."

Indeed, it wasn't bizarre at all. Lyrule had been surprised, sure, but Zest was a handsome man. She could certainly see the appeal. Unfortunately...Lyrule also knew what Zest had said just moments ago.

For his daughter's sake, he wasn't planning on remarrying. Knowledge of that left Lyrule unsure how best to respond.

As Lyrule stood there, torn, Winona pushed her aside and cheered Jeanne on. "It's not odd at all. Age doesn't have squat to do with love. Besides, I'm sure he'd prefer someone younger over someone his age anyway."

"D-do you think so...?"

"Of course. They always say wives and carpets are better new, don't they?"

"W-Winona!"

As a delighted look spread across Jeanne's face, Lyrule pulled Winona aside and whispered in her ear. "What do you think you're doing, going and giving her ideas like that?!"

"What's wrong with that?"

"Wh-why, Mr. Bernard just told us that he wasn't thinking of remarrying, didn't he?"

"That's his problem. Doesn't have anything to do with Jeanne, does it?"

"Well, um, maybe not, but..."

Even so, Winona was getting Jeanne fired up about a man unlikely to return her affection.

In Lyrule's opinion, that was a pretty cruel thing to do, but Winona didn't slow down, pushing her aside once more and offering

Jeanne a suggestion. "Y'know, this could be your chance. Why not try cooking the guy's dinner for him tonight?"

"M-me? Cook?"

"Sure. It was gonna be our job, but I don't see anything wrong with you takin' over. I'm telling you, a lovely young wife who can cook is a surefire hit with the fellas."

"A lovely young wife… B-but as much as it shames me to admit it, the only time I've ever cooked was when they taught us how to make field rations at the Knight Academy, and that's not exactly something fit to serve to others…"

"No worries. You've got a top-notch assistant right here—Lyrule!"

"M-me?!"

Lyrule hadn't expected to get dragged in, and her eyes went wide.

Winona continued pointing at the hapless blond as she went on. "I mean, just take a gander at her. All that warm, inviting softness, why, it's like her whole body's screamin' that she was born to be a lovely young wife. Plus, she's got huge honkers."

"Wh-what does that have to do with anything?!" Lyrule exclaimed.

"You're right…! She *would* look fantastic in an apron!"

"Not you too, Jeanne!"

Jeanne's sudden agreement left Lyrule shocked. Before Lyrule had time to recover, Jeanne snatched her hands and made an ardent plea. "U-um! If you don't mind, Lyrule, please, make me into a lovely young wife like you!"

"I'm not even married!"

As such, it was a hard request for her to fulfill.

And yet—

Oh dear…

—Jeanne's pleading gaze was the exact sort of thing Lyrule was weak against. She couldn't bring herself to turn the other woman down. It was also beyond Lyrule to admit that Zest wasn't interested and that any effort on Jeanne's part would be wasted.

Caught between two complicated options, Lyrule sighed. "…Putting the part about being a wife aside, I'd be happy to help you learn how to cook. I…I am good at preparing food, after all." One way or another, dinner would have to get made, so Lyrule didn't mind helping Jeanne out.

Jeanne squeezed Lyrule's hands and cried "Thank you so much!" from the bottom of her heart.

The only thing Lyrule could respond with was a forced smile. She couldn't even figure out what to do about her own love problems. How was she supposed to help bring another's to fruition?

Once they finished their conversation in the storage room, Jeanne went to Zest and explained her inadvertently caused misunderstanding. Then, after apologizing profusely for the trouble she created, she declared that she would help the other two look after him. Zest told her not to worry about it, but Jeanne knew that she couldn't back down if she wanted her plan to work.

"No, no, I insist," Jeanne persisted. Eventually, she practically forced poor Zest to let her join Lyrule and Winona.

After cleaning up the house, the three women headed to the Dulleskoff market to buy dinner ingredients.

"So this is what a market is like?!" Jeanne's eyes gleamed as she looked over the myriad colorful foods on display. "Wow, they really do sell all sorts of things here."

Seeing how excited she was, Lyrule inquired, "Jeanne, have you never been to a place like this before?"

Jeanne nodded, a little ashamed. "I've walked through them, but this is my first time actually looking closely at all the goods. My maid, Elaine, handles all my day-to-day shopping, you see…"

"Ah." Lyrule nodded.

Put simply, Jeanne wasn't just bad at cooking but at shopping, too.

Jeanne didn't know how to find the freshest vegetables, the choicest cuts of meats, or the cheapest shops. Lyrule would have to teach her all that, too.

Now understanding just how steep her task of helping Jeanne was becoming, Lyrule again asked a question. "Well, why don't we start by deciding on the menu. Is there anything you'd like to make for Mr. Bernard?"

"O-oh, I don't know. I'm sorry, I don't know the names of many dishes."

"What about something you remember eating and liking yourself? If you tell me what it was like, I'm sure we can re-create it," Lyrule said.

Jeanne took a moment to think about the suggestion. Finally, she replied, "There is one thing, I guess. Elaine made this dish the other day that was incredibly tasty and elaborate. It would be nice to make something like that."

"What exactly was it?"

"Um, it was a rectangular thing of minced meat about yea big with vegetables and eggs mixed in."

When she saw the shape Jeanne was making with her hands, Lyrule realized what she was getting at. "Oh, that sounds like a meat loaf."

"You've heard of it?" Winona asked.

"It was in the cookbook that Adel once brought me from the imperial capital as a souvenir. It's supposed to be a common meal for nobles down there to eat," explained Lyrule.

Winona grinned. "A young, metropolitan wife who can make dishes from the imperial capital, eh? Doesn't get better than that."

"Right? With meat loaf, you don't just grill the meat. You grind it up so you can shape it. It gives the dish a very refined feel," Lyrule said.

"Sounds like we've got a winner. A one-dish meal feels a little sparse, though. Anything else you can think of?" pressed Winona.

Jeanne took another moment to think.

Suddenly, her eyes went wide. She'd thought of something. "This is just a rumor Elaine heard, so it might not be true, but there's been talk of a miraculous food that can cure any ailment. Allegedly, it has a divine flavor unlike anything that came before it, and a single bite of it will cause its taste to linger on your tongue for a full three days. If such a thing really exists, I'd love to be able to get some for Commander Bernard…"

"I-is there truly a dish that amazing?!" Lyrule asked.

"Sounds sketchy," Winona remarked. "It's got the same cultish smell to it as that company my husband told me about that sold lamps that could grant wishes, charms that'd grant you eternal youth just by sticking them on your body, and stuff like that. What's this stuff called?"

"If I remember right, it was…mayonnaise?"

Lyrule choked.

"What's wrong?" Jeanne inquired worriedly.

"N-n-nothing, nothing at all!"

As Lyrule shook her head rapidly to try to hide how stunned she was, she sifted through her memory. As she did, she recalled how Masato had distributed mayonnaise across Dormundt and claimed it was a gift from God as part of his scheme to get the city to surrender without having to shed a drop of blood.

"Well, no wonder it seemed cultish. 'Cause it came from a cult."

"W-Winona, be quiet! Shh! People outside of Elm Village aren't supposed to know that!"

After shutting Winona up, Lyrule turned back to Jeanne.

"Actually, I'm afraid mayonnaise doesn't have all those amazing effects you said. It's really just a sauce."

"Ah. Well, that's a shame."

"Still, it is very tasty. I'm sure Mr. Bernard would love to have some. I even know the recipe, so would you like to try making some?"

"Really?! Please, teach me your ways!"

"Of course." Lyrule nodded. In her mind, a menu was forming.

Mayonnaise didn't really work as a stand-alone dish. What's more, an entrée of meat loaf alone really lacked some greens. As such, Lyrule suggested to the other two that they could round out the meal with a steamed vegetable salad.

With a plan set, the three women divided up the labor. Lyrule and Jeanne would get the vegetables, and Winona was in charge of the meat.

A little while after they split up…

Jeanne brought Lyrule a large white radish. "Lyrule, look at this wonderful daikon! What do you think?"

It was plump and firm, and its leaves were magnificently large. However…

"Hmm. It certainly looks impressive, but…" Lyrule took a close look at its leaves. "Oh, I knew it. It isn't as heavy as it looks, and it's already bolted."

"Is that bad?"

"If you leave daikon in the ground for too long, they begin flowering, and the roots will get cracked. The flowers are stealing up all the roots' nutrients, you see. Once that happens, it makes the daikon taste hard and dry. The ones over there are smaller, but because they've ripened correctly, they'll be a lot tastier."

"Ah, so bigger isn't always better? I would never have guessed… How do you know so much about food?" Jeanne queried.

"Well, back in my village, I was always in charge of cooking."

"Wow! I suppose that lovely young-wife energy you give off isn't just for show!"

"I'm very sure it is."

From there, Lyrule continued teaching Jeanne what to look for in vegetables, and the pair quickly made their way through the shopping list. Together, the two managed to buy just about everything they needed. For some reason, though, Winona still wasn't back with the meat.

Wondering what was going on, Lyrule and Jeanne made for the butcher section of the market. There they discovered Winona standing in front of the jerky hanging from one shop's eaves with a troubled expression.

"Winona, what's going on?" Lyrule asked.

Winona pointed at the dried meat. "Take a gander here."

"Why? Is there something wrong with the jerky?"

"What's wrong is there's nothing *but* jerky. Nothin' fresh anywhere."

"Oh, you're right…"

The only things hanging from the eaves were cuts of cured meat.

The shopkeeper, a well-built, older woman, came out and explained Dulleskoff's situation to them. "Sorry about that, gals. The whole area around the city is a big old breadbasket, so we don't get much fresh game in these parts. Dried stuff's so much more cost-efficient to transport, so none of the nearby villages want to go to the trouble of bringing us livestock. The Amartya Trading Company sometimes has wild boar in stock when they're lucky enough to catch one, but even then, it's so expensive it never makes its way down to public markets like ours."

It was only then that Lyrule realized she couldn't think of a single time she'd seen fresh meat for sale in Dulleskoff.

Winona's shoulders slumped. "Haa… I never imagined fresh

meat'd be that scarce. That's a bummer. Wild boar are so tasty this time of year… And nutritious, too! Eating liver's great for making you get better."

"It is?" Jeanne asked.

"That's the sayin' back in our village, at least. Great for replenishing lost blood and all. Dunno how true it is, though. Dr. Keine'd probably be better to ask there," admitted Winona.

"That really is disappointing, then…," Jeanne said, dejected.

"Yeah, but if there isn't any for sale, then there's not much we can do about it. Let's just get some of the smoked stuff and head back," proposed Lyrule.

However, Winona immediately shot the compromise down. "Screw that! You're giving up too easy!"

"…Winona?" Lyrule looked over at the *byuma*, not sure what she was talking about. Winona turned to face Jeanne. "Jeanne, was it?"

"Yes, that's right."

"Anyone ever tell you that love is the most important ingredient?"

"I've heard the saying, yes…"

"Well, it's true. Now, you know how to do that? You know what specifically you gotta put in a dish to fill it up with love?"

"…Blood?"

Oh my! Lyrule thought.

"Close!" Winona replied.

"I-it was?!" yelped Lyrule, startled.

"What you need is the resolve not to be afraid of sweating and bleeding. You gotta be ready to go to any lengths for the person you care for. That sentiment right there, that's the best spice there is."

"Y-you're right!" Jeanne exclaimed.

"………"

Jeanne was thoroughly convinced, but Lyrule eyed Winona suspiciously.

Winona sounds serious...

That was a bad sign. There was no telling what Winona would say next, but it wasn't going to be anything good. Lyrule had known her long enough to be absolutely certain of that.

And sure enough, her premonition was on the mark.

Winona wrapped her arm around Jeanne's shoulders. "And to that end, let's go hunt us up some wild boar!"

Her suggestion was downright absurd. And to make matters worse...

"Of course! I'm an excellent hunter!"

"Whaaaaaat?!"

Seeing Jeanne wholly on board with Winona's nonsense sent Lyrule into a tizzy. Meanwhile, Winona continued on full speed ahead. "Now that we've got that settled, the first step is to hitch us a ride."

"I have a carriage over at the barracks; why don't we use that?" Jeanne proposed.

"H-hold on just a minute!" Lyrule cried. "Are you two serious?!"

"Of course," Winona replied. "It's boar season right now, so their livers are all soft and juicy."

"I know, but that doesn't mean it's a good idea to run off hunting on the spur of the moment like that!"

"No, Lyrule," Jeanne interjected. "I want to do whatever's in my power to make a delicious meal for the commander... I may not know how to pick out vegetables, but I learned how to hunt boar as part of my survival training. How am I supposed to become a lovely young wife if I don't give this my all?"

"Last time I checked, lovely young wives don't usually run off to the mountains to hunt boar!"

At that rate, Jeanne was going to get completely sucked in. Lyrule had to think fast if she was going to talk the lovestruck woman out of going. "B-besides, it's already starting to get late. Even if you leave now, it'll be dark by the time you get back. Think of how hungry Mr. Bernard will get if you make him wait that long for dinner."

"Ah… You're right," said Jeanne, finally seeing reason.

"Boo. All I wanted was to celebrate spring with some cold beer and some fresh boar stew…," Winona moaned.

"So you had ulterior motives after all…," muttered Lyrule.

Suddenly, a thunderous racket echoed out from across the market, interrupting the conversation. It sounded like something was being trampled and crushed underfoot. People started screaming.

"Wh-what the hell is that thing?!"

"Someone call the Knight Order! Hurry!"

"It's coming this way!"

"Ruuuuuuuuuuun!"

A wave of people came charging toward them to flee the still-ongoing sounds of mayhem and destruction.

"Wh-what in the world is happening?" Lyrule asked.

"The empire didn't come and attack us, did they?!" Jeanne cried.

The sudden commotion caused the three of them to freeze in place.

An older man shouted as he came running toward them. "Don't just stand there! Run!"

"U-um, what exactly is going on?" Lyrule asked him.

"Amartya just got this gigantic boar in, but it escaped, and it's going on a rampage!"

The moment the words left the elderly man's mouth, Lyrule felt a tremendous gust of wind blow past her on either side. She felt an ominous, knowing hunch come over her as she looked to see that Jeanne and Winona had vanished in the blink of an eye.

"Oh, I knew it! They're gone!"

They had charged directly toward the source of the chaos.

By the time Lyrule finally caught up to them—

"Got your fresh boar right here!"

—Winona's exuberant voice was already echoing through the market.

"That was incredible. Who are those two?!"

"They took down that massive boar with just a sword and a billhook!"

"Whew! Lookin' good there, ladies!"

"………"

Pushing through the gathered crowd, Lyrule made her way to the pair of troublesome women.

When she got to its center, she found a massive boar probably ten feet tall, as well as Jeanne and Winona standing victoriously atop it. Upon sensing Lyrule's gaze, Jeanne pulled her blood-soaked sword out from the boar's gut and beamed as she waved it at her like one would a hand.

"Look, Lyrule! Now we have all the ingredients we need for our metropolitan meat loaf!"

Despite Jeanne's radiant smile, Lyrule couldn't bring herself to meet the swordfighter's eyes. At the moment, Jeanne was the spitting image of a savage outland barbarian.

Shortly after Jeanne and Winona took down the rampaging boar before it could hurt anyone, its owners from the Amartya Trading Company came running frantically after it. As they explained it, the boar was bigger than they had anticipated, and the hammer at their meat-processing plant had failed to knock it out properly. That was how the great beast had escaped.

As a knight in charge of maintaining law and order in the city, Jeanne immediately gave them a harsh reprimand for their negligence. She declared that the Knight Order would conduct a thorough safety inspection of the Amartya Trading Company's facilities later.

The Amartya merchants, for their part, were nothing but apologetic. As far as they were concerned, they were just glad that Jeanne and Winona had stepped in before anyone got killed. As thanks for the assistance, they offered the fierce pair of women the freshest cuts of meat. Surprisingly, Jeanne immediately turned them down.

Her wages came from the peoples' taxes, so it was only reasonable that she worked to protect them. She hadn't done anything worthy of gratitude, and she thought it improper of her to accept it. However, it was true that Jeanne needed that meat for her dinner.

As such, she offered them a compromise. She was willing to take a few cuts, but she would pay them its fair market value instead of accepting it for free. Because the boar was so much larger than expected, the merchants hadn't even been sure how they were going to store it all, so they were more than happy to agree to such terms.

Thus, thanks to a stroke of good fortune, Jeanne, Winona, and Lyrule managed to get their hands on exactly what they'd been lacking. They made sure to hurry back to Zest's house before the boar flesh spoiled.

Once they got to the kitchen, the trio divvied up the roles like before, with Winona grinding up the meat and Lyrule and Jeanne in charge of preparing the vegetables and mayonnaise. Unfortunately, they quickly ran into trouble.

"You've never used a kitchen knife before, Jeanne?"

"During my survival training, I was always on the team that

gathered the ingredients. Don't worry, though. I am a knight, after all. I know my way around a blade better than most."

"Well, I suppose that is true."

"Of course it is. You worry too much, Lyrule. Hyah!"

"WHAT ARE YOU DOING?!"

"Hmm? I'm just cutting off the stems..."

"It's dangerous to swing the knife down that hard. You'll chop your fingers off!"

"It'll be fine. I am a knight, after all."

"That sort of overconfidence is a disaster waiting to happen. You have to start being careful *before* an accident happens, not after. And you don't want to hack away at the vegetables like that. Instead, you want to slice them carefully and pull them along as you go. And whenever you're using a knife, always make sure to hold your other hand in a cat's paw."

"A what, exactly?"

"A cat's paw. You curl your finger in like this, so you don't cut them. Then use that hand to hold the vegetables in place."

"Um...like I'm doing meow?"

"Adding cat noises really isn't necessary..."

"M-my apologies...!"

Part of it was probably nerves due to Jeanne's inexperience, but it also seemed like she just wasn't great at any sort of delicate endeavor.

Lyrule felt like she was going to have a heart attack just watching the redheaded knight. One thing in particular that scared her was the prospect of Jeanne trying to peel carrots. When Lyrule attempted to do it for her, though, Jeanne insisted that she wanted to do it herself.

She was trying to fill the meal with her feelings for Zest. As such, she sought to make as much of it herself as possible.

In the end, everything Lyrule had been worried would happen did. Not only were the carrots peeled so poorly they looked like burdock, but sure enough, Jeanne ended up nicking her thumb, so their color was closer to red than orange.

However, Jeanne just kept pouring her love into the cooking, never once getting discouraged, never once giving up, and never once complaining.

Seeing how dedicated she was made the ache in Lyrule's chest grow stronger. Zest wasn't planning on remarrying. Jeanne's feelings and efforts wouldn't sway him. And Lyrule herself had known that all along.

Winona had pulled Lyrule into this whole mess, and she'd ended up helping Jeanne out, but…letting Jeanne work so hard without even warning her made Lyrule feel like she'd done something cruel. For this reason, Lyrule made up her mind to tell Jeanne everything.

"Um, Jeanne…"

"Yes? What is it?"

"Actually, it's about Mr. Bernard…"

As they put the meat loaf in the oven and waited for it to bake, Lyrule told Jeanne the truth. She explained about the conversation Zest and Winona had right before Lyrule and Winona discovered Jeanne in the wardrobe.

Jeanne listened to it all in silence. When Lyrule was finished, she murmured, "I see…" Her eyebrows slumped, and she let out a little sigh.

Lyrule's apologetic face was so crestfallen it was like she was the one who'd just heard the news for the first time. "I'm so sorry… I wanted to tell you, but Winona was being so irresponsible and got you so excited that I could never find a good chance…"

Jeanne gave the other young woman a forced smile. "You're a very kind person, Lyrule, but…you really don't have to worry about it. To be honest with you, I already suspected that Commander Bernard wasn't thinking of remarrying."

"You did?"

"There…were signs. When men who aren't married…and those who are but pursue women anyway…talk to me, I can generally gauge their interest in me from their body language and how they look at me. Commander Bernard always seems relaxed, no matter who he's speaking with."

Lyrule was familiar with what Jeanne was talking about. After all, the long-eared girl was quite attractive herself, so it was fairly common for people to show that kind of interest in her. Such a thing was entirely natural. Just as Lyrule was attracted to Tsukasa, most everyone instinctively sought the affection of others. That was simply the way the majority of people were wired.

However, Jeanne was right. Lyrule had never gotten that vibe from Zest. It was as though he didn't need that kind of connection with the opposite sex at all. He was complete as a person all on his own. Jeanne had picked up on that and had grown suspicious that the commander didn't need her in his life. At least, not that way.

Yet…

"But that's fine. It is what it is," Jeanne declared, resigned.

"Huh?"

"This is…the first time in my life I've ever felt this way about a man. I know that he's worried about his daughter, and I understand that a younger woman courting him might prove annoying. Even so, I think that if I don't get a little selfish about what I want, I'll regret it for the rest of my life."

Jeanne's cheeks flushed scarlet as she made her bashful declaration and laid her feelings bare.

Faced with such a bold avowal, Lyrule—

"Regret it…for the rest of your life…"

—couldn't help but think of her own circumstances.

What about her? Would she regret it? The answer was obvious.

"Ah! Lyrule, look!"

Jeanne leaped up from her chair and dashed over to the brick oven. "It's finished! See how delicious it looks?"

A savory aroma wafted up from the meat loaf atop its metal platter as Jeanne showed it to Lyrule. It was a perfect rectangle and full to bursting with flavor. The moment the two cut into it, succulent juices would no doubt come exploding out.

Lyrule gave it a big nod. "It looks lovely. *Very* metropolitan."

Afterward, Jeanne, Winona, and Lyrule sliced up the completed meat loaf and brought it to Zest's bedroom along with the salad and some bread.

Upon seeing his dinnertime menu, Zest let out an amazed sound. "Oh-ho... Meat loaf, huh?"

"Oh, so you've heard of it?"

Still seated on his bunk, Zest answered Winona's question with a nod. "My girl can't get enough of it. Says she won't eat plain old roasted meat anymore 'cause it's 'bumpkin food.' Honestly, she can be a real handful sometimes."

"Ha-ha. She'll grow out of it, don't you worry." As Winona made small talk, she placed a wooden board atop the railing on Zest's bed as a makeshift table and rested his dinner upon that. "Go on, eat it while it's hot."

"Don't mind if I do." Zest did as instructed and took a bite. "...This is great! The flavor's all rich, but it doesn't taste greasy at all. What's your secret?"

"Boars are nice and lean this time of year," Lyrule replied. "So when you grind up their meat and mix in their livers, you get a nice layered flavor that isn't overly fatty."

"Livers are great for replenishin' blood," Winona added. "Perfect for someone with injuries like yours. Jeanne worked real hard preparin' it for you."

"She did?" Zest inquired, almost doubtful.

"Oh, absolutely. Isn't that right, Jeanne?" Lyrule added.

Suddenly finding herself thrust into the spotlight by the unexpected wingwoman that was Lyrule, Jeanne's entire body tensed up, but she managed to force herself to nod timidly. "…Um, was it to your liking?"

Zest bobbed his head with enthusiasm. "Best darn meat loaf I've ever had… I can't let my daughter find out I've been eating like this, or she'll hate me for having sent her back to my folks'."

He gave Jeanne a lighthearted smile.

Seeing Zest in good humor brought similar expressions to Lyrule's and Winona's faces as well. Jeanne remained the odd one out, however.

When she spoke, her face was still as stiff as a board. "The only reason it turned out so well is that Lyrule taught me everything. If I had been on my own, the results wouldn't have been even half as good." With a discouraged look in her eyes, Jeanne confessed that the marvelous meal was beyond anything she could have accomplished alone.

Lyrule couldn't conceive of any proper reason for such an admission, so why had Jeanne done so? It was confusing, and Lyrule opened her mouth to say something in Jeanne's defense. Whatever words she'd meant to form got jumbled and caught in her throat, however.

Jeanne slowly raised her head and stared straight at Zest. She was so tense it almost hurt just looking at her, and when Lyrule saw that, she couldn't find anything to say.

Then, after the silence persisted for a moment, Jeanne made her decisive statement. "But I'll practice hard from now until I can make delicious meals all by myself. And I'll learn how to shop for ingredients, too. So...would it be okay if I came and cooked for you again tomorrow—and the day after that?"

There was only one reason an unmarried woman would want to come to a single man's house and prepare food for him. It was as blatant of a proposition as they came.

Even Lyrule and Winona were shocked. Neither of them had expected Jeanne to be nearly so proactive. In the end, though, the person most surprised by the knight's aggressive tactic was Zest.

His subordinate, a woman young enough to be his daughter, had basically just confessed that she had romantic feelings for him. However, with age came perspective. Surprised as Zest was, he quickly regained his composure, put down his silverware, and sat up straight.

"That kind sentiment's plenty enough for me."

He gave Jeanne a small bow. It was a clear rejection.

Surely Jeanne had been expecting that sort of reply, but her expression still looked like she was concealing a deep pain. "...So you're really not going to remarry out of concern for your daughter?" Jeanne's voice trembled as she choked out each word.

"That's part of it, yeah, but..." Zest paused to make sure he met Jeanne's eye. "Listen, you're young and beautiful, and you've got your whole life ahead of you. It'd be a shame for you to shack up on the spur of the moment with an old fart who's got a kid. Go on and save your heart for someone better."

The commander smiled warmly. It was the sort of expression a parent would wear as they watched over a child.

...The two weren't even on the same playing field. In Zest's eyes, Jeanne was no different from his actual daughter. To him, *she was just a kid*. Zest's response made that unquestionably clear.

Having to hear Zest's harsh kindness made Lyrule wish she was anywhere else—

"No."

"…?!"

—but what truly struck her speechless was what Jeanne said next.

"That isn't a good enough reason for me to give up."

The Jeanne who'd appeared on the verge of tears had vanished. Instead, there now stood a red-haired woman with eyes that held a burning intensity bordering on anger.

"Someone who was so considerate of me…who would gaze at me so gently, even as he warned me to stay away… I can't abandon my feelings for someone like that so easily. You of all people should know that, Commander!"

"…!"

"I'll work hard to get your daughter to like me! I'll get better at cooking! And as for my age, I'll eventually be an old lady, too! So…if you're going to reject me…please, at least reject *me*…!"

His daughter was one thing.

If that had been Zest's only reason, Jeanne might have been able to give up on him. There was more to it than just that, however. Out of concern for Jeanne, Zest felt it was his job as her senior to stop her from making a big mistake.

From Jeanne's perspective, though…that was the height of arrogance. A reason like that would never be enough for her. Her feelings weren't the kind that could be swayed so easily. As someone who'd undoubtedly loved his late wife, Zest should have been able to understand that.

Jeanne's insistence caused Zest to hang his head and softly murmur in understanding. "Yeah. Yeah, no, you're right. Putting on airs and telling you not to feel that way was downright selfish."

That wasn't kindness. A man Zest's age should have known better. After dutifully acknowledging that he shouldn't have made light of Jeanne's affections, he raised his head back up and looked at her.

Jeanne's whole body tensed again. This time, Zest was going to

©Sacraneco

turn her away for real. She trembled in fear and reflexively closed her eyes.

Much to Jeanne's surprise—

"…Man, you've got me in a bind. How'm I supposed to turn down a lovely young lady who thinks so much of a lunk like me? Can't think of a single reason why I should."

—what came out of Zest's mouth wasn't the rejection she'd been bracing herself for.

"Huh?"

Jeanne snapped to attention, and when she did, she realized something. Zest was looking at her, deeply so, in a way he never had before.

The wounded man took another bite of his meat loaf. "…This really is fantastic. How'd you feel about making it again for my girl next time?"

Zest's stern expression crumbled away.

It wasn't a definite answer one way or the other. Instead, he was saying that he wanted to learn more about her. In short, he was interested in seeing where things went.

"O-of course! It would be my pleasure!" Jeanne replied with a nod and a radiant smile.

Then, all of a sudden—

"Wah?!"

—Lyrule, who'd been watching it all play out with bated breath, couldn't hold herself back any longer, and she wrapped Jeanne in a big embrace.

"Thank goodness, oh, thank goodness…!"

"L-Lyrule? Why are you crying?"

"Mmmm….!"

Lyrule didn't answer Jeanne's confused question.

She couldn't.

Jeanne's feelings had struck a deep chord with her. Lyrule knew all too well how agonizing it was to love someone.

Her throat trembled from all the emotions welling up from her chest, and she couldn't get the words out. Seeing that, Jeanne took a moment to reflect on how fortunate she was to have met such a kind person. As she returned the hug, she gave her heartfelt thanks to her empathetic friend.

"Thank you, Lyrule. Thank you so much for everything..."

"Hoo boy! Quite the show we got treated to today!" On the way back from Zest's house after splitting up with Jeanne, Winona let out a pleased whistle as she thought back on the day's events. "Makes me feel like a kid again!"

"That was so nerve-racking I feel like I barely survived..." Lyrule had never imagined that Jeanne would confess so quickly. Perhaps knights really were made of sterner stuff. Just watching things from the sidelines had been murder on Lyrule's heart.

Winona agreed with Lyrule's sentiment. However... "Ha-ha-ha. Still, she never woulda moved the guy's heart if she hadn't been so forward and gutsy."

"You think?"

"Yeah. Zest just saw Jeanne as a kid, so she had to power through that false impression with brute force. That was some impressive stuff she did." After commending Jeanne, Winona turned to Lyrule with a mischievous grin. "You might wanna take notes."

"...Was I really that obvious?"

"You pick up a thing or two after bein' a woman for three decades. Plus, c'mon. I'm basically your mom, remember?"

"That's true…"

Lyrule wasn't particularly surprised. Winona came across as self-centered, but she actually paid a lot of attention to the people around her.

As the two women walked down the road, Lyrule came clean and confessed her affection for Tsukasa. "It's been weighing on me all this time. I mean, we're from entirely different worlds. By all rights, we never should have met. Wouldn't it just be a bother if I imposed on him with my feelings?"

"If that were enough to make you give up, you wouldn't be agonizing over it so much, right?" reasoned Winona.

"…!"

"Being from different worlds, having a big age gap, none of that stuff matters. Y'know, even people from the same world kick the bucket and leave people behind all the time."

"Winona…"

"No point worryin' about the distant future. You'd have to be a *real* god to know how things're gonna play out. All that matters is what you got in your heart here and now…and havin' the resolve to risk it all on that. Go all out. Even if the worst scenario comes to pass, at least you won't have any regrets."

Winona's husband died young, so her speech carried particular weight. The blissful days she'd spent with her husband had ended too soon, yet she held no remorse. Not once had Winona come to bemoan spending the time she had with the man she loved.

"So? You got that resolve?"

I…

After parting ways with Winona, Lyrule headed to Tsukasa's office.

She needed to give him her report on the day's events and request that Jeanne take over Zest's care.

But on her way there—

"Ah…"

"…!"

—she stumbled across a petite girl.

The young woman was wearing a red hat, and her chestnut hair was done up in three braids.

It was Ringo Oohoshi.

"G-good evening…"

Ringo averted her gaze and gave Lyrule's awkward greeting a nod. In an instant, the air between them grew strained. Lyrule was certain Ringo was aware of her feelings. So when Ringo tried to pass Lyrule by, she called out to her.

"Um! Ringo!"

"Weh?!"

The Prodigy scientist clearly hadn't expected that. Her shoulders jolted, and she turned around.

"You've probably realized by now. How…I feel about Tsukasa."

Ringo paused for a moment, then nodded. That was no surprise. Lyrule took a deep breath and looked at Ringo head-on.

"I…don't plan on losing."

"…!"

"You've done so much to help us, Ringo…but even though I'm really grateful to you, I can't give up on these feelings…"

This was the answer Lyrule had settled on.

Tsukasa and the other Prodigies weren't supposed to be in their world in the first place. If Lyrule woke up the next day to find that they'd vanished like smoke, she wouldn't be the least bit surprised. Even if such a thing did come to pass, Lyrule never wanted to regret the time she'd spent with the Prodigies or the fact that she fell for Tsukasa.

Brimming with resolve, Lyrule made a firm proclamation to the other girl who harbored the same feelings for Tsukasa. "So...once your work here is done, and you all go back to your own world...I'm going to confess to Tsukasa..."

It was Lyrule's way of keeping things fair. She didn't know if Tsukasa would end up picking her, Ringo, or neither of them at all. Still, she did understand that she didn't want to have any sort of unfair advantage over her friend and savior, whose feelings for Tsukasa probably long pre-dated hers.

"I'm sorry for bringing this up out of the blue, but it's something I needed to tell you."

Having said all she wished, Lyrule turned her back on Ringo and resumed walking toward Tsukasa's office.

However—

"You...can't...!"

—Ringo called out to stop her.

"I...can't?"

Not understanding what Ringo meant, Lyrule parroted her words back as a question.

Ringo bobbed her head up and down anxiously. She looked like she was on the verge of tears. "I-it's not...fair..."

"Not fair...? What's not fair?"

It was then that something utterly ridiculous squeaked out of Ringo's mouth. The words were far louder than anything Lyrule had ever heard the inventor say before.

"I—I—I...don't have huge breasts like you do!"

"Wh-what?!" Lyrule, bewildered, let out a hysterical cry herself. "B-breasts?!"

"Th-that's...right! There's no way I can win against your massive chest... You're being a bully."

"Wait just a minute. B-breast size doesn't have anything to do with it, does it?"

"I-it does. Bearabbit t-told me that guys like girls with big boobs."

"W-well, that's certainly true for some people, but Tsukasa isn't a pervert like that. A gentleman like him wouldn't decide based on breast size!"

"Th-then get rid of yours!"

"Now you're just acting unreasonable!"

All of Ringo's usual shyness was gone, and her eyes burned with a fierce intensity.

It just went to show how strong her love for Tsukasa was.

If she was going to accuse Lyrule of being unfair—

"Besides, if anyone's got an improper advantage, it's you, Ringo!"

—then Lyrule had a thing or two to say for herself.

"You've been friends with Tsukasa for so much longer than I have, and you know so many things about him that I don't, and on top of that, you can build just about anything. How is any of that fair?! You help him out with so many things, and you're *unbelievably* cute! There's no way Tsukasa doesn't share your feelings!"

"C-cu—"

Ringo's face went so scarlet it looked as though steam was about to burst from her head. Usually, being called cute would be enough to make her turn tail and scurry away on the spot. At this moment, Ringo was anything but her usual self, however. Even though her cheeks were so red they could burst into flames, she held her ground.

"Th-there's no way that's true. Between a runt who stinks of oil all the time like me and someone who's pretty, good at cooking, and has a nice body like you, it's obvious who Tsukasa would go for!"

"Not at all! You don't stink of oil, and even if you did, it would just be proof of how hard you're working to make things easier for everyone! There's no way Tsukasa would hold that against you. Besides, I've only known him for a short while, so of course he likes you more than me. It doesn't make any sense for you to call me unfair!"

"I-it does too... You two make a way better couple!"

"No, no, Ringo, you and Tsukasa are perfect for each other!"

The two of them were standing face-to-face in the hallway, neither willing to back down an inch.

Or rather, perhaps they were doing nothing *but* backing down.

...What in the world *were* they doing?

Neither of them was exceptionally cut out for conflict, so the argument quickly devolved into a complete mess.

After their quarrel went on like that for a little bit, Ringo spoke with conviction. "...Fine. If you're going to keep teasing me like that, then I'll just have to confess to Tsukasa before you get the chance!"

"But that's so underhanded!"

"Nuh-uh. It's your fault for being so pretty."

"Th-then, *I'll* just have to confess before *you* get a chance!"

"Don't you copy me!"

"You copied me first!"

"Grrr........."

"Hrrr........."

The two of them pouted menacingly at each other.

Then, all of a sudden—

"What are you two making a fuss in the middle of the hallway for?"

—they heard a voice from off to the side.

It was a dignified, androgynous voice that both Lyrule and Ringo were well acquainted with.

""Eh?""

When they turned to look, they found the object of their affection, Tsukasa Mikogami, standing beside his exchange student, Nio Harvey.

"Ts-Tsu..."

"Tsukasa?! H-how long have you been there?!"

"Nio and I were having a late dinner, so we just came up the stairs."

"D-did...you hear our...conversation?"

"No. Not any specifics, in any case. However, I did catch my name once or twice. Did you two have something you needed to talk to me about?"

"U-uh..."

"U-um..."

Lyrule and Ringo glanced at each other.

Because of where they'd stopped in their conversation, they were both trying to figure out if the other was going to make a decisive move.

However...

"Um!"

"U-uh..."

As she restlessly looked back and forth from Ringo to Tsukasa, Lyrule found herself at a loss for words. Ringo appeared to be in much the same boat.

They'd been all gung ho about being the first to confess just moments ago, but now that they were faced with Tsukasa's red and blue eyes, they couldn't get the words out.

Each was hoping the other would strike first. And they could both tell from the other's gaze that the feeling was mutual.

Then, while they were already weakened—

"Something on your minds?"

—Tsukasa was the one to deal the finishing blow.

"""_____"""

©Sacraneco

Lyrule's and Ringo's eyes spun in their sockets—

""I-it's nothiiiiiiiiing!""

—and they fled the scene together at top speed.

Acting on one's resolve was sometimes easier said than done. After all, courage was built on the accumulation of the actions a person had taken in the past. Getting yourself worked up might make you think you were ready to do something, but it hardly made for much of a foothold in reality. It would crumble in the face of a stiff breeze.

As it was, Ringo and Lyrule still had plenty of hurdles left to overcome. That fact became painfully clear while the pair made their expeditious retreat.

"What was that about?"

Tsukasa tilted his head to the side as he watched the two of them leave.

I could have sworn they mentioned my name...

He wondered if, perhaps, he'd misheard. After standing still for a moment and considering the situation, he decided, "Well, if it's important, I'm sure they'll get back to me at some point."

Choosing not to worry about it anymore, Tsukasa set off in the opposite direction of Ringo and Lyrule.

Hmm?

"........."

Beside him, Nio Harvey was standing stock-still and staring after Lyrule and Ringo. There was no emotion in his eyes. They looked like little glass beads.

"Nio?"

Nio's golden fox ears twitched when he heard his name, and he looked over at Tsukasa. "Y-yes? What is it?" He sounded a little surprised, but his eyes had regained their usual friendly gleam.

"Did you need something from them?"

"Hmm? Why do you ask?"

"…It's just that you were watching Ringo and Lyrule so intently, I figured you might have some business with them."

"No. Not that I can think of, at least." Nio tilted his head in confusion. It didn't look like he was lying.

Maybe he'd just been spacing out from fatigue. Tsukasa knew that he'd been pushing a lot of his odd jobs onto Nio's plate.

As such—

"I have a meeting with someone after this, so you should take the rest of the day off."

—he encouraged Nio to head back to his room and get some rest.

"You're still working, Mr. Tsukasa, even at such a late hour?"

"Yeah. The country's foundations are largely stable now, but there's still a lot of work to be done before we can hand control of the government over to the people."

"That's right. You mentioned something about…elections? Where every person in the nation gets a vote on who should lead the state?"

Tsukasa nodded. "You split the country up into regions, and through elections, each region selects a representative. Entrusting the Republic of Elm's reins to a National Assembly made up of those representatives is our current provisional government's primary goal."

"But…isn't that basically just voting on who gets to be nobles? Won't things get out of hand when all the farmers and merchants and carpenters and everyone else all go and throw their hats into the ring?"

"That's definitely a concern. We'll probably have to set up an election-deposit system and other rules to prevent things from descending into chaos. In my opinion, though, I would be pretty happy if the populace ended up taking to politics so proactively."

"Really?"

"Absolutely. The moment people stop proactively engaging with their democracy is the moment it starts decaying from within. After all, a democratic nation's populace is the mechanism by which it purifies itself of rot. If the masses grow negligent in their responsibility, then the entire system falls apart. That's why it's imperative that people need to be aware of the rights and responsibilities they carry constantly. Instead of lamenting the system's decay, they need to acknowledge that it is a direct result of the fruits of their labor. When the folks lose sight of that fact, they cause democracy to crumble."

"So because they don't have a king to push that responsibility onto, them living or dying is all their own fault? Wow, at first it sounds like equality for all would be really good for commoners, but in reality, living in a democracy is actually a lot more work than living in a monarchy..."

"That's right. But you have to remember that responsibilities aren't the only things they earn. They gain honor, too."

"How so?"

"For example, let's say that there was a prosperous era where nobody starved, and people were free from the fires of war. If that happened in a monarchy, then the king would get all the credit to himself.

"When that comes about in a democracy, however, the honor for that accomplishment belongs to all. Great cultural triumphs will be owed to all the nation's people who came together to love their neighbors, raise the downtrodden, and support one another.

"It might last a decade or even only a year, but that's fine. It will be a shared success, sustained by the efforts of all involved. That will be something humanity will forever be able to point to with pride. 'There was an era, a proud moment in time,' they will be able to say, 'when humankind lived together hand in hand.'"

Nio seemed bewildered at the explanation. "But…is that even possible?"

One did have to wonder if commoners were capable of creating a land where no one went hungry or died cruelly at the hands of others, and everyone cooperated and lived in peace.

Tsukasa gave him his answer. "I don't know."

Perhaps it was nothing more than an unreachable ideal. As a politician, Tsukasa had seen the cruelty of others' souls more closely than most. He knew that, by nature, humans were wicked and sinful. Conversely, that was precisely why…

"But for me, I believe it's a goal worth risking everything in pursuit of."

It was true. Humanity was evil by nature. History had borne that fact out time and time again. Perhaps paradoxically, people also possessed the kindness required to love others. Even the most heinous dictators and criminals still had mothers, fathers, children, and friends. All had someone they loved and who loved them in return.

Tsukasa had a dream.

He hoped everyone could someday realize just how noble that emotion they carried within them was. He wanted them to comprehend just how wonderful humankind could be. Once each person realized how much potential they had, that seemingly impossible ideal would become a reality.

"…I'm sorry; I'm getting carried away."

Realizing how impassioned his speech was becoming, Tsukasa reined himself in. For now, his aspirations were a goal better suited for his original home.

This world, on the other hand, was immature. War ran unchecked, and its political discourse hadn't even reached the point of developing formal systems of public law. It wasn't ready for such a lofty concept.

Tsukasa could explain it all he wanted, but it was unlikely anyone would genuinely grasp what he was saying.

As such, the Prodigy politician decided to end his monologue on the matter there. "Anyway, I'm keeping someone waiting, so I really do need to be off."

Nio gave Tsukasa a quick bow. "O-of course! Good work today, Mr. Tsukasa!"

"You too," Tsukasa replied, then began making his way up the stairs to his office.

As he did, Nio called out to him from behind. "By the way, Mr. Tsukasa!"

Tsukasa turned around, and Nio continued with a certain degree of determination in his voice. "I...I might not have the will nor the power to dream so big. But...I think it would be wonderful if my beloved homeland could become a kind, noble place where people help one another out regardless of their statuses! And if I can use what I learn here to make that happen, nothing would make me happier!" Nio's eyes gleamed with vigor and hope as he spoke of his desire for the future.

Tsukasa smiled broadly and offered the little *byuma* encouragement from the bottom of his heart. "...You're right; that would be wonderful. And I look forward to watching you make it a reality."

Tsukasa, too, hoped Nio would bring about such a wonderful tomorrow. If that happened, Elm and Freyjagard might be able to enjoy true, unreserved friendship.

"I'll do my best!" Nio replied. He wagged his tail happily as he trotted down the stairs.

...He's got enthusiasm, he's got the drive, and he's got ideals.

It was hard to find anything to complain about in such a decent, talented individual.

The things Nio was learning during his exchange program in Elm would no doubt go on to be a beacon of hope for the entire continent's future. As such, Tsukasa knew he needed to protect him. Not just for Elm's sake, but for Freyjagard's as well.

With his resolve renewed, Tsukasa continued up the steps. When he got to his office, he opened the door and promptly apologized to the girl waiting within.

"…Sorry about the wait, Shinobu."

"That's Nio's a good kid."

The room was lit by nothing but a single candle.

Tsukasa's desk sat amid mountains of books and documents, and Shinobu had been leaning against it as she waited for the other high schooler.

"You could hear us?"

"I am a journalist, y'know. I can hear a pin drop from a mile away."

"I don't think many of your professional peers share that particular talent."

"…Y'know, Nio kinda reminds me of the old you."

"Does he? I can't say I remember a time when I was ever that honest." Tsukasa shrugged as he sat down at his desk. Then he thanked Shinobu. "I apologize for calling you here at such an odd time, by the way."

"No worries, no worries. Not like I was busy… So? Given the late hour, I'm guessin' it's something you'd rather avoid having people overhear."

"Quick on the uptake as ever, I see."

Tsukasa unlocked his desk drawer and took out a softball-size object wrapped in cloth.

He placed it on the desk and removed its covering. Inside…was a hard black shard that glistened and shone in the candlelight.

"Is that…?"

"I asked Winona to bring it over from Elm Village. It's a sample of the mineral-like tissue all over the Lord of the Woods's body. The thing is…it bears a striking resemblance to the substance that covered Duke Gustav."

"—!"

"At the time, we had just learned that dragons and beastfolk existed, so discovering a monster didn't really catch our attention, but…it's been on my mind ever since I saw Gustav in that form. So I took this sample and one of the few crystals left over after Gustav turned to ash and had Bearabbit analyze their structural makeup. The results…were intriguing, to say the least."

"How's that?"

"These crystals aren't inorganic. *They're organic matter, with nucleotide base pairs in the standard double-helical structure.*"

"So…it's not a rock; it's a hunk of meat?"

"That's right. Closest in structure to human flesh. And when we took the DNA from this shard and compared it to the one from Duke Gustav's ashes, we discovered that they were a perfect match."

"…What does that mean?"

"Take a look at this."

Tsukasa took a stack of papers out of the same drawer and handed them to Shinobu. They weren't made of the parchment typical for that world but were simply pure-white printing paper made with Ringo's technology.

"What's this?"

"A report on the experiments I had Keine perform that involved introducing the material to the bodies of a pair of mice, one orally and the other via transplant."

"…!"

Shinobu quickly flipped through the documents.

The pages detailed how, a few days after the experiment began, the mouse with the transplant descended into a state of abnormal agitation and became so violent it actually destroyed its cage. Shortly thereafter, the heightened blood pressure from the rage caused its blood vessels to rupture. Then, when they examined the corpse…they discovered that it had undergone a *57 percent increase in skeletal muscle* compared to before the introduction of the ebony material.

"When she saw the bizarre test results, Keine said that the mouse 'appeared to have evolved,'" Tsukasa explained.

"It was trying to become some non-mouse 'thing,' but it couldn't withstand the change and died? …What *is* this black stuff?" Shinobu asked.

"I'm afraid I don't know. It could be something naturally occurring in this world; it could be a secret weapon of the empire…all we have is speculation. The only thing we're certain of is that there are many concepts in this world that we don't understand yet. The fact that we're even here is the prime example. That said, there's one man who undoubtedly knows far more about that truth than we do," said Tsukasa.

"Imperial Grandmaster Neuro el Levias, huh."

"Back at the summit, he hid what he knew about the memetic concept of the evil dragon. Why is that? We know about a children's story where seven heroes came from another world to defeat an evil dragon ruling over the continent, but if that's all, then I don't see any reason to lie about it. In other words, it's incredibly likely that Neuro knows more about the evil dragon than we do and that this secret information can be found in the Freyjagard Empire. I want you to go and dig up whatever you can on that, as well as anything else related to the legend of the Seven Heroes or the original Seven Luminaries."

"'Cause we need to see the whole picture before we know whether we can trust the grandmaster, right?"

"Exactly. Grandmaster Neuro has presented us with a way home, but…we don't even know why we were called here yet. If we leave without ever learning the reason, I'm certain it would fill us with regret. But if we want to figure it out, I feel we need to uncover more about the lore behind the Seven Luminaries and the Seven Heroes so we can figure out what exactly this evil dragon is. Can I count on you?"

Shinobu gave Tsukasa's request a big, firm nod and eagerly thumped her chest. "I'm with you all the way. Just leave it to me!"

Tsukasa gave an apologetic expression. "…I really am sorry about this. As Japan's prime minister, I'm well aware how foolish it is to endanger our relationship with the one man who knows how to get us home, but…I've grown too invested in this world."

However, Shinobu just poked the white-haired boy on the forehead. "What're you taaaaalkin' about?" she shot back. "All of us care about this place, dummy. Plus, remember what that person talking through Lyrule said? '…You must save this world.' Doesn't that make it sound like something real nasty's about to happen here? Sure, we're gonna leave this planet eventually, but that doesn't mean it's none of our business what happens to it. We gotta look out for it for Lyrule and all the people of Elm…and the people of Freyjagard, too."

"…Of course. You're absolutely right. I'm counting on you, Shinobu."

"Sha-sha. ♪"

CHAPTER 3

❧ The Prodigy Businessman and the Trade Conference ❧

The night sky was starless. The sea of water was dark. The curtain of clouds was black.

Sandwiched between them, however, the horizon line was glowing red.

Fire.

The ship, with its massive sails, was engulfed in burning crimson. And the flames weren't the only thing rising up into the sky.

Shouting. Cannon fire. Dying screams.

It was the sound of combat. There was a battle taking place.

Right in the middle of it all…was a *byuma* girl with red hair. She was the slave purchased by Prodigy businessman Masato Sanada.

It was Roo.

She dragged her wounded, bleeding body across the vessel, desperately hoping to escape the scorching tongues of the blaze. Unfortunately, they were on the sea in the dead of night.

There was nowhere to run.

Roo soon found herself cornered on the edge of the deck. As she stared down despairingly at the inky ocean, a shadow fell over her. She turned around and saw a large man with a sword wet with blood.

She didn't close her eyes. No, she fixed her scarlet glare straight at him. It was an act of challenge, a curse.

Roo hated this person. Taking people's money by force instead of cunning was an act of base barbarity. These savages were just as bad as the ones who'd once torn her from her family. Unfortunately, the thieves didn't give half a damn about Roo's feelings on their piracy.

The kind of person who casually inflicted violence on others typically wasn't inclined to give anything—only take.

A blade came crashing mercilessly down. It sliced up flesh, chopped through bone, and scattered black blood beneath the scarlet flames.

How did things get to such an ending?

It all started back at the four-nation trade conference held in Port City Laurier of the former Gustav domain.

Situated directly across the sea from the Azure Kingdom and the Lakan Archipelago Alliance, Port City Laurier was by far the largest commercial hub in the former Gustav domain.

One day, the Republic of Elm had invited ambassadors from its three surrounding countries to Laurier's city hall to hold an important conference regarding trade between nations.

"Thank you all for taking time out of your busy schedules to be here today. Now, this conference today will shape the future of your four lands—Freyjagard, Azure, Lakan, and Elm. Shall we begin?" Masato swept his gaze over the four representatives seated in the city's hall's conference room as he announced the summit's beginning. "I, Masato Sanada of the Republic of Elm's state religion, the Seven

Luminaries, will serve as today's mediator. If anyone objects, please raise your hand… Since there are no objections, we can continue. Next, I will introduce the conference attendees, starting with the representatives. First, we have Duke Heinrich von Rosenlink, director of the Freyjagard Empire's mint."

The handsome *hyuma* man sitting at one end of the square table stood. "And hellooo to you all. A pleasure to be working with you, my friends."

His blond hair was very long, and he smoothed it back with his hand and shot them all a wink.

Heinrich von Rosenlink.

He was relatively young, only in his thirties or so, and his slender features gave him a rather attractive profile. He had well-groomed hair, long eyelashes, and several showy jewels adorning his body. In his hand, he clutched a single crimson rose. However, while his excessive ornamentation made him come across as foolish, his status was no laughing matter.

The Imperial Mint was the body that single-handedly controlled the Freyjagard Empire's finances, the most massive powerhouse on the continent, and the Rosenlink family had retained sole control of its leadership for several generations. As such, their influence extended over every business on an imperial plot. It was no exaggeration to say that Rosenlink's whims were what determined if the empire's people would be eating meat or potato skins for dinner.

He was, without a doubt, the most qualified person in the empire to attend that conference.

Masato gave Rosenlink's greeting a small round of applause, then moved on to the next delegate. "Next, we have Shenmei Li, vice chief of the Lakan Archipelago Alliance."

"Oh, hello."

The black-haired, fox-eared *byuma* woman sitting opposite

Rosenlink gave her greeting without standing. She was wearing a lascivious dress that resembled a cheongsam.

The Lakan Archipelago was a group of more than ten islands, each ruled by a powerful family. Together, they formed the Lakan Archipelago Alliance. The head of each clan would come together and collectively decide on a chancellor to serve as their king, and a vice chief then supported the chancellor. When a chancellor died, the vice chief would also serve as interim chancellor until the next time the family leaders could meet. In short, they were the second most powerful people in Lakan.

In addition, Shenmei Li had also amassed a vast fortune on her own and was Lakan's most prominent merchant. She knew economics inside and out. Between her authority and her talent, she, too, was well qualified to have a seat at the conference that would decide their four nation's economic fates.

"Then, we have Sergei Pavlovich, minister of foreign affairs for the Azure Kingdom."

"…Hmph."

The Azure Kingdom, much like Le Luk, was blanketed by perpetual snow due to the spirit ley lines it was built atop. Sergei slid back in his chair and crossed his arms. His sole reaction to Masato's introduction was a lone harrumph.

It was a rude response, to be sure, but that stern expression of Sergei's—which looked as though it had been forcefully chiseled out of stone—had the effect of cowing his opponents into submission. Any timid diplomat who went up against him would find themselves unable to properly voice the points they needed to make.

Perhaps his gruff demeanor served as a sort of negotiation tactic in and of itself.

Finally, Masato introduced the fourth person at the table, the representative from the Republic of Elm.

"And lastly, from our own Republic of Elm, we have Vice Minister of Finance Elch."

He was a young *byuma* male with chestnut hair and lupine features. No, it wasn't some other person who happened to have the same name. It was the very same Elch who'd been fighting for independence alongside Masato and the others since the very beginning.

"I—I look forward to working with you all."

"Ohhh my, what a looker," Shenmei remarked. "And so youthful! Hey, young man, how old are you?"

"I—I…"

Elch stiffened up. He wasn't used to being in official conferences. Masato quickly stepped in to back him up. "I'm sorry, but there are still several introductions to get through. If you could leave the personal conversations for later, Vice Chief Li, that would be much appreciated."

The look of dejection that crossed Shenmei's face didn't tarnish her beauty in the slightest. "Oh boo. What's wrong with a little flirting? …Now that I see, though, you aren't half bad yourself. And that sharp look in your eyes—goodness, you're just my type. What do you say, want to fool around a bit after this? I'm staying in Freyjagard for a little while."

"Ha-ha. That's quite the offer, but again, we have business to get to," Masato asserted.

"Tch. Country hicks. Can't control yourselves, even in official meetings."

Right when things were starting to settle down, Sergei of Azure shot Shenmei a biting remark.

Shenmei responded in kind. "Excuse me? If we're the countryside, what does that make your nation? You haven't anything but snow and bears. Plus, what's with that ridiculously stuffy outfit you're wearing? You might still have blizzards over in Azure, but here in civilization, we're well into spring."

"I'll have you know that Azure's customary formalwear is the skin of an animal you hunted yourself."

"How barbaric."

"Don't think I'll let that slight against our people stand, vixen! You want me to carve you up next?!"

At that point, Masato had to step in to pacify Sergei and Shenmei. "All right, everyone, let's just take a deep breath."

People were fighting before the conference had even properly begun. War had existed for as long as borders. There had never been any guarantee that everyone would get along, and small disputes were largely unavoidable.

Knowing that, Masato made no efforts to denounce them. Instead, he skillfully soothed the strained tensions while allowing both sides to save face. Thanks to his vast experience with meetings where two sides didn't see eye to eye, he could do so with just a few words.

Within seconds, Masato had the conference back on track. "Next, I'd like to introduce the members of our respective business communities who are here with us today."

A number of wealthy merchants and government officials from each of the four countries stood behind each seated delegate.

Masato started introducing them one by one.

As Elch watched him skillfully list off their names, he swallowed nervously.

Here we go...

At the moment, Elm had yet to hold its first elections. It had no official cabinet, nor did it have any cabinet ministers. That left many essential government responsibilities unaccounted for.

As such, the Seven High School Prodigies who claimed to be

angels of the Seven Luminaries decided to each temporarily head up a ministry that corresponded to their particular talents.

The Ministry of Finance, naturally, fell under Masato Sanada's jurisdiction. He was the one who'd appointed Elch as vice minister.

When Elch first had heard the news, he was completely blindsided. *"M-me?! A vice minister?!"* he'd exclaimed.

"Yup. And as Elm's provisional vice minister of finance, you're gonna be the one in charge of the four-nation trade conference."

Flustered by the unexpected promotion, Elch had quickly tried to argue against it. *"Huh…? W-wait, WHAT?! Why me?! I thought you were gonna run all the talks about money and stuff!"*

However, Masato had clearly expected Elch's consternation and found it deeply amusing. He replied with a wicked smile. *"Nah. I'm just gonna be the mediator."*

"B-but why?!"

"The plan is: We're gradually shifting governmental responsibilities over to people from this world. If you guys keep havin' us wipe your butts forever, it'll be no different than when you were with the empire."

"F-fair enough, but…"

Elch had no rebuttal for that.

Masato was completely right. If they kept depending on the Seven Prodigies from another world for everything, then they weren't exactly self-reliant. After all, they were just as capable and virtuous as anyone else. That was the guiding principle that had driven the revolution. Relying on Masato and the others forever would defeat the whole purpose.

The Republic of Elm's people needed to get to the point where they could protect their proud lifestyles, even once the Prodigies returned home.

"For this conference, I'm gonna be completely hands-off. It's up to you guys to finish on top."

Elch could understand where the Prodigies were coming from with their decision. They weren't holding back to be mean or cruel. They were doing it because it was in everyone's best interest.

But even though Elch understood the choice…he couldn't reconcile in the slightest how the Prodigies could put someone like him in charge of helping manage a fledgling nation.

"*Y-you're joking, right? I'm just some kid from the sticks! I can't help run a country…!*"

"*Why not? You can read and write. That puts you ahead of half the other guys in this world already.*"

"*B-but finance is about managing the entire country's money, right? In that case, just pick someone like Jaccoy! Aren't there plenty of merchants at Elm Trading who are all way more qualified to deal with money stuff than I am?*"

Jaccoy had gotten completely outplayed by Masato, but the fact remained that he was a merchant so skilled he'd once held a stranglehold over an entire domain's economy.

Elch couldn't compare with talent like that.

However—

"*Nope. Not a one.*"

—Masato had immediately shot Elch's opinion down.

"*You're kidding!*"

"*Dead serious, my man. Those guys are merchants, not bureaucrats.*"

"*So?*"

After Elch had tilted his head to the side in puzzlement, Masato explained. "*Both jobs deal with money, but the mindset you need for each of 'em is totally different. For a merchant, makin' money is everything, but that's not what bureaucrats are about. The vice minister of finance is in charge of the nation's purse strings. They're not in it for profit. If you aren't willing to spend money to help the people out, you ain't fit for the job. There's a lotta people who'd be smart enough to make*" coin hand over fist, but dumb enough not to realize how they were hurting international relations and their own people's welfare in the process. But you, you've got what it takes."

"I do?"

"Remember back when we first got better, how you chewed us out at the feast your granddad threw for us?"

"Urk..." Elch had looked awkwardly away at having his old screwup—or at least, what he saw as one—thrust in his face. "Th-that's just 'cause I didn't believe you guys yet..."

Masato laughed. "Hey, don't look so down about it. I'm not blamin' you. Hell, I'm giving you a compliment."

"Huh?"

"There's not a lot of guys who'd be able to keep the village's finances in mind and say what needed to be said while everyone else was celebrating. But anyone who can't isn't cut out to watch over a country's coffers. A democracy's treasury is the taxes—the lifeblood—its people entrust it with. Folks who don't keep the needs of the masses at the top of their mind while they're running the numbers don't have the right to touch so much as a coin of it," Masato had declared.

"...!"

"Don't worry, I'll fix you up with a team of people who know their economics backward and forward. Make sure you talk to them and borrow as much of their knowledge as you can. Still, it's gotta be a guy like you holding the keys to the vault. Someone with the willpower and self-control to do his job no matter what the people around him are sayin'."

That was why Masato was entrusting Elch with the vice minister of finance job. It wasn't careless nepotism, not in the slightest. The expert businessman had chosen Elch because of the character traits the young *byuma* man had demonstrated.

At being handed such a heavy responsibility, Elch had looked down and thought on it for a moment. *"A-and…you're really not gonna help us?"*

"You can choose to rely on me or not. Makin' that decision is part of the job, too."

"…All right. I'll do it."

Elch's mind was made up. As thanks for saving their lives, the seven strangers who'd gotten stranded in their world had given them all sorts of gifts. The Prodigies had helped Elch and everyone else out enough to repay that debt and more, but they couldn't keep relying on the incredible septet forever.

This world's denizens might be inexperienced, they might stumble, but they had to start walking independently.

That was the sense of responsibility that now drove Elch.

Now, back in the present…

Elch sat at the four-nation trade conference with the weight of the Republic of Elm's future resting on his shoulders.

At the moment, they were discussing tariff rates on various goods, limits on certain imports designed to protect local industries, what kind of insurance Elm would offer on domestic assets in the event of a war, and other similar matters.

There was one question their opponents were trying to answer: What kind of trading partner would this new nation on their continent prove to be?

With each inquiry and demand they made, Elch took advice from Jaccoy and the other advisers behind him and gave decisive answers.

All in all, it was an impressive display.

He'd studied up and put in the hours to prepare for this.

Each question he answered helped prove that his labor hadn't been in vain. Before long, all the stiffness he'd suffered during the introductions had melted away, and his face was brimming with confidence.

Then the discussion moved on to the most critical itinerary item of the day.

"Now, the next matter we'll be discussing is the new 'goss' currency the Republic of Elm plans to mint, as well as the exchange rates thereof."

When the mediator, Masato, mentioned a new monetary system, Elch felt as though all his fur was standing on end. It was like an electric current just shot through the air.

The entire room instantly tensed up, and the look in the other three delegates' eyes was completely different than it had been before. They all understood full well just how important this subject was.

"Vice Minister Elch, take us away."

After Masato took the tense room and piqued everyone's attention, Elch stood from his seat and spoke. "Before we get into the discussion, I'd like to first take a moment to show you all what exactly goss is. Roo, would you mind?"

"'Kay! ...No, no. 'Kay *sir*."

On Elch's instruction, Roo pitter-pattered around the table in a maid uniform and passed each delegate a shiny gold coin.

Those pieces were examples of the goss that were going to become the Republic of Elm's national currency.

As he eyed his sample, Freyjagard's delegate Rosenlink let out a cry of amazement. "Goodness me. The rumors of your technological prowess hardly do you justice. Why, I've never seen such perfectly circular coinage in all my years."

That world had yet to develop technology capable of producing metallic money with such accuracy. Rosenlink wasn't the only one marveling at the fruits of Elm's technology, either.

Lakan Archipelago Alliance's vice chief, Shenmei Li, peered intently at her coin and posed a question to Masato. "It really is something else, yes. One thing, though. Who's this adorable young thing engraved on it?"

"That's a portrait of our deity, God Akatsuki."

"Oh, so this is what he looks like. Kind of a cutie, isn't he?"

"I'll be sure to let him know you said that. He'll be delighted."

Elch found himself exasperated at Masato's characteristically snide response, but he started in on his explanation of the currency regardless. "What you're each holding is a thousand-goss gold piece, our highest denomination. We'll also be minting hundred-goss silver coins, as well as one- and ten-goss copper coins for paying smaller sums."

"Ah, I see. So you based it off the empire's gold and rook."

"Exactly. The precious metal content is the same as the empire's money as well."

The decision to follow a system similar to the imperial one had been instituted to make the transition easier on the masses.

At that point, Sergei of Azure responded to Elch's explanation—

"Hmph. True, they're well-made...*for trinkets, that is.*"

—with a contemptuous scoff.

"...Would you care to elaborate on that, Ambassador Pavlovich?" Masato invited.

"I really have to explain? As a currency, they're utterly worthless." Sergei threw his sample coin down on the table, then continued. "It should go without saying, but coinage is more valuable than the raw material of its component metals. And that added value comes from people's faith in the nation that issued it. But a country's trust is derived from its long history. Why should I believe a fresh-faced society of peasants?"

"He has a point," Shenmei of Lakan agreed. "'Equality for all,' was it? A government of the people for the people, with no nobles or commoners? …I must say, I have my doubts about how long it will last. Why, it would be little surprise to wake up tomorrow and find your nation to have vanished in the morning like the moon's afterglow. Would any of you be able to trust a country such as that?"

Shenmei turned to the Lakan merchants behind her, and they echoed her sentiment.

"Not a chance."

"Seems like a little much to even call it currency, to be honest."

When Elch heard that, he, Jaccoy, and the other Ministry of Finance members standing behind him all put up their guards.

"And so it begins…"

"Yeah."

Later in the conference, they were going to discuss the quantities and rates that the other nations and companies would build up foreign exchange reserves of Elm's new currency at. In preparation, the foreign people were trying to drop the goss's perceived value. That way, they could negotiate more favorable rates for themselves.

It was a massive problem for Elm.

"It's all right, though. This is within expectations."

Elch and the others had seen it coming and had devised a plan accordingly.

Unshaken by Sergei and the Lakan delegation, Elch stated, "We understand your doubts, both about our lack of history and about our radical, unproven democratic system of government. After taking your concerns into account, the initial rate we request for foreign exchange reserves…"

Then he dropped the bomb.

"…is one unit of Freyjagard Empire gold to one unit of Elm gold."

"The HELL you say?!"

Elch had just declared that imperial and Elm currency were of equal value.

To that, Sergei loosed a violent bellow with his eyes nearly popping out of his skull, and Shenmei quietly shot a steely glance Elch's way. "...Kid, were you listening to anything we just said? You've given us little reason to trust Elm, and without trust, your coins are nothing but lumps of metal. Why would we value them as highly as Lakan ira or Azure celis, let alone the currency of Freyjagard, one of the most highly esteemed nations in the world?"

"Would you mind taking that thousand-goss coin you have there, tilting it, and taking another look at the zeros?" Elch requested of Shenmei.

"Hmm...?"

Shenmei and the others did as instructed and held their coins at an angle.

That's when they spotted it.

"Wh-what's this?!"

"H-how is Elm's name floating up inside the zeros?!"

"By engraving the surface of the coins unevenly, we can make letters and images appear on them through a process called lenticular printing. It's a divine technology conferred unto us by the Seven Luminaries, and it doesn't exist anywhere else in the world.

"This means that Elm's currency is *functionally impossible to counterfeit*, meaning you can always be certain that you're working with the real deal. Consequently, *we lack the ability to produce low-grade coins secretly and claim they were mere counterfeits if we're ever called out on it*. Our monetary system is one you can put absolute faith in, *Vice Chief Shenmei*," Elch declared with confidence.

"Urk..."

Shenmei's jaw twitched.

The Lakan Archipelago's islands had been independent nations for many years before coming together in alliance. As a result, each ruling family owned the equipment required to mint currency, and they were constantly battling counterfeiting problems. That wasn't all, either. The infamous incident where the previous Alliance government had taken advantage of that fact to lower their coinage's purity without telling their trade partners, then claimed they were falsified pieces upon having their scheme discovered was well-known. The whole fiasco had dealt severe damage to the Lakan Archipelago's reputation.

Elch had implicitly referenced that episode to give his words a second meaning. Reading between the lines, his message was "At least our country's money is more trustworthy than yours, lady."

The fact that it was the previous chancellor who'd caused the scandal notwithstanding, Shenmei had no rebuttal to such a maneuver. She had no choice but to shut up.

Sensing his position weakening, Sergei turned elsewhere for aid. Specifically, Rosenlink, who was still gazing curiously at the goss sample. "H-hey, Rosenlink! Don't just sit there, tell this uppity whelp where he stands! He's trying to claim that his upstart nation carries the same value as Freyjagard's illustrious history!"

Sergei was trying to rile up the imperial representative so he'd take Sergei's side.

However, Rosenlink instead cocked his head and said something wholly unexpected. "Hmm? Why should I tell him anything? The Freyjagard Empire has no complaints about the rate he proposed, I'll have you know."

"WHAAAT?! Wh-what's the meaning of this, Rosenlink?!"

"Come now, come now. It's nothing to get so excited over, is it? We of the Freyjagard Empire have seen the power and felt the Seven Luminaries' technology's might. Painful lessons, to be sure, but lessons well learned. In terms of credibility, we trust the Republic of Elm quite a lot. In fact, I'd say we're getting the better end of this particular deal."

"Y-you snake! What happened to the man who railed so vehemently against the Blue Grandmaster's spineless foreign policy?!"

"Please, my good Mr. Pavlovich, no competent statesman lets his personal feelings get in the way of official business. There's no love lost between us Bluebloods and those four ill-bred grandmasters, it's true. Our families have been the bedrock of our great nation for centuries, a fact that they utterly fail to show proper deference toward. Oh, they claim to have played pivotal roles in getting our esteemed emperor his throne, but I for one don't trust them as far as I can throw them. But that's one thing, and this is another. Nothing to do with each other in the slightest. But if you're not interested in the rate, then, *well*, Lakan and Azure are more than welcome to sit this trade out and watch from the sidelines."

"Rrr…!"

"…Do be warned, though, Elm is a nation that wrested its independence from Freyjagard on merit alone. Who knows, perhaps the rest of the world is looking at them with much more expectant eyes than you are, and maybe the exchange rate will grow less and less favorable for you as you wait. But I'm sure a brilliant merchant who made her name known across all three of our nations doesn't need me telling her that, does she, Ms. Li?"

"…Hmph. Spare me the condescension."

Even though Elm rebelled against Freyjagard and snatched away its land, the director of its mint had chosen to side with the rebellious nation.

Sergei and Shenmei were both clearly shaken by the unexpected development.

Meanwhile—

Nice, nice… He's doing exactly what he promised.

—Elch clenched his fist beneath the table.

Rosenlink was claiming that he trusted Elm because they'd fought against each other. In reality, that was only lip service. Faith wasn't what Rosenlink and Elch shared. It was a secret agreement.

One Freyjagard gold coin for one Elm gold coin.

That was the arrangement that Elm's Ministry of Finance and the Imperial Mint had colluded on beforehand.

It had been evident from the get-go that the two weaker countries would try to use the conference to lower the goss's value. That was why Elch had conspired with the empire. In exchange for some favorable terms, Freyjagard had agreed to back Elm up at the meeting.

Once the biggest fish of the group accepted Elm's terms, the other two would have no choice but to fall in line. After all, the size of the markets and governments involved meant that the Freyjagard Empire's foreign exchange reserves request would dwarf that of the other two countries put together. In other words, things had been decided before the delegates even took their seats. It was exactly like how Masato had once driven Jaccoy to ruin and forced him to pay reparations.

Elch had been watching Masato for a while now, and in that time, he'd learned a thing or two. For one, trying to use logical arguments to win people over during the conference itself was the worst possible course of action. Changing another's opinion in just a few short hours was inconceivable.

No, you needed a forum to take measures and forge agreements in advance so you could reach your desired result before anyone even arrived. The real battle took place before the conference. The meeting itself was merely where you revealed your hand. Now Elch's preparation was paying off in spades.

Once they realized they weren't going to be able to get the empire on their side, the Azure and Lakan delegates turned around and started quietly talking to their advisers. Then they revised some of the documents sitting in front of them and disappointedly informed Elch that they would accept his stated rate.

Upon hearing the news, Rosenlink joyfully clapped his hands together. "Then it sounds like we're all settled!"

"Hmph," Sergei growled.

"More or less, yes. We're all in agreement over here," Shenmei agreed.

"Well, all righty then! Now that we've concurred on a rate, let's move on to deciding how much we're each going to trade for, shall we?" After speaking, Rosenlink called Roo over and placed a piece of parchment atop the silver tray she was holding. "Between our government and our businesses, the Freyjagard Empire would like to request an exchange of this much currency."

The other two countries followed suit, taking the request forms they'd amended after talking it over with their merchants and advisers earlier and placing them atop Roo's tray.

"This is what we want… Not as much as we planned, seeing as you set the rate so high."

"Hurry up and look this over."

Roo brought the forms to Elch. He scanned them—

"…———?!"

—and was struck speechless.

You're kidding… They're asking for several times more than we expected…

He immediately shot Jaccoy a look and showed him the forms. Jaccoy's eyes went wide.

"What do you think, Jaccoy?"

"Hmm… Good question. Give me just a moment."

Jaccoy took the forms and showed them to the rest of the Ministry of Finance.

They were all surprised as well, but they quickly got to work shuffling documents around and murmuring among themselves. A short while later, they whispered something in Jaccoy's ear, and he came back over to Elch.

"*Sorry for the wait. Based on our rough calculations, it should be fine to accept those proposals.*"

"*Are you sure? If we produce too many coins…that'll make each one worth less, won't it? It'll cut into the value we get out of minting them…*"

"*Quite right. However, our estimates tell us that the demand for Elm's currency is going to be tremendous. If we don't get at least this much money into circulation, we could experience deflation and miss our chance to expand into new markets, which would be a great shame. The more our currency spreads and gains popularity worldwide, the better a position it gives Elm in the international community.*"

"*…Makes sense.*"

Jaccoy and the others were right.

As a developing nation, this was Elm's best chance to get recognized by the international market.

The greater penetration goss could achieve, the more their seigniorage would increase in the future.

If that happened, it would be a great asset to Elm moving forward.

Logically, Elch knew all that. And yet…

…Is this really gonna work out?

He just couldn't shake his nagging doubts. It was the first time he'd ever had to make such an important decision. He wanted Masato's advice. Surely, the Devil of Finance could show Elch the correct path to take.

Self-doubt nibbled away at the *byuma*'s heart.

However—

C'mon, don't be a dumbass.

—Elch quickly scolded himself for that weakness.

All they did was help the Prodigies when they were injured and nurse them back to health. Just how long did they intend on continuing to make them repay a debt that small? They couldn't keep relying on the septet forever.

When the Prodigies returned to their world, it was the duty of Elch and everyone to keep them from having to worry about the people they were leaving behind. Understanding that, Elch forced himself to make up his mind on his own.

"Very well. We've looked over your requests and have no objections to their contents."

"Wonderful!" Rosenlink cried. "Shall we write up the contract and make it official, then?"

"However, there is one thing. These sums for exchange are higher than we expected, so it will take us some time to prepare the currency. Is that acceptable?"

"As long as you honor the delivery date, we have no complaints," Shenmei replied.

Sergei agreed. "…Speaking for Azure, we're fine with that, too."

"Freyjagard's got no objections, either, of course!"

"We appreciate your understanding… Masato?"

Elch called Masato over and handed him the request forms.

Masato took them. "We all finished here?"

"Yeah. Do it."

Masato gave Elch's reply an appreciative smile, then turned to the delegates. "In that case, allow me to go draw up an agreement based on these contents. While I'm doing that, we've prepared a light lunch for you all, so please feel free to enjoy yourselves and make conversation while you wait. After you eat, we can all confirm, sign the accord, and bring today's meeting to a close."

Masato bowed, then exited the room.

After leaving, Masato headed to another chamber to formally document all the matters that had been ratified in the conference.

As he walked, he murmured compliments to Elch for having been able to team up with Freyjagard and stave off Azure's and Lakan's aggression. "…Heh. So he worked things out with the duke ahead of time, huh? Well, I guess after watching me in action for so long, he picked up a few dirty tricks of his own."

It was like night and day compared to how Elch had once gotten railroaded by Neutzeland's market monopoly. Slowly but surely, he was learning. The sight filled Masato's heart with joy.

"But…this time, *your opponents were one step ahead of you.*"

Masato was sure of that. He respected Elch's hustle, but in the end, he'd gotten played. Elch should have been more suspicious of the fact that the Azure and Lakan delegations had put in such huge orders after nitpicking the rate so aggressively.

At this rate, Elm's gonna fall into their *trap headfirst.*

Indeed, Elm and Freyjagard weren't the only ones who'd made a secret alliance. After watching the conference, Masato understood as much quite well. However…he wasn't going to tell Elch and the others that. Doing so would negate everything Masato hoped to accomplish, and they wouldn't learn anything.

…Still, I can't say I love sittin' back and doing nothing when I know we're gonna take a beating.

Elm was flourishing, and the Prodigies' road home was well within sight. Before long, they would have to hand over their roles and responsibilities to the nation's people. That was the decision Tsukasa had made, and that was what they were sticking with.

There's still a way we can bail 'em out if it looks like things are gonna go completely belly-up, though.

There were several, as it happened. All of them hinged upon the Prodigies still remaining on this planet, however. Just because they were sending Elm's people to the school of hard knocks didn't mean they had to let them get knocked out.

Then, a few days after the four-nation conference, the situation unfolded precisely the way Masato had expected and sent the Elm Ministry of Finance into panic mode.

The price of raw gold had exploded far beyond what any of them could have imagined.

"What the hell's going on?!"

After charging into the room in Dulleskoff City Hall assigned to the Ministry of Finance, Elch shouted his first words.

"Th-the cost of gold bullion just shot up. Not just in Elm, but across the whole continent..."

"I know that already! What I'm asking is: Why? What made its market value quadruple over the last two days?!"

"Our members on the ground are looking into it as we speak! We should have more information soon, but—"

The moment the words left the staffer's mouth, a portly, middle-aged *hyuma*—Jaccoy—came charging in with a stack of papers in his hand through the door Elch threw open. "I have news! We found out what companies were buying up all the gold bullion in the Archride province! It was the Qinglong Gang from the Lakan Archipelago, Snegurochka from the Azure Kingdom, the Odin Company from the Freyjagard Empire, and several other foreign firms..."

To put it bluntly, it was all companies who had merchants at the conference acting as advisers!"

"…!"

Hearing Jaccoy's report sent a stir through the ministry members.

After intentionally requesting vast amounts of gold-intensive foreign exchange reserves, the foreign companies had bought up all the gold on the market and were planning on bleeding Elm dry by selling it to them at exorbitant prices.

Naturally, doing so was a gross violation of their contract. The agreement they all signed at the conference explicitly prohibited that kind of insider trading and listed harsh penalties for anyone caught doing so.

They think we're just gonna sit back and let them blatantly rig our market like that…?! Elch thought, indignant.

"Get out there and force the businesses who sold them the ore to show you their contracts! Once we see those settlement dates, those scumbags'll be finished!" Elch ordered Jaccoy.

Unfortunately, Jaccoy just gave him an anguished shake of the head. "That…won't work, I'm afraid."

"Why not?"

"Take a look at this. It's the contract one of the local Archride province companies signed."

Jaccoy handed Elch one of the sheets of parchment he was holding. Elch snatched it out of his hand and looked it over. The blood drained from his face. "The contract is dated a week before the conference…?!"

But how's that possible?

The only reason Elm required more gold was that they agreed at the conference to trade far more currency away than they'd been expecting. That need hadn't existed a week before the meeting. In other words, it didn't constitute insider trading.

"So they just predicted we'd accept their demands and bought up the gold ahead of time?" Elch asked confusedly.

Masato, leaning against the wall and watching over the proceedings, let out a cynical laugh. "You really think they'd take that huge gamble in advance?"

"Huh? Masato?"

"Nah—there's an easy, risk-free way to get the same result."

"Oh yeah? What's that?"

Masato responded by shifting his gaze from Elch to Jaccoy and replying with a question of his own. "Jaccoy, you used to manage a company; why don't you try this on for size? Here's an example. Let's say I came to your business and told you I wanted to buy a hundred pounds of gold bullion. And let's say you accepted. But then, when we drew up the agreement…you found out that *I'd dated it a week in the past.* What would you do?"

"Ah…!" Jaccoy immediately went pale.

"That's right—you'd let it slide. Parchment ain't free, after all. It'd be one thing if the new date screwed up your quarterly taxes, but as long as it fell within the same season, a couple of days here or there wouldn't make much of a difference to you."

"That's…certainly true."

In this world, settlement dates generally weren't seen as particularly important.

As long as it didn't cause problems with their taxes or their books, most merchants would prioritize saving on paper costs and locking in the deal.

After all, the kind of parchment used for necessary contracts like that was by no means inexpensive, and fussily pointing out the mistake ran the risk of souring your trade partner's mood and getting the deal thrown out altogether. Elm's enemies were abusing that blind spot to commit fraud.

"Even if we grilled the gold sellers and got them to admit that the trade took place after the conference, our opponents have signed contracts to back up their story. It'd be impossible to expose them."

"Dammit…!" Elch ground his teeth at Masato's statement.

It was true. The other nations had hard evidence on their side, so calling them out would accomplish nothing. They could merely argue that Elm had intimidated their domestic firms into making baseless accusations, and that would be the end of it.

What can we do…?

As Elch racked his mind, Jaccoy offered him a suggestion. "The price of gold is rising, even as we speak. If things go on like this, we won't be able to produce enough coins to meet all three countries' demands. Shouldn't we place a halt on trading gold and prohibit people from taking any out of the country?"

Elch, however, shook his head. "…No, we can't. That'd be no different than freezing assets."

The trade conference the other day hadn't just been about their new currency. The four nations had also signed an agreement guaranteeing property rights of foreign assets on domestic soil.

Freezing resources without proof of misconduct was a clear violation of that accord. If they tried to pull a stunt like that, Elm would come under fire and be accused of being a lawless nation that couldn't keep a promise for even a week.

"Vice Minister! If that's the case, what if we supplemented our thousand-goss gold coin shortfall with hundred-goss silver coins and ten-goss copper coins? Look here at this copy of the contract we signed! It says that 'one goss shall be traded to the Freyjagard Empire at a rate of one goss to one rook, to the Lakan Archipelago at a rate of one goss to one and one-third ira, and to the Azure Kingdom at a rate of one goss to one and one-quarter celis,' but it doesn't specify anything about gold or silver coins, so doesn't that mean it's fair game?"

"…It's probably fair game, but basic math says that we'd need to mint ten times as many silver pieces or a hundred times as many copper ones to make up the same amount. If we did that, we'd hit the melting point in no time…"

In financial terms, a melting point was the threshold where *the value of the precious metals in a coin exceeded its face value*, thereby incentivizing people to melt it.

If they tried to produce enough silver and copper currency to make up for their shortfall of gold, the market would naturally respond to their orders by causing the price of silver and copper to skyrocket. The moment those prices crossed the melting point, they'd start losing money with every piece they produced.

Plus, most people used silver and copper coins in their day-to-day shopping, not gold ones. Distortions in their values would cause significant disruptions to ordinary folks' lives. That alone meant that they could only do so as an absolute last resort. It simply wasn't a pragmatic plan.

"Elch, you want me to lend you a hand?"

Upon suddenly hearing his name called, Elch turned and looked at Masato. From the look on Masato's face, it was clear that he wanted to help out so badly he was practically crawling out of his skin.

"…Why're you offering help before I even ask for it?"

"I-it's just, I mean…it's annoying, having to sit out."

Masato needed to avoid giving them advice. He wouldn't always be there to look after them, so they needed to build up experience independently. Even though Masato knew that, it didn't change the fact that he was still the one-man army of a president who made sure to attend *every meeting of every company he presided over*. Silently watching over people just didn't sit right with him.

More than anything, he wanted to step in and clean everything up on his own. That desire was written all over his face.

It only went to show how deeply Masato cared about Elch and the nation as a whole. Elch was grateful that the Prodigy businessman felt that way, but that was precisely why he had to refuse.

"We know perfectly well that we can't keep counting on you guys forever, y'know. Sorry I'm such a slow learner, but you're gonna have to watch your student struggle for just a little longer."

"The vice minister is absolutely right. It would be pathetic of us to depend on you angels all the time."

"Elm's our country, after all. We have to be the ones to put in the work."

All the other ministry members shared Elch's sentiment.

They all remembered the speech Tsukasa gave during the founding of the republic. Until they could stand on their own two feet, they would never truly be free. That was why they were racking their minds. Everyone was trying to figure out what they should do.

"When times get bad, the important thing to do is identify the absolute worst-case scenario and be willing to take a couple hits to avoid it. Trying to aim for the best possible outcome when you're already down never ends well." An old lesson of Masato's echoed in Elch's mind. Now, what was the worst-case scenario here, the result that Elm needed to dodge at all costs? The answer was simple.

"...We can't afford to default on the currency exchange."

Once Elch arrived at that, he quickly gave Jaccoy his instructions. "Jaccoy, go send complaints to the foreign companies and demand explanations from them."

"W-will that accomplish anything? They'll just play dumb, won't they?"

"Even so, we need to show them that we won't take their blatant fraud lying down. If we stay quiet, they'll think they can push us around."

"...Good point. I'll get on it at once!"

Next, Elch turned to the remainder of the staff. "As for the rest of us, we're gonna get that raw gold, or we'll die trying! We don't have the luxury of worrying about price right now!"

"B-but given the current market rates, we don't have the budget to purchase enough of it! If we spend too much here, it'll put our future public works projects in jeopardy!"

"Right now, the number one thing we want to avoid is breaking the agreement we made at the trade conference. If we can't come up with those coins by the deadline, it'll erode trust in the republic. Plus, we'll have to pay a massive fine. I don't care what we have to do; we're getting that gold! No ifs, ands, or buts! If we have to melt down Freyjagard and Lakan coins to get there, then that's what we'll do! And as for the public works projects, I know it sucks, but we're gonna have to move back some timelines."

It pained Elch to have their screwup negatively affect other departments, but…if people wanted to call him incompetent, they were free to do so. They wouldn't even be wrong. Regardless, Elch refused to let himself hurt the Republic of Elm's reputation.

To prevent that, he made one more choice. He turned to Masato. "Masato, we're short on hands here. Can you go explain the situation to Tsukasa for me?"

"Got it. I'll take care of the busywork, too, so you guys just focus on dealin' with the problem."

"You're a lifesaver…!"

Masato nodded, then started heading for his office, situated right next to the Ministry of Finance's room. "All right, Li'l Roo, let's bounce. Grab those documents for me on your way out."

However—

"………"

—Roo just looked at the floor with a severe expression. She made no move to follow him.

"Li'l Roo?"

When Masato called her name a second time, Roo finally realized he was talking to her and looked up with a start. "Ah…sorry. Roo was just…thinking." Then, after apologizing, she continued, "Elch looks like he needs help, so Roo's gonna stay behind and help him. Roo's really good at counting money!"

"You sure? Well, it's not like I need any backup on my end, and having another person over here who can help out with calculations'd probably make things easier on 'em. Go for it."

"Roo'll work hard!"

And with that, the Elm Ministry of Finance began working to fight through their international baptism by fire, the gold price inflation by foreign firms. They needed to protect the Republic of Elm's good name. Given the situation, they could hardly blame vultures for starting to circle.

Unfortunately…

At that point, none of them truly realized that the situation their republic was in was far graver than any of them could have possibly imagined.

What's…? What's going on…?

To trade for the gold that they needed, they first headed to Laurier's commercial district. When they got there, though, Elch was struck dumb. None of the foreign companies that had been buying up gold were looking to sell any.

At first, Elch thought it was just a hardline negotiation tactic to drive up the price. That wasn't the case, however. No matter how much he sweetened his offer, the foreign traders just kept obstinately shaking their heads. Not one was remotely interested in even considering the notion.

"We need it for other ventures," they all claimed.

Curiously, none of the merchants' faces betrayed any ambition. It was businesslike practicality down the line. In fact, it was almost as though...*the gold wasn't theirs.*

Why don't any of them seem interested...?!

Elch and the others had been under the assumption that companies were buying up gold to sell it at a considerable markup. They had thought that as long as they could come up with the money, they could still get their hands on the raw gold. Their expectations had quickly been dashed, however. Not one of Elch's people could get so much as a negotiation started.

The bizarre turn of events left Elch baffled. Deep in his gut, though, he already had a vague notion as to the truth of this conundrum.

In Drachen, the Freyjagard imperial capital, there stood a grand mansion in the nicest part of the city.

Inside it, one of Rosenlink's servants came and informed him that Elm was running around desperately trying to amass gold. As Rosenlink played with the rose in his hand, he gazed out his northern window, toward the Republic of Elm off in the distance, and smiled gloatingly. "Sounds as though the market's being quite the fickle mistress. Wouldn't you agree...Shenmei?"

Shenmei Li, the beautiful woman sitting atop the nearby bed, gave Rosenlink's feigned innocence a tittering laugh. "You say that as if you're not the one who lit this particular fire. What a scary man you are."

It was true.

Elch's hunch had been right on the money.

The gold market getting cornered wasn't the result of companies trying to profit off of insider trading. No, it was a devious scheme conducted by Azure, Lakan, and Freyjagard to shatter public confidence in the Republic of Elm.

"Elm's dogs can scurry around all they like; it won't make a lick of difference. Officially, the companies bought up all the gold, but in truth, it was our states. There's no private enterprise at work here—this is war, waged with gold and silver."

No matter how many trading companies Elm went to, it wouldn't do them an ounce of good. After all, the merchants didn't even have ownership rights over that gold bullion. None could sell the stuff, even if they wanted to. This was especially true because the actual owners were the governments of the nations the traders operated out of.

"If they fail to amass the gold and default on their contract, public trust in Elm will collapse into nothing. And if they forcibly seize the gold or restrict exports, they'll violate the property rights agreement they just signed, and that will cause faith in them to crater as well. It's damned if they do, damned if they don't. Once nobody trusts them anymore, we'll be able to buy up their new currency for pocket change. We'll have them by the neck, and that'll let us force through whatever favorable treaties we want... You're a bad, bad man, you know," Shenmei cooed.

"...It's hardly my fault they're so brainless. Even though the Four Grandmasters' incompetence let them found a nation, it's nothing more than a colony of half-wits. How could a group like them ever hope to govern a country? Don't they know that education and grace run in their veins? Peasants like them *exist* to be ruled by us Bluebloods... Isn't that right?" Rosenlink turned his gaze to the young female maid who brought him the information earlier. "What is it you uneducated, unrefined people are good for?"

"........."

The maid walked over to him, knelt, and began licking his boots.

She knew that Rosenlink had the power to destroy not just her but her entire family. He'd already proven as much on that day when an idle whim inspired him to take her fiancé from her by pinning an imagined crime on him and sending him to the executioner's block.

That was why this poor woman was utterly subservient to him.

Rosenlink looked down at the maid with satisfaction. "…Precisely. You worthless creatures exist to crawl on the ground, cater to us Bluebloods, and lick our shoes. That's what it means to be a peasant."

As far as the Rosenlink family, who'd maintained sole control of a critical imperial office for generations, was concerned, that was an unshakable, inviolable law. To them, the Republic of Elm, with its declarations of equality for all, was a blight that needed to be stamped out.

Rosenlink spoke once more. "Elm isn't the only one in the wrong, mind you. Ever since our war-loving kaiser took the throne, his needless valuing of military glory has damaged even a nation as mighty as our Freyjagard Empire. Naming those mangy, lowborn mutts as the Four Grandmasters? It's a crying shame, I tell you."

That was a mistake that needed correcting.

"After his defeat at Elm's hands, though, the Blue Grandmaster's fall from grace is all but assured. With that, and with my scheme destroying Elm's credibility, hopefully, the kaiser will finally open his eyes. He'll realize that blood is the be-all and end-all and that we noble Bluebloods are the only ones fit to rule. And when that happens…we'll finally be able to show those Four Grandmaster wretches where they stand. Like *so*."

"Agh!"

A muffled scream rose up from beneath Rosenlink's boot. He was trampling down on the maid's fingers nearly hard enough to break her bones. However, the woman didn't fight back. Even with her bones creaking from the pressure, she just kept on licking Rosenlink's shoe.

The sight of her miserable figure filled Rosenlink with obvious glee. The scene was a microcosm of Freyjagard's corruption and the true nature of autocracy in general. It made for a society where people were forever divided into the rulers and the ruled. There was no justice there.

When people held power over others, they would invariably use it for cruel ends. That psychological tendency had been proven in the Stanford prison experiment, a famous exercise where everyday people were split up into guards and prisoners. In that test, it had taken less than a week for the "guards" to start mercilessly abusing the "prisoners" with relish.

Being able to freely control other beings who resembled yourself was a pleasure just as addictive as any narcotic. For generations, the Bluebloods had enjoyed that as though it was a matter of course. Such an institution would warp the psyche of just about anyone.

Like a group of patients with the same mental disease, the entire ruling class was sick.

However, there was no one there to admonish them, nor any doctor who could heal their malignant souls.

"I do love a strong, clever nobleman." Shenmei Li leaned in seductively and whispered in Rosenlink's ear. "When you take power, I do hope the Li clan can rely on your support."

"But of course. We of noble blood are, if nothing else, patrons of the beautiful."

Azure. Lakan. Freyjagard.

Those were the three countries that had bought up gold as part of their plot to obstruct Elm from issuing their new currency.

At that moment, though, not a single person in the Republic of Elm had realized that it wasn't just foreign companies engaging in insider trading. It was a calculated, national-level plot to devalue the Republic of Elm itself. Not a single person aside from Prodigy businessman Masato Sanada, that was.

He'd grown wise to the plan during the trade conference. As a result, he had a pretty good idea of how things would develop from there. Unfortunately, he also knew that he needed to help foster growth in Elch and the other ministry members, so he kept his mouth shut and went to request a budget revision from Tsukasa as they'd asked him to.

Tsukasa readily agreed. "Got it. I'll swap out the budgets and allocate emergency funds to cover your excess expenses from the gold price hike."

From atop the sofa, Masato gave Tsukasa a wry grin. "Swap 'em out, huh? So you already had a new one ready to fire off?"

"I was the one who advocated transferring our work over to this world's people. It would be irresponsible of me not to have contingencies ready to back them up with."

Tsukasa had a habit of always being prepared for anything. It was very like him.

He might not have been at the trade conference, so he couldn't have predicted the particulars, but taking measures to prevent budget overages from causing administrative problems was well within his capabilities.

"'Can't keep leaning on us forever'—is that how he put it? I do like the sound of that," Tsukasa remarked enthusiastically.

Masato nodded and responded in kind. "Yeah, and he's bein' a good influence on the others, too."

"That just goes to show how you picked the right people for the job."

"Well, sure. Who the hell do you think I am?"

Back on Earth, Masato was the leader of the largest business conglomerate in the world, the Sanada Group, and he was the president of every one of its member companies. It was safe to say that Masato knew a thing or two about human resources.

Even back when they were fighting against Neutzeland in Dormundt, Masato's keen eye had already picked up on Elch's latent talent. Elch wasn't suited to the life of a merchant, but he would make a damn good bureaucrat.

"A person's sense of responsibility is the bedrock of their character. Without that, they've got nothin' going for 'em. Right now, all Elch's got are drive and bravado, but...he's got that bedrock, and skills'll come in time. He's gonna make for an honest, reliable civil servant someday. Winona raised him well."

"Then I'll be expecting great things from him," Tsukasa responded.

Masato was never wrong about those kinds of things.

Tsukasa nodded...then murmured, "That aside..." with a look of exasperation on his face. "We brokered the peace deal just days ago, but it would seem they're coming after us already."

"The Bluebloods, was it? Those noble diehards who're pissed off that the emperor picked a bunch of nobodies to be his Four Grandmasters?" confirmed Masato.

"That's right. As I understand it, the empire is divided between the Four Grandmasters, who hold true power, and the Bluebloods, who despise them for encroaching on their privileges," said Tsukasa.

"The way they see it, it probably looks like we just kicked the Blue Grandmaster's ass, so they think it's their chance to win back their power. Neuro's from another world like we are, though, so I can't imagine anyone from this world poses much of a threat to him... Hang on, why *is* Neuro workin' for the Freyjagard emperor? The grandmasters were supposedly the ones who won him the throne, but he seemed pretty fine throwing away land like it was nothing. Didn't feel like he was all that loyal to the empire *or* the emperor."

"Who knows? He claimed that he came here because his original planet became uninhabitable, so it's entirely possible he just supported the emperor so he could steal a cushy job out from under the nobles. Either way, thinking about it isn't going to get us anywhere."

Tsukasa had a point. The Prodigies weren't Neuro, after all. Masato nodded in agreement.

When you observed someone to discern how they felt about something, it was all too easy to end up mistaking your unsubstantiated assumptions for the truth. Tsukasa and Masato lived and breathed politics and business, so they knew just how dangerous that could be.

Because of that, Tsukasa steered the conversation back to the Ministry of Finance. "...Do you think Elch will be able to thwart the three nations' plan?"

"Not a chance" was Masato's immediate answer.

"You sound sure of that."

"The guy's smart, and his instincts are sharp. He'll probably be able to figure out that the gold price spike is because Azure, Lakan, and Freyjagard are setting a trap for Elm and that it's not just a couple companies trying to turn a quick profit. But askin' him to find a way out at this point is puttin' too much on his shoulders. The guy's still too pure for that."

Masato knew. Elch's honesty was one of his great virtues, and it was one of the things that made him a great bureaucrat. This time, though, the enemy was crafty. There weren't any *proper* ways to get out of their trap.

Now that Elm had been snared, freeing themselves through conventional means was impossible. If they wanted to escape, it was going to take some twisted, irrational thinking. Elch wasn't ready for that yet.

His coworkers were no better, either. True, they were no strangers to trickery, but...this was their first time working as public officials. It was going to take a while to acclimate to the new environment.

It was difficult for Masato to imagine any of them being able to solve their problem. After all, the solution would take a very particular kind of person to find. It would take someone the complete opposite of Elch, someone self-serving and immoral. A real picaro.

Although... Maybe she *could...*

As the thought passed through Masato's mind, he chuckled. "Nah, that's expecting too much."

"Hmm?" Tsukasa inquired.

"Nah, nothing to see here. Just a guy who's too proud of his kids. But back to the matter at hand, Elch can't topple their scheme, but he's not thoughtless enough to let his pride get in the way of doing his job. I imagine he'll call me in before long."

"Then I'm counting on you to help them out when that happens."

"Oh, for sure. Wouldn't be able to sleep at night if I knew I let them get had."

A week had passed since the abnormal spike in gold prices.

Thanks to the foreign companies' utter refusal to do business with them, Elch figured out what was going on just like Masato predicted he would.

The gold *wasn't* theirs.

That initial vibe he'd gotten had been completely correct.

"We got played... Azure, Lakan, and Freyjagard must've all been in on it. After Duke Rosenlink made his secret arrangement with us, he turned right around and leaked all our plans to the other two nations. They knew everything, and they still put on that little show for us."

"""".........""""

The Ministry of Finance members, who'd made their way back to their office in Laurier, all nodded at Elch's breakdown. None of them had found any success at their respective destinations. Not a single one of the foreign companies was willing to part with the gold they'd amassed. Negotiations couldn't even be started.

That reaction, or lack thereof, had led everyone else to much the same conclusion as Elch. This was no insider trading. There were national forces at play there.

"But why would they do that?! What do they have to gain?!" one ministry member yelped.

"We made a contract with those three countries to exchange a bunch of our new currency. If we break it, we'll have to pay them a massive fine. Maybe that's what they're after?" another offered.

"That's certainly part of it," Jaccoy responded. "But...their primary objective is probably to destroy public trust in Elm as a nation. It's like the Azure delegate said at the conference—a currency's worth is determined by the value of its base metals combined with people's faith in the nation that issued it. Without trust, our exchange rates will take a steep dive."

By buying up gold, the other countries would be able to fine Elm for breach of contract, sell them the gold bullion at an exorbitant markup, and buy up their new currency for dirt cheap because nobody trusted Elm anymore.

At worst, there was the possibility that they'd get branded a premature upstart of a nation and have their currency issuance rights forcibly wrested from them. Elm's foes were trying to drain every last drop of marrow from Elm's bones. The staffers grimaced in frustration. One of them punched a desk.

"That blond narcissist bastard...! Getting the better end of the deal, my ass!"

"He was planning on double-crossing us all along!"

"Vice Minister, we should send complaint letters to all three of those countries right now!"

"…I'm afraid that's not a good idea," Jaccoy asserted.

"Why?!"

"Even if we did, they'd just insist that it was the companies who bought all the gold, so we should take it up with them. The foreign powers will likely come after us for making false allegations."

Elch nodded in agreement. "Jaccoy's right. That's exactly why they used the companies as intermediaries. All our complaints'll do is fall on deaf ears."

"Th-then what's our course of action?!"

"………"

Elch responded by balling up his hands and pressing them against his forehead in thought.

They'd been able to buy a little of the gold they needed from domestic companies, but the foreign investors had snatched up the vast majority of it. Between the amount they managed to scrounge up and the amount they procured in advance, it barely came out to half the total quantity needed. At that rate, there was no way they could fulfill their end of the contract.

Elch and the others needed to find some way to snatch the precious metal out of the foreign companies'—or rather, the foreign governments'—hands.

That much was clear. The question was, how? Elch couldn't think of a single way to do it.

"I don't suppose anyone has a brilliant idea?"

"""""………"""""

He tried asking the rest of the staff for insight, but all he got back was an awkward silence. Most of them had been skilled merchants before joining the Ministry. However, all that knowledge did was let them see just how masterful their enemies' trap was.

Defaulting on the contract was obviously out of the question. Freezing the foreign companies' assets would be a violation of their agreement. Buying back the gold wasn't a viable option, either. The companies knew they didn't have the rights to the stuff, so they wouldn't even entertain the notion of selling it.

Negotiating with the governments responsible was undoubtedly a barren course, too. The foreign bodies would just insist that the gold belonged to the companies and that the whole situation had nothing to do with them.

Elch and his team were boxed in from every side. There was nothing they could do and no way to escape.

Frankly, the only way for them to save Elm would be to have not signed the currency exchange agreement in the first place. Unfortunately, that ship had long since sailed. All that remained was to sit in silence.

"Got it." Seeing their reaction, Elch let out a defeated sigh. "...I guess that's that, then. No point in being stubborn if it's just gonna hurt our country. It stings, but...looks we need to get Masato to bail us out."

The others all nodded quietly.

It was pretty pathetic to have to come crawling back to Masato after they said all that stuff about independence, but some things in life were more important than pride. At that point, it would be better just to leave things to the angels before the situation got any worse.

The finance administration was in unanimous agreement on that point.

All except for one anyway.

"Wait a minute!"

At that moment, the situation took a turn that not even Masato, the man who'd seen through the entire conspiracy, had expected.

"Roo knows a way! A way we can do it!"

And it did so at the hands of the slave girl he bought—Roo.

With surrender on the horizon, one voice cried out in dissent.

The ministry members all looked in astonishment toward the source of the protest…then faintly chuckled when they saw it was just Masato's *byuma* slave girl. While she was technically Masato's disciple, she was still just a kid at the end of the day.

As such, the gathered assembly of bureaucrats all wrote it off as a childish joke. "C'mon, kid, the adults are talking right now," one of them chided her.

However, Elch cut them off. "Hold on."

He and Roo had studied under Masato simultaneously, so he knew just how large the gap in Masato's expectations for the two of them was. Elch understood how much more talent Masato saw in Roo than in him.

He didn't know what exactly Masato had seen burning in Roo's young eyes, but if he believed in her, then she must have been harboring considerable talent.

"…Roo, you got an idea? If you do, I'm all ears." Elch figured it wouldn't cost him anything to at least hear her out.

Roo replied in a hesitant tone. "So um, y'see. When Roo heard that merchants in those other countries were buying up lots and lots and lots of shinies and trying to sell them to us for lots and lots of money, she thought it was really strange. 'Cause…there was no way that'd ever work out good."

"What do you mean?"

"Well, like, we don't need lots and lots and lots of shinies, right?

We need lots, but not lots and lots and lots. So they gathered up lots and lots and lots, but we don't need that much."

"…Oh, I get it."

"V-Vice Minister? What's she talking about?"

Elch translated Roo's young words into something the confused staffers might have an easier time understanding. "Basically, she's saying that they scooped up every last scrap of gold bullion in the marketplace, but that's way, way more than we need to mint our new coins. They're gonna have mountains of it just rotting away in storehouses."

Roo bobbed her head. "Yup. So someone's definitely gonna sell it off first. There's no way their plan can work out good."

Thanks to Elch's elaboration, the rest of the Ministry of Finance finally caught on to what she meant.

However…

"That might well be true, but didn't we decide that this wasn't just insider trading?"

The staffer had a point. They'd already ruled out the possibility that it was a group of companies trying to buy up gold bullion to sell it off at an enormous markup.

"Even if we assume she's right, it doesn't matter any—"

"It's the same."

"Huh?"

Roo cut him off. Now her tone was firm and unfaltering. "Maybe it was merchants who bought up the shinies, or maybe it was important guvver-mint people, but either way, it's the same. 'Cause…it's not like they all get along."

"!"

"There's gonna be someone who wants more, more, more, all for themselves. There's gotta be."

When Roo pointed that out, everyone else gasped.

She was inarguably correct.

The relationship between Azure, Lakan, and Freyjagard was by no means a good one.

And with the current, infamously belligerent Lindworm administration, international relations between them were only growing tenser by the day.

If a group of people like that was presented with a delicious apple pie, would they be able to split it three ways amicably? Was their relationship that genial?

Each staffer present asked themselves that same question, and each one there arrived at the same conclusion.

As if.

There wasn't a snowball's chance in hell.

"Sh-she's right. It'd be weird for a snooty bunch like them to get along and divvy things up equally."

"Yeah, it wouldn't surprise me if someone broke ranks and screwed the other two over. It'd surprise me if they *didn't*."

"But wouldn't they write up a contract to prevent that?" one of the female staffers asked.

Elch shot her theory down, though. "…Probably, but even if they did, it wouldn't be worth the parchment it was written on. Their big excuse is that the companies are buying up all the gold on their own, remember? The governments could never make such an agreement between them public, and that means it's unenforceable."

Contracts only worked in worlds that had laws. However, theirs was a lawless scheme conducted in society's underworld. Any contract they made would be an accord between people involved in tricking others and trapping them into agreements they couldn't fulfill.

A child's scribblings were more likely to be honored. And so…

"What Roo's talking about is definitely plausible."

"""………"""

The rest of the staff nodded in agreement.

Just as Roo had said, odds were good that someone would screw up their enemies' plan out of self-interest. The whole finance staff was certain that it was possible and, at the same time, amazed at how such a young girl could be so insightful.

It was no wonder that Masato himself held her in such high esteem. Once again, Elch found himself awed at his classmate's talent.

Unfortunately...

"But if we pin all our hopes on one of them screwing the others over, and none of them actually do, then it's curtains for us."

Roo's insight was keen, and the future she predicted might well await them. However, in the unlikely event that none of Elm's enemies broke step, the republic would end up in the worst possible scenario.

When Elch considered that possibility, he knew that their best option would be to ask for Masato's advice and support as soon as possible rather than gambling on their opponents turning on one another.

"...Looks we need to get Masato's help after—"

No sooner had the words left his mouth than—

"Wh-wh-wh-what? Huh?! Why?!"

—Roo flew into a panic.

"Wh-why do we need that?!" she frantically insisted.

Elch, thinking that perhaps she was just upset because they weren't using her plan, gave her a quick answer. "I just said, remember? If we simply wait around for the bad guys to screw up, and they don't, it'll be too late. People's trust in our nation is at stake here, so we can't afford to take a risk like that."

It was the same response he gave her before, and that only served to consternate Roo even further.

She replied with an expression like she couldn't understand a word Elch was saying. "B-but why wait around? It doesn't make any sense!"

"I-it does make sense. None of the other countries have actually broken their silent agreement yet, right? Sure, someone probably will, but for now, it's all just a theory."

"So? That doesn't matter."

"Huh?"

This time, it was Elch's turn to get confused.

Roo wasn't making any sense. Elch looked into her eyes, trying to figure out what the young girl was trying to tell him…

"It doesn't matter if Roo's telling the truth or not. Why should we care? We just want the shinies. So all we have to do is find the person who wants more, more, more and tell them that they're going to be in trouble. Then they'll go ahead sell us the shinies."

…and shuddered.

The moment he realized what Roo was intimating, his whole body trembled with fear. As far as Elm was concerned, it didn't matter if anyone broke ranks or not.

What was important was that they *might*.

Because that possibility existed, all they had to do was falsely accuse one of their three foes of doing so, and they could get one of the others, or perhaps even both, to cave for real. Roo had suggested this without a shred of shame and as if it were the most logical conclusion in the world.

"Did Roo say something wrong?" the little girl asked.

"N-no…"

As Roo cocked her head to one side, puzzled, Elch and the other ministry members' admiration turned to fear.

When they realized that one of the other nations might violate the agreement and sell off their amassed gold first, they all thought the same thing.

Ah, I see. That does seem likely.

Roo's mind had been the only different one among the bunch. She hadn't even considered how likely or unlikely it was. The veracity of the situation had never once crossed her mind. To Roo, it didn't matter. The only thing of consequence was that she could make one of her opponents believe it was true.

No normal child thought that way. No normal *person* thought that way.

Doing so took a particular natural disposition—the temperament of a picaro.

Many of the Elm Ministry of Finance people were merchants, and because of that, there was something they were sure of. In the not-too-distant future, Roo would be a formidable trader herself...as well as a terrifying villain.

That's not all. Everyone also understood that the young girl's plan was their best shot at solving their current predicament.

"Vice Minister!"

"...I'm right there with you."

With no moves left to play, turning to Masato had been their only option. It was regrettable, but they had accepted it because they had no choice. But now...things were different.

Just as Roo pointed out, there was no way the other three nations truly trusted one another. A few baseless rumors were all it would take for suspicion to take root in their hearts, and once planted, doubt was a weed that was impossible to uproot.

That would be plenty to topple the temporary foreign alliance like a house of cards. Roo's plan was almost guaranteed to work. And with that being the case, the ministry members knew it would be wrong of them to turn to Masato without giving it a try.

"Looks like Masato's gonna have to sit this one out a little longer. Roo, we're adopting your strategy!" Elch declared.

"Hooray!" Roo threw her arms up in a full-body display of joy.

Elch grinned hesitantly at how innocent she looked, then started thinking. "Which means the next question is: Who to con…?"

Jaccoy piped up with a suggestion. "I believe we'll want to target Mr. Sergei of Azure."

"Why's that?"

"Process of elimination. Ms. Shenmei is a skilled merchant by trade, so choosing her as our target is an intimidating prospect. And as for Mr. Rosenlink, he played us for fools, and if we went to negotiate with him, it would expose the fact that we knew about it. Once that happened, he would undoubtedly come to question why we would bring such an offer to a man who once betrayed us. That could cause any number of problems for us. But with Mr. Sergei, we could tell him that Freyjagard broke ranks and came to us looking to make a deal. But because they betrayed us once already, we can't trust them, nor do we want to. We could tell Sergei that's why we want to partner up with Azure instead. 'Freyjagard betrayed us, and now they're trying to betray you, so we should work together.' Creating a mutual enemy will make it easier to get them to collude with us."

"Ah. That makes sense." Elch nodded. It was no wonder that Jaccoy had once made all of Dormundt his prey.

He was being forced to walk the straight and narrow after losing to Masato and coming under the Seven Luminaries' rule, but Roo's words must have awoken the wickedness lurking in his mind. However, the fact that he saw things differently from Elch was precisely what made him such a reliable ally.

"Then it's decided! We're heading to Azure to negotiate with Sergei! Ready a ship!"

""""Yeah!!!!"""""

Sergei had returned to Azure, so that was where the Elm Ministry of Finance headed to break the three nations' siege.

There, up on the northern continent, they arranged a meeting with the man in question.

In it, Sergei stood firm in his claim that the gold acquisition was all being carried out by independent companies, so he and his government had nothing to do with it, but Elch responded by spinning him the exact yarn Roo and Jaccoy had come up with.

In short, Elch told Sergei about how the Freyjagard Empire broke the three nations' secret pact and came to Elm on their own, looking to exchange gold for favorable trade agreements. Naturally, them doing so would cause the price of gold to plummet, and Azure and Lakan stood to suffer tremendous losses.

Not a word of it was true, of course. And yet…that didn't change the fact that it was undeniably plausible. The three nations' united plot was by no means strong enough to withstand the suggestion of such a betrayal.

"Rrrrrgh!"

At first, Sergei looked ready to laugh off Elch's claims as baseless rumors, but as Elch went on, sure enough, the blood began draining from the Azure minister of foreign affairs' flush-red face.

For a killing blow…

"And we have the proof right here."

"Wha…?!"

The moment Sergei saw the fake order form Elch had prepared as a prop for the meeting, his panic reached a fever pitch. Just as Roo had pointed out, the truth was by no means a universal constant.

A different "truth" existed in each person.

Upon witnessing the falsified document, Elch's lie became reality for Sergei. He bellowed with rage, standing up so hard it made his chair topple over. "That dickless punk! He conned me!"

"So you admit that it was your three governments, not the independent companies, who were inflating the price of gold?"

"Urk—"

A pained expression crossed Sergei's face as he realized the blunder he just made.

Undaunted, Elch went on. "Oh, don't get me wrong. I'm not here to criticize you for that."

"What?!"

"If you want to talk about cons, then Elm and Freyjagard secretly conspired to advance the trade conference according to our interests. We're in no position to judge you. But the one thing I can't stand for is Freyjagard coming out as the sole winner after they betrayed us. You're right, Rosenlink *is* a dickless punk, and we want to see him get what's coming to him. That's why we came to Azure."

As Elch emphasized how much he hated the empire and the empire alone, he slid a second sheet of parchment across the table.

Sergei took it, puzzled. "What's this…?"

"An order form for gold bullion. The Republic of Elm wants to buy what we need for our new currency from Azure."

Sergei's eyes went wide. He scanned the document intently. "This is a lot lower than the current market price…"

"Well, sure. That price is only there because you all illegally inflated it. You can't honestly expect us to respect it."

"…W-well, but…"

Sergei faltered, reluctant to part with the gold for so much cheaper than its going rate. However, the moment he failed to reject the offer outright, he'd already fallen into Elm's trap.

Elch smiled at Sergei's reaction, then leaned in for the finishing stroke.

He placed his hand atop the order form and scornfully made to retrieve it. "If you're not interested, that's fine, too. We'll just head to the Lakan Archipelago and make them the same offer. If you think you can get the going rate for your gold on the open market, then, by all means, be my guest. But once our offer's off the table, you'll be spending every waking minute praying that the empire doesn't hold a fire sale and cause the price to crash even lower."

The effect his words had was instantaneous.

"H-hold on a moment!" Sergei grabbed Elch's arm before he could take the order form back. "F-fine! We accept your terms! Take our gold, I insist! Felix, go fetch me a pen and ink!"

"A-at once, sir!"

His face pale, Sergei shouted over to his majordomo waiting over to the side and accepted Elm's terms in their entirety.

After concluding his meeting with Sergei, Elch headed back through Kroniskov, the Azure Kingdom capital, and made straight for its port.

"Vice Minister! How'd the negotiations go?!"

"…See for yourself."

Elch went up onto the ship where Roo and some other Ministry of Finance members were waiting for him and flashed them the document Sergei had signed agreeing to sell Elm the gold he obtained through the Azure trading companies.

They all let out cries of joy.

"We did it!"

"With this, we'll have all the gold we need…!"

"You showed up big time, little miss!"

"Tee-hee."

Roo, the architect behind the plan that just saved Elm from the brink of defeat, basked in their praise. Her tail wagged back and forth as the finance administrators tousled her hair.

As Elch watched Roo from a little ways off to the side…he found himself reminded of just how terrifying she was. Thanks to the false charges she levied against the Freyjagard Empire, that innocent little girl had caused smoke where there was no fire and forced Azure out into the open.

Elch didn't think Roo had done anything wrong. Rosenlink of Freyjagard tricked them first, after all. Turnabout was fair play. However, the only reason he felt that way was because of Rosenlink's deception. If not for that, would they still have gone along with Roo's plan? Would they have been able to do so without having it gnaw at their consciences? Elch wasn't sure.

If Elch could help it, he didn't want to have to trick or hurt anyone. Conversely, Roo, the one who came up with their plan, had no such qualms whatsoever. That much had been made unmistakable because *she'd never once mentioned who they should frame.*

As far as Roo was concerned, it didn't matter.

Even though Elm had been duped, that anger didn't even factor into her calculations. The only important thing was whether her method would achieve the intended results. That was the only thing Roo had focused on.

What wondrous powers of concentration the little *byuma* had. What an unerring sense of purpose. That was no doubt what people were talking about when they spoke of "talent." At the same time, however, there was something Elch couldn't help but wonder.

Wasn't a young girl with such massive reserves of potential…just as dangerous as a child with a knife who didn't know how to use it?

…Masato, you know that, right? Are you just helping her sharpen her blade or teaching her the right way to use it, too?

Elm got the gold they needed. They won. And yet, for some reason, Elch felt a terrible sense of foreboding.

In all likelihood, he had his days as a hunter to thank for that. Living in constant peril had given him a keen sixth sense for when his life was in danger.

While the Ministry of Finance was scurrying all across creation to try to scrape together the gold they needed, Masato holed himself up in his room so he could burn through the mountain of odd jobs and clerical work he'd taken off their hands.

By the time things settled down for him a bit, Elch and the others had already nearly arrived in Azure for their meeting with Sergei.

After taking a bath for the first time in two days and waking up from his thirty-minute catnap, Masato cocked his head to the side.

...*Elch's SOS is late.*

Masato had been sure that they'd come asking for help by now. The longer they stubbornly held out, the fewer ways he'd have to assist them when they finally came calling.

He got up from the sofa he'd been napping on, used his hand to corral his hair into some semblance of presentability, and headed for the Ministry of Finance to check up on things.

"Yo, Elch, what's the...? Wait, huh?"

Much to Masato's surprise, all he found inside were two young staffers when he opened the door. Typically, there would be at least ten people packed in there. It felt downright deserted.

"Why, if it isn't Mr. Masato! Did you have something you needed from us?"

"No, not really, I just..." Masato swept his gaze around the room. "Looks like it's kind of a ghost town around here. Are Elch and the others still runnin' around trying to find gold?"

"Oh, you're looking for the vice minister?" The staffer's expression lit up, and he began talking animatedly. "Well, listen to this! You know the slave girl you rescued?"

"Who, Li'l Roo?"

"Yes, her! When the rest of us were at a complete loss and feeling utterly hopeless, she was the one who showed us the answer! She came up with an idea to use false rumors about the Freyjagard Empire betraying the other two countries and secretly trying to sell us gold to break up our enemies' alliance!"

"Wha…?"

Masato was so shocked that the words got caught in his throat.

The staffers nodded in satisfaction at his response. She was so young, yet she saved them from the brink of defeat regardless. It made them happy that an angel was sharing their shock.

"I must say, it's no wonder she caught your eye, Mr. Masato. I'm excited to see what she'll come up with next! Ha-ha-ha!"

Little did the ministry workers know that Masato didn't share their sentiment. In fact, their thoughts were wholly opposite.

The staffers were full of admiration and respect for Roo's precocious deeds. Masato, on the other hand…was full of worry and despair.

"WHEN?!"

"Huh—?"

Masato rushed up to the ministry workers and shouted so loud it hurt their ears.

"When?! When'd they leave?!"

"W-wait, what?"

"Answers! Now!!"

"O-of course! They set out two days ago…!"

"Where to?! Azure?!"

"Th-that's right, but why—?"

"Dammit, that means they're there already…!"

Neither of the staffers had ever seen Masato so panicked.

"What's going on?" they asked, but Masato didn't answer. There was no time for meaningless chatter.

He pulled his cell phone from his pocket and tried calling Elch.

However—

"That idiot must've been so busy he forgot to charge his!"

—it didn't connect.

Ringo had taken the liberty of remodeling all their phones. A recent satellite they'd launched had drastically increased their network coverage. The Azure Kingdom was well within signal range.

The only reason the call wouldn't go through was because Elch's phone ran out of power. That meant the GPS locator would be useless, too.

"Shit, shit, shit!"

"M-Mr. Masato…?"

As he swore, Masato moved on to plan B. This time, the name he tapped on his contact list was Tsukasa's.

The call connected immediately, and Masato didn't so much as wait for Tsukasa to greet him. "Tsukasa, shit's bad! I need a warship, now! And we've got that satellite from the missile guidance system, right? Tell Ringo to start scanning the sea route between Elm and Azure ASAP!"

Afterward, Masato, the confused staffers, and a group of soldiers they borrowed from Tsukasa headed out across the waves.

Why was he in such a panic? Nobody else on the vessel knew for sure. As they traveled the midnight sea, they quickly came to understand, however. The sight in the distance made it painfully obvious.

On the horizon sat Elch's ship, burning crimson atop the jet-black waters. Imperial Mint Director Heinrich von Rosenlink had predicted their every move.

Well, it wasn't quite fair to say he'd foreseen what Elm's Ministry of Finance would do. It was more the case that he simply knew just how flimsy his own alliance was.

That was why he kept Shenmei Li close at hand and also why he'd sent spies to follow Sergei when he returned to his homeland. The spies' instructions were simple: If Elm has contact with Azure, make the preparations necessary to eliminate them by force.

Elch and the others failed to realize just how wicked the measures their partner in peace had prepared were.

As a result, Elch's ship had been attacked and torched. As for survivors…

"………"

How long had she been out for? Before she realized what was happening, the girl lost in the darkness found that her consciousness had returned to the light. As she woke, blood and ego rushed back through her body, and she slowly opened her eyes.

"Hey, Li'l Roo. You're up."

There, she saw the young man who was both her savior and her teacher looking back at her with a relieved expression.

"…Uh…wh…?"

The girl—Roo—was confused.

How had she ended up lying down? Why was Masato watching over her?

She didn't know.

The last thing she remembered was…

"_____!"

Roo's mind turned, and the memories came flooding back. All at once, she recalled what had happened before everything went dark.

It had looked like the pirate was going to cut her down. Right before he did, though, Elch had come rushing through the flames and tackled him. With the pirate thrown off-balance, Elch wrested his sword from him and turned it on its owner.

Unfortunately, the respite that bought them only lasted a moment.

No sooner had Roo been saved than the pirate ship turned its cannons on the vessel from Elm, and the deck collapsed.

Elch had immediately grabbed Roo tight, but the floorboards were done for. The two were plunged into the sea, and the impact from the fall had struck Roo unconscious.

"T-Teacher...! A-agh..."

"There's no need to push yourself. It's nothing serious, but you're still bruised all over. You should just take it easy for now."

Hearing that calm, collected voice made Roo realize that Masato wasn't the only one looking down at her. There was a young man with mismatched eyes, as well—Tsukasa Mikogami.

After Roo was knocked out, Masato and the others hadn't just nursed her back to health. They had brought her all the way back to Dulleskoff.

"We caught the fleeing pirates, so we have a pretty good handle on what happened. Your ship was attacked by a group of mercenaries under the employ of Mint Director Heinrich von Rosenlink," Tsukasa explained.

"Is...everyone okay?" Roo asked.

"Thanks to Merchant's quick thinking, the Ministry of Finance made it out without any casualties. They're all awake and recovering."

Then Tsukasa broke the news to the poor girl—seven of the sailors on their ship didn't make it. In all likelihood, they'd died trying to stop the raiders from boarding.

"And what about the papers?! What about the contract for the shinies?!"

Tsukasa shook his head. "...I'm sorry."

That contract was the physical embodiment of all their hard work. Elch had tried to protect it, but it had ended up going missing when he fell into the water.

Ringo Oohoshi's military satellites were good, but not even they could pick out a single scrap of parchment bobbing around the entire ocean.

Without the contract to prove that the deal had been made, the Azure companies would never give them that gold.

Naturally, the remaining staffers had immediately rushed to Azure to try to explain the situation. But when they tried to get the contract reissued…they were utterly unsuccessful. Sergei flipped on them, claiming that he didn't remember ever having signed anything of the sort. Curiously, he'd looked quite afraid as he made the statement.

Imperial spies must have gotten to him while Elch and the others were beset upon at sea.

Once Roo finished listening to the whole story, fat tears began pouring from her big, catlike eyes. "Waaaah… *Hic*, waaaah… I'm sorry, Teacher…"

"Hey, Li'l Roo, you don't have anything to apologize for. That bastard from the empire is to blame here, not you."

"Exactly. That man will get what's coming to him; we'll make sure of that. You can rest easy."

As Roo sobbed, Masato and Tsukasa gently tried to comfort her.

Going to negotiate with Sergei had been Roo's idea. Even so, she was hardly to blame for Rosenlink's debased actions.

However, Roo violently shook her head at their consolations. "If Roo had just thought a little more, none of this would have happened. If she'd used her head, nobody would have died…"

"———!"

The words gave Tsukasa an insight into Roo's wisdom, momentarily startling him. She wasn't just sad, nor did she merely feel guilty. Roo knew what she should have done and understood that she'd fallen short of that mark. *That* was what she was sorry about.

It had tormented the young girl the whole time they'd been talking, ever since she first woke up. And if that was the case…then comforting her would be meaningless.

Masato knew precisely what he needed to say.

And so—

"That's right."

—he affirmed Roo's regrets.

"You were too focused on getting the gold, and you got complacent the moment you figured out how to. The scope of our enemies' plot shoulda told you how far they'd go to protect it. But you never even considered that Freyjagard might predict another betrayal. Not once did you think they might be watching the other two to see if we made contact, and you didn't realize that they'd take such extreme measures. All those regrets you feel, that's stuff you shoulda been able to see coming."

"…Yeah."

"There was a predictable threat, and you ran right into it. You screwed up."

"……Uh-huh."

"Great. Now reflect on that. What happens next time?"

Roo briskly wiped away her tears with her bandaged arms, then looked straight at Masato with a fire burning in her eyes.

"Roo's…not gonna mess it up…"

"That's my girl."

Introspection wasn't about wallowing in self-pity. It wasn't something you did with your head hung down. You were supposed to look straight ahead and etch an unwillingness to ever make the same mistake again into your soul.

Satisfied that Roo understood that, Masato smiled and tousled her red hair. "You think on that long and hard while you're cooped up in here, 'kay? But once you're better, your days as a handmaid are over. From now on, I'm putting you to work as my personal assistant."

"...! 'Kay!"

With that, Masato and Tsukasa left Roo's hospital room. As they headed toward their respective offices, Masato gave Tsukasa a shrug. "...You hear that? The kid's *reflecting on what she did.*"

"Yeah, that was quite a surprise..."

"Man, when I was her age, I was a piece of shit. I wouldn't know I'd done somethin' wrong until my parents started shouting at me. And hell, even when I apologized, it was only ever to *get 'em off my case.* I never actually got that what I'd done was bad."

"I was similar. Between that and the fact that Roo unraveled the three-nation siege, she's shaping up to be quite a terrifying young lady."

"Tell me about it. I bagged myself one hell of a student."

Roo's piercing discernment allowed her to identify what was important in any given situation quickly. It was a rare talent.

There were plenty of examples where it had served her well. The way she'd spotted the weak point in their enemies' alliance was one such instance. Another was when she'd noticed how consignment trading allowed Masato to secure goods and labor at the same time. Most important of all was that Roo had *found Masato Sanada in the first place.*

However...her ability extended only to the present and the past. She couldn't see anything beyond that. Foresight, or the ability to predict future events, was something you gained through hard-won experience.

"Li'l Roo can take a scrambled-up puzzle and put it back together in no time, but if you hand her a puzzle that's missing a piece, she doesn't know how to picture what's on it yet. If I leave her to her own devices, her talent's gonna eat her alive... After that scare, I'm gonna have to keep a closer eye on her for a little while."

As Masato's mouth curled into a pained smile, Tsukasa came to a sudden stop beside him. Masato looked back, confused. "I'm sorry," Tsukasa apologized. "This was all my fault. I shouldn't have been so insistent about us handing our duties over to the locals."

A dejected expression worked across Masato as he shot Tsukasa's apology down. "Come off it, man, we both know that ain't true. They chose to fight to protect their country of their own free will. You tryin' to apologize for that is like spittin' in their faces.

"'Sides, if you wanna talk about who the biggest dumbass was, it wasn't Li'l Roo for not seein' the attack comin', and it wasn't you for wanting 'em to step up to the plate. Nah, it was the guy who couldn't deliver when master politician Tsukasa Mikogami put him in charge of the Ministry of Finance. I'm to blame here."

As he spat out the words, Masato turned to hide his expression from Tsukasa. "I talk a good game about being able to read people, but I misjudged Li'l Roo's talents. I knew her greed made her strong, but I figured she was still just a kid. Never expected she'd be able to come up with the idea of *leveling false accusations against her enemies to throw off their step*. Pathetic, right? At the end of the day, even I'm just a slave to my biases and preconceived notions."

As Masato laid bare his failure, his tone grew more pained. Much like Masato himself had said, foresight was something that came from the accumulation of one's experiences. He'd recognized Roo's talents, but in all his life as a merchant, he'd never once encountered anyone with skills surpassing his own. As a result, his main point of comparison for Roo was what he was like at her age.

Masato couldn't help it, but that was what made him deny it.

For a second, the possibility had floated through his mind, but he'd written it off as expecting too much from her. Doing so had been a bitter mistake. No amount of regret would get the guilt out of his system now.

So what could he do?

There was only one answer.

"This is my mess. I gotta clean it up."

"Merchant..."

"Don't try to stop me."

Tsukasa tried to say something from behind Masato, but the Prodigy businessman shut him down cold.

"Y'know, Tsukasa, I'm pretty self-aware about the kind of power I've got. That's why I can usually just laugh it off when people swipe my money, steal my women, or when my business partners screw me over. But this time, that imperial bastard laid a hand on my employees. He fucked with my *family*. And you don't just get away with that. From here on out, I'm handling things my way."

He looked back over his shoulder and turned his bloodshot, rage-filled eyes toward Tsukasa.

Upon seeing them—

"Fine."

—Tsukasa agreed to let Masato take care of everything related to the new currency project.

Tsukasa knew there was only one thing that could make his usually levelheaded friend go berserk: having his employees get hurt.

To Masato, his subordinates were the most important thing in the world. Far more so than laws or morality. So whenever anyone wronged them, Masato didn't show them a shred of mercy. He wouldn't rest until he stripped the offender of everything they had.

In all likelihood, that was probably part of the reason he'd devoted himself so wholeheartedly to the world of finance. Tsukasa suspected that Masato's obsession stemmed from his father's suicide, but whatever the reason, nothing could stop him once he got like that.

Considering the relationship between Elm and Freyjagard, Tsukasa hoped that Masato would avoid taking things too far. Still, he knew that if he tried lecturing Masato, there was a danger that the two of them would end up fighting.

Understanding that, Tsukasa nodded and settled for a gentle reminder. "Just make sure that this doesn't come back to bite us, okay?"

To that, Masato merely scoffed. "Dead men don't do a lot of biting." Ending things there, Masato headed back to the Ministry of Finance on his own.

As Tsukasa watched his friend go, he let out a sigh. If he left Masato to his own devices, the young man was liable to end up crippling the Freyjagard Empire's economy just to get at Rosenlink.

When such disasters occurred, it was always society's weakest who took the brunt of the blow. The strong used the weak as shields. If you wanted to cut down the mighty, you needed to be willing to trample over the corpses of the weak to do so.

That was doubtless what Masato intended to do.

Tsukasa respected his friend's feelings but couldn't allow that to happen.

...Looks like I'll need to get involved after all.

So he decided to work out a plan to prevent that. He refused to let Masato's rampage harm Freyjagard's innocents. In a sense, Tsukasa had to clean up after Masato's mess.

However, he didn't find that fact annoying.

On the contrary, he rather enjoyed it.

He appreciated how Masato's pure, unadulterated rage allowed him to abandon his own profits and interests for the people he cared about.

Tsukasa knew that he could never be like that.

To him, Masato's fury was a thing of beauty.

Which means it's my job...to make sure it finds its way to the right people.

©Sacraneco

After splitting off from Tsukasa, Masato headed directly for the Ministry of Finance.

The young Devil of Finance already knew of two possible ways to break the deadlock.

The first...would be to use Ringo's technological prowess to excavate and process a large amount of raw gold from a vein in Elm. During Bearabbit's geological survey, he discovered a massive, untouched deposit in Buchwald, so that would be easy enough to pull off.

However, that plan had one significant drawback—the deposit was simply too big. Based on their initial calculations, it contained about ten times the gold that currently resided within Elm's borders. If its existence became public, their neighbors wouldn't just sit quietly by.

With that much precious metal at stake, a war would almost certainly break out.

Because of that, Tsukasa had chosen to keep the deposit's presence a secret. At the moment, only the Seven High School Prodigies knew about it. However, that problem only existed if the people from this world got involved.

If the Prodigies had Ringo excavate in secret, they could get their hands on the gold just fine. They could then claim it was one of God Akatsuki's divine miracles, and people would probably believe them.

Through this method, Elm could fulfill the currency exchange agreement while releasing only the bare minimum amount of gold they needed into the world, avoid causing any unnecessary damage to the economy, and most importantly, avoid provoking their neighbors' greed. It was assuredly the cleaner method of the two.

Unfortunately, Masato had no intentions of taking it.

He had at first, though. Masato had been fully ready to wrap up the whole situation with a little bow. Unfortunately...his enemy, Rosenlink, had done the unthinkable. By endangering the lives of Masato's people, he had taken a step he couldn't rescind.

Now, Masato had no reason to show the imperial any mercy. Without a moment's hesitation, he settled on plan B. He wanted to burn Rosenlink to the ground.

...Hmph. I knew it from the get-go, but this "public servant" stuff doesn't suit me one bit.

As Masato derided himself for using his government status to satisfy a personal grudge, he opened the door to the Ministry of Finance.

The atmosphere inside was dark and gloomy. Everyone's shoulders were slumped with exhaustion and dejection.

"Masato..."

Elch caught sight of the high schooler and looked up with apology plain in his eyes.

"Yo, what's with all the long faces in here?" asked Masato.

"I'm sorry... We couldn't get it done without you..."

Masato responded—

"Hoof!"

—by giving Elch a light kick to the groin.

"Hurnbglsrbguxl?!?!"

Even though it was light, the stiff leather of Masato's boot crashing into Elch's balls caused the young man to collapse to the floor in agony.

Tears welled up in his eyes as he shouted in protest. "Wh-what the hell was that for?!"

"It'd be one thing if you were a pretty lady, but I ain't interested in hearing a grown-ass man whimper and moan. Besides, it's not like apologizing to me is gonna change what needs to get done."

"…!"

"You still got something you need to do, don'cha?"

Masato's words made Elch and the rest of the staff look up with a start.

Masato was right. They were the Elm Ministry of Finance. In other words, they carried the weighty responsibility of managing all the republic's monetary affairs. They could screw up or apologize all they liked. That responsibility wasn't going anywhere. Nobody was coming to replace them.

This was something that only those assembled here could do. They had to finish what they started.

However…

"Yeah, you're right. We still have obligations to uphold. But there's only a week left before the currency exchange, and we can't fulfill our responsibilities on our own."

As such, it was clear what they needed to do. Elch looked Masato straight in the eye—

"Masato, please, lend us a hand…!"

—and, in his capacity as vice director, decided to ask the Devil of Finance for help. That was the only way they could do what was required.

Masato nodded in satisfaction and thumped Elch's back hard enough to sting.

"Yeah. I got this."

Jaccoy spoke up, still uneasy. "B-but, Masato, the situation is dire! Sergei of Azure keeps insisting that he never sold us that gold. Is it even possible for us to prepare the coins we need before the deadline?!"

Surprisingly, Masato's expression didn't darken in the slightest as he offered his outrageous answer. "Oh yeah, no sweat. Hell, we could make ten times that amount with room to spare."

""""T-ten times?!"""""

The staffers began clamoring in disbelief. Even for an angel, was that even possible? Was he going to spin gold out of nothing, as they had with gunpowder?

Such a miracle wasn't at all part of Masato's scheme, though.

Perhaps Ringo Ooboshi could have pulled off something along those lines. But while all they could picture were *ways to come up with more gold*, the plan Masato had in mind went beyond their wildest imaginations. It was a nasty, full-on attack, but it was guaranteed to bring reliable results.

Masato began giving orders. "Listen up, if this is gonna work, I need you all to move fast. Jaccoy! Take the Findolph team and go buy me the items on this list! Chop-chop!"

When Jaccoy scanned the order form Masato handed him, he tilted his head in confusion. "I-I'm afraid I don't follow... Are you planning on opening a clothing store?"

"There's no time to explain, but you'll find out soon enough. Just go and get 'em."

"O-of course!"

"Elch! Take the Buchwald and Gustav teams with you to Azure and dig up everything you can on Sergei Pavlovich's economic situation!"

"You mean, like...his personal finances?"

Masato nodded. "Yup. And I'm gonna need to be able to get in touch with you from across the sea, so make sure you keep your damn phone charged."

"Y-yeah, got it... But what's all this gonna do?"

"Answer me this. Have you ever known me to do anything pointless?" Masato gave Elch a fearless smile. The grin helped Elch remember.

"Never…!"

Masato was a guy who repeatedly pulled impossible stunts like they were nothing and beamed all the while.

"Archride team, you're with me. We're takin' a trip down to Freyjagard to see Shenmei Li. *Assuming she's got the skills to back up that track record of hers, she should listen to reason.* But it's like Elch pointed out: We're short on time! From here on out, there's no breaks till the finish line. If you think you're sleeping this week, think again!"

""""Yes sir!!!!""""

With a new course charted, the Elm Ministry of Finance whirred back to life under Masato Sanada's leadership. There were only seven days left until the currency exchange. Squads rushed off to Elm, Freyjagard, Azure, and Lakan, everyone doing their best to get the job done.

Five days had passed since Masato took direct control of the ministry.

The deadline was a mere forty-eight hours away now.

As the Elm Ministry of Finance scrambled, Sergei Pavlovich's mansion in Azure had a visitor. Between his well-groomed, almost feminine blond hair and the rose he was toying with, it was all but impossible to mistake his identity.

It was the director of Freyjagard's Imperial Mint, Duke Heinrich von Rosenlink.

He leaned back in the visitor's sofa and crossed his long legs as he spoke to Sergei, who was sitting across from him. "I see you chose not to reissue the contract, Mr. Pavlovich. I'm glad you took our warning to heart."

Sweat beaded on Sergei's forehead as he vehemently denied the claims. "D-don't get me wrong, Azure and Elm never made any secret arrangement in the first place! When those fools came to me talking nonsense, I threw them out and told them that if they came back, I'd stuff them and hang them on my wall! Whatever your useless lackeys told you, they got it all wrong!" he bellowed, pointing at the men standing behind Rosenlink, the ones who'd been stationed in Azure to monitor Sergei's actions.

They also organized the mercenary attack on Elm's ship after Sergei met with Elch. While the boat burned in the sea, they came to Sergei, told him what had happened, and warned him not to reissue the agreement when Elm invariably came asking him to.

A scornful smile played at Rosenlink's lips. "Oh? How odd. They tell me you made no efforts to keep your voice down when you were shouting about how Freyjagard betrayed you first."

"I—I have no idea what you're talking about! I never said anything of the sort! Besides, what proof do you have, labeling me a traitor?! This is slander! These baseless accusations make my patience wear thin! If you don't have any business with me, then get out!"

Sergei rose off his couch and pounded on the table between them as he blustered. Rosenlink gazed at him with eyes full of disdain. The only way Sergei knew how to negotiate was by intimidating his opponents into submission.

How limited. How inelegant. What a useless man.

In contrast to the scorn Rosenlink felt for the man before him, though, his smile was the very picture of friendliness. "Okay, okay. Then we'll just call it a misunderstanding and leave it at that."

"It's true, though!"

"Yes, yes, whatever you say. You valiantly turned down Elm's shameless demands and set them on the straight and narrow. How splendid. Truly, we of the empire are fortunate to be blessed with such a good friend."

"Hmph…!"

Right when Sergei settled back down on his sofa, however, Rosenlink's tone grew sterner. "But even though things ended without incident thanks to your resolute decision-making, the fact does remain that these proceedings have exposed a potential hole in our alliance. Such gaps must be patched, and that's the reason I came to your fair country today."

"Patched? How do you mean?" Sergei inquired.

"Oh, it's simple, really. We just need you to leave your gold in our custody. If you don't have it on hand, then you won't be tempted to sell it."

"Y-you condescending punk! Treating me like a child...!"

Rosenlink's plan was no different than a parent putting the nice china out of their child's reach. Sergei's anger was entirely reasonable.

"All right, all right, calm down," Rosenlink replied. "Do let me finish. Azure wouldn't be the only one doing it. Freyjagard would be in the exact same boat."

"What?"

"In exchange for letting us take custody of your gold bullion, the Freyjagard Empire will entrust the Azure Kingdom with an equal amount of its own."

"Huh...?"

Rosenlink's plan was basically to have them swap gold bullion one-to-one.

Sergei tilted his head to the side, unable to comprehend the meaning of such an exchange.

"What would that even accomplish?"

"The important part is that it isn't a trade but a temporary lease of an identical sum on either side. When you lease something, you have a duty to return it. You can't just say, 'Oh, I'm sorry, I sold it,' and expect that to slide. No, no. If either of us fails to return the borrowed gold, there would be considerable penalties involved."

"So that's it...!" At that point, Sergei finally understood what Rosenlink was getting at.

By temporarily exchanging ownership rights of their gold and setting up contractual obligations to return it after the date of Elm's currency exchange, Rosenlink was making it impossible to sell the stuff during that time frame.

"We'll set the return date as the day after the currency exchange. That way, we can prevent any more *unfortunate misunderstandings* from taking place."

"H-hmm..."

When Rosenlink finished talking, Sergei pretended to consider the other man's proposal carefully. Rosenlink was keen enough to understand that was just for show, however. Sergei wasn't intelligent enough to carefully contemplate anything.

Right now, the only thing he was pondering was the meaningless reluctance he felt at the prospect of readily agreeing to Rosenlink's plan. Nothing more.

All it would take was a little push to get him to do exactly what Rosenlink wanted.

"By the way, it was actually Ms. Shenmei who came up with this plan originally. She and I already signed a similar lease agreement. Azure is the only one left. What do you say? Unless you're planning on doing something underhanded, I don't see any reason to refuse."

And sure enough, Rosenlink's assertion that "everyone else had already done it" was enough to get Sergei to agree. "...Hmph. Fine. I'll go along with this scheme of yours. I was never planning on betraying you in the first place, and I can't say I enjoy being the subject of unfounded suspicion."

"Much appreciated, Mr. Pavlovich. With this, our alliance is truly unbreakable."

And at that moment, the final method Elm could use to secure the gold they needed by the deadline disappeared for good.

With his meeting with Sergei finished, Rosenlink and his lackeys left the room and headed down the long marble hallway to leave the mansion.

As they walked, one of the lackeys angrily cursed Sergei's name. "Damn that brazen oaf! First, he gets tricked by Elm's cajolery, and now he lies to our faces about it?!"

It would have been one thing if Sergei had just played dumb, but what really ground the man's gears was how Sergei had lied and called him useless.

His master shrugged as he walked beside him. "Oh, settle down. Thanks to your hard work, things ended without incident, so let's just be happy with that."

"Without incident... Milord, surely you don't mean to let that man off the hook?!"

"That was the plan. Is there some problem?"

"M-Milord, I must object! That man, that traitor, tried to betray the glorious Freyjagard Empire! Why should he get to enjoy the fruits of our scheme without having to suffer for that slight? Why, he might even get carried away and claim our achievement for his own!"

Rosenlink agreed. Knowing Sergei, he probably would.

There was a good chance that he'd even end up going to his king and tell him that *he* was the one who came up with the three-nation plot to entrap Elm.

However, Rosenlink had known that all along. "Good. Let him."

"What?"

"I see no issue with allowing a shallow simpleton with no talents beyond ranting and raving to get ahead in the world. It's in our empire's interests, no? I'd love nothing more than for him to amass more power and influence still. Each time he advances his stature in life, the Azure Kingdom grows that much weaker."

"………!"

"Besides, his debt will come due in time. Freyjagard will bring Azure to its knees someday, and his incompetence will be an invaluable asset in facilitating that."

When people in other countries rose to positions of authority they were ill-equipped to handle, it was something to be celebrated.

Rosenlink had no reservations about helping such a man succeed.

After all, what better ambush could there be than a person who was stupid and industrious situated in the enemy's own ranks?

Rosenlink understood that full well. That was why he was letting Sergei's betrayal slide. He knew the day would eventually come when he took everything Sergei held dear.

However…

"But that's still a ways off. For now, our focus lies with Elm. By trading ownership rights of the gold, we successfully removed it from play. No matter how Elm struggles, there's simply no way for them to get what they need for the currency exchange meeting in Laurier in two days. When they fail, public trust in their nation will plummet. They'll have no choice but to accept whatever scraps we offer them." Rosenlink chuckled to himself as he reached for the door at the end of the hallway.

Through it, there was a reception area for people waiting for an audience with the minister. It was the quickest way to get to the mansion's front entrance.

When Rosenlink opened the door, he was greeted by a most unexpected face.

"Hmm?"

"Oh?"

Two people were sitting on the sofa in the reception area.

One of them was a tall young man with black combed-back hair.

He was one of the angels who'd founded the Republic of Elm, as well as the mediator from the trade conference in Laurier a short while back—Masato Sanada.

The other was the *byuma* boy who'd attended that same conference as Elm's representative, Elch.

Rosenlink was taken aback for a moment, but he quickly recovered and greeted them as if they were old friends. "Well, well, well! If it isn't an angel of the Seven Luminaries and Elm's vice minister of finance! What a strange coincidence, meeting you two here! I must say, I imagine it's been a rough few days for you all. Who'd have imagined that the price of gold would explode right when you needed it to mint your new coins? The market can be a harsh mistress."

Masato shot the imperial a sarcastic smile. "Yeah. Thanks to you."

"Oh? What do you mean by that? As I've explained to your people time and time again, the gold price increase was all the work of individual companies. My government and I had nothing to do with it whatsoever. Although, *heh*, given that an angel had to come here himself, I take it the uneducated band of peasants wasn't up to the task of running a country?"

"...!"

"Nah, we never expected them to be perfect from the get-go. Me bein' here was well within expectations... Though I am kicking myself for not gettin' involved before you pulled your little stunt."

"Hmm? And what stunt might that be?"

As Rosenlink continued playing dumb, Masato dropped his voice an octave and bared his quiet fury. "You did a real number on my people out on the sea the other day."

Rosenlink responded with an expression that seemed almost amused and an affected tilt of the head. "Dear me. Are you talking about the tragic pirate attack that took place between Elm and Azure a few days ago? As I've already made quite plain, Freyjagard had nothing to do with that, either."

"You know we have full confessions from the perpetrators, right?" pressed Masato.

"All baseless nonsense, I'm sure. People like that will tell you whatever they think you want to hear," countered Rosenlink, maintaining his facade.

"Piracy in and of itself is a capital offense. Between that and the casualties, those raiders are getting the death sentence. You're telling me you don't feel even a shred of guilt about that?"

"Why are you so insistent that I was pulling their strings?" Rosenlink sighed and gave his shoulders an exaggerated slump. "I must say: It's really quite rude. Are you saying you trust the word of brigands spewing baseless garbage to escape punishment over Freyjagard's official statement? That's low, my friend. It's a slight I'm afraid I can't overlook. You would accuse me—a man grieving for your fallen sailors and working night and day to enforce the law and public order atop the waves—of allying himself with pirates?! Why, I've never been so insulted in all my life! If you're going that far, then I must insist that you produce proof that I was the one who gave them their orders. And *definitive* proof, mind you!"

As Rosenlink demanded that Masato provide evidence of his culpability, he strode up to Masato so close he could feel Rosenlink's breath.

"You do have a method of validating your accusations, don't you? I mean, you would have to. Saying all that without a shred of information to back it up, *well*. The international community won't look kindly on an uncouth upstart nation casting baseless aspersions of piracy against a lauded Imperial Duke."

"........."

"Where's this proof of yours? Come on, let's see it. Come on, come on, come on, come on, come on!"

"................."

As Rosenlink challenged the charge leveled at him, his tone grew increasingly spiteful and mocking.

Masato just stood there silently. What else could he do? He had no proof firm enough to pin down a man who shrugged off confessions by the perpetrators themselves.

Silence was his only resort, his only option.

Upon seeing that—

"...Bwah, bwa-ha-ha-ha-ha-ha-ha-ha-ha-ha!!!!"

—Rosenlink let out a maniacal cackle.

"Nothing, then?! How utterly pathetic! And I'm to believe this waste of space is an angel?! Ah-ha-ha-ha! It's perfectly laughable!"

"M-Milord?!"

Watching their master drop his usual affectation and reveal his true self sent Rosenlink's lackeys into a panic.

Rosenlink paid them no heed, however, instead choosing to prod Masato in the chest with his index finger repeatedly. "Cat got your tongue, hmm? 'Our government had nothing to do with the gold price spike.' 'The pirate attack was just a sad stroke of misfortune.' Ah-ha-ha-ha! What idiot would believe that farce?! Please, that many coincidences in a row, all benefitting us? Obviously, it was all our doing!"

"Milord, listen to what you're saying!"

Rosenlink's underlings went pale as sheets and tried to get him to shut up.

"Oh, it's fine." Rosenlink waved them off unconcernedly, then looked at Masato with contempt in his eyes. "Even dullard commoners could figure out that we were the masterminds behind all of this. But even so, they lack the proof to accuse us of anything! That's why he's just standing there with his mouth clamped shut! Why, I can stand here and confess to everything, and not a word of it will stand as evidence! 'I have no idea what you're talking about,' I'll just say! 'I'm afraid you must be mistaken'!"

Rosenlink's utter lack of shame was enough to make Elch snap. "You lying son of a—huh?!" However, just as he was about to grab Rosenlink by the collar, Masato reached out his arm to stop him. "Why?!" Elch protested, but Masato kept his hand raised.

"Heh, at least you aren't as ignorant as your little mutt, 'angel.' He's right—everything I'm saying is a complete and utter fabrication. But planning and scheming to let your falsehoods go unquestioned is precisely what diplomacy—why, history itself—is all about!"

History was written by the winners, no matter how ugly and cruel the actual reality was. That was just as much the case here as it had been on Earth. Museums proudly displayed works of art their nations pillaged in war. Leaders would extol the values of peace atop land they stole from their enemies with violence and slaughter. Society was quick to condone such actions and leave things like truth and justice as mere afterthoughts, cheap trinkets that the victors could repaint and change to their tastes. In essence, victory *was* the truth. And as such, nothing they pinned to Rosenlink would stick.

Masato knew that. The longer he stayed silent, the more elated Rosenlink grew.

"I imagine you came here today to try to swindle that dimwit Sergei again, but you're a day late and a rook short. With the key to his treasury safely in my hands, he couldn't betray us if he wanted to! And Lakan is no different. Struggle all you like, that gold is forever beyond your reach! What are you going to do, angel? Where are your miracles now?! Ah-ha-ha-ha!" Confident of his victory, Rosenlink cackled with glee.

Masato's answer was swift.

"AAAAAACHOO!!"

"………"

With a mighty sneeze, he launched a fat, point-blank payload of mucus-rich saliva directly into Rosenlink's face.

"Whew! Ah, my bad. I've been working like a madman these past few weeks, and I think it's makin' me come down with something. But hey, you're the one who got all up in my face, so you only have yourself to blame."

"Wh-why, you little shit!!" shrieked Rosenlink.

"M-Milord! You mustn't!"

Rosenlink's face flushed red with rage, and his lackeys had to quickly run over and stop him before he could swing his raised fist at Masato. "Unhand me! This *rat* dared to sneeze in my noble face!"

"Milord, please, calm down! You can't strike a foreign leader!"

"Your pal's got a point there," Masato said as he grinned. "Plus, all your yapping's drawn quite a crowd. Dunno if you'd be able to keep this many people quiet, y'know?"

"…!"

The words brought Rosenlink back to his senses. He looked around. As was to be expected from the clamor he was making, many of the mansion's maids were staring at him with troubled expressions. Rosenlink awkwardly cleared his throat, now understanding that he'd gotten carried away.

Upon seeing that, Masato gave him a pacifying smile in the most condescending way he could. "Besides, there's no need to get all worked up. Our deadline's just around the corner one way or the other. Gotta save some of that energy for the big day, am I right?"

"Oh yes, I'm looking forward to the settlement date quite a bit. Until then, enjoy your futile struggle!" Anger flashed across Rosenlink's face, but he merely spat out one last threatening remark before heading for the entranceway and exiting the reception area. The double doors slammed behind him as he left.

Filled with anger and left with nowhere to direct it, Elch slammed his fist into the table. "Dammit! That bastard showed his true colors…!"

When he did, the table shook, knocking Elch's LCD phone onto the floor.

The moment it did, Elch turned to Masato as though something had just dawned on him. "H-hey, you can set it so these things remember conversations that happen around them, right?! Did you piss him off on purpose so you could record his confession?!"

Masato was a shrewd guy. Maybe that was why he'd let Rosenlink go off like that. However, Masato just tilted his head in confusion. "Huh? Why would I do that?"

"Wh-why…? To prove all that evil stuff he did, why else?!" Elch insisted.

"That wouldn't prove squat. This world doesn't have audio recording tech, so if we tried to use it to pin the blame on Rosenlink, he'd be able to weasel his way out of it for sure. Plus, even if we did get the bastard to confess, it wouldn't amount to much."

"It wouldn't?"

"Nah. He'd just give some bullshit apology and pay some reparations to Elm and the dead sailors' families. And the money wouldn't even come out of his own pocket. He'd get off scot-free."

In Masato's eyes, that was utterly unacceptable.

"…He's not escaping that easy. Not by a long shot."

"M-Masato…" When he saw the dark flames smoldering in Masato's eyes, Elch gasped.

Masato responded with a reassuring smile. "Don't worry, just watch. We're gonna take that long-haired prick and make his blood run cold."

"Sir, you have some merchants from the Berkutsk Trading Company asking for an audience."

After Rosenlink had left, Felix the majordomo passed along the information he got from the maid working in reception.

Sergei tilted his head. "Berkutsk? Never heard of them. What do they want?"

"They say they're here about the Dmitri Glass Atelier's overdue payments for some wholesale silica."

Sergei clicked his tongue. "…Tch." So that was it.

It happened three years ago.

Even though Sergei knew nothing about fine art, one of his noble friends had gotten him hooked on crafting. Back then, he'd decided to sponsor a glass workshop in exchange for them putting some of his original works up for sale. Unfortunately, the world wasn't ready for Sergei's genius, and he ended the whole venture firmly in the red.

Not only did Sergei fail to turn a profit, but he also hadn't even come close to recouping his costs. As a result, he was saddled with a tremendous due that he'd yet to pay off. And that wasn't the only place he owed money, either.

Thanks to his personal excesses and several similarly failed business ventures, Sergei was up to his eyeballs in debt. Surprisingly, he generally didn't spare that fact much thought, however. After all, he was a powerful cabinet minister of the Azure Kingdom. No bill collector could possibly threaten him. As such, Sergei saw little reason to repay his obligations at all.

To him, other people's coffers were bottomless piggy banks he could draw from as he liked. But now, his next visitor was committing the outrageous act of demanding repayment.

How dare they. Absurd, egotistical anger welled up in Sergei's heart. "Those lowly traders think they can demand money from me? Azure's minister of foreign affairs? The nerve."

"Shall I turn them away, sir?" asked Felix.

Sergei shook his head. "No, let them in. I want to give them a piece of my mind."

Wasting no time, Sergei got to pondering what he should make these upstart money lenders do. Kneel before him? That went without saying. It was only reasonable, given the grave offense they were guilty of. Then he would grind his boots into their heads. That would brighten his mood back up for sure.

Much to Sergei's surprise, the ones who appeared before him as he indulged in his egotistical daydreams—

"Yo. It's been a couple weeks, Minister."

—were none other than Masato Sanada and Elch from the Republic of Elm.

Sergei's eyes went wide. He bellowed at the butler who'd escorted them there. "Wha—?! Y-you two...from Elm?! Felix! What's the meaning of this?!"

"I-I'm dreadfully sorry, sir... I'm afraid I didn't know..."

"C'mon, man, we both know you'd never have let us in if we told 'em we were comin' to get you to reissue the gold sale agreement."

As Masato nonchalantly barged into the room, Sergei rose from his sofa in rage. "Silence! I never made any such deal! In fact, I have no idea what you're even talking about! Felix, throw these fraudsters out this moment!"

"A-at once, sir!"

Felix did as instructed and grabbed Masato by the shoulder. However…

"You sure that's a good idea, bud?"

"?!"

"You were there when they signed the papers, so you know who's tellin' the truth here. When that fact comes to light…you sure you wanna be the guy who has to take responsibility for throwing a foreign representative out on his ass under false pretenses?"

"I—I…"

Felix shrank back at Masato's threat.

"What the hell do you think you're doing?!" Felix's heartless master continued roaring. "Get him out of here!"

Sweat beaded up on the majordomo's forehead. He was stuck between a rock and a hard place.

His ray of salvation came when Masato finally spoke. "Eh, whatever. If you wanna stick that badly to your story that the deal never happened, then have it your way."

Upon hearing him nullify their agreement, Sergei's eyes went wide, too. "What was that…?" He wanted to make sure he hadn't misheard.

Masato's second answer was the same as his first. "I'm saying it's fine. You win. Azure never agreed to sell gold bullion to Elm… After all, it's not like the deal was ever that legit to begin with. We got you to sign it by flashing you a counterfeit contract, so you're well within your rights to cancel it."

Sergei tilted his head to the side.

Why was Masato confessing to this? He was intentionally putting himself at a disadvantage.

No matter the angel's reasons, Sergei was more than happy to have that accord vanish. He agreed without a moment's delay. "Th-that's right. I'm glad to hear you're willing to see reason. That agreement is null and void!"

"Yup, that's fine… *But not honoring your legitimate contracts, now that's a whole other can of worms.*" A chilling smile spread across Masato's face as he sat down on the sofa across from Sergei's. "When we told the maid at reception why we're here, that was God Akatsuki's honest truth. Your debts are coming due, friend. *We're here to collect every last celis we lent you.*" Masato pulled dozens of parchment sheets out of his bag and slid them across the table to Sergei.

"Huh?" Sergei replied, not entirely understanding what was happening. It was a natural reaction. After all, he had never once borrowed Masato's money. Why was he making such an absurd claim? "What nonsense are you going on about…? Whaaaaat?!?!"

When Sergei reflexively glanced down at the forms, however, his eyes went wide with shock. Each sheet was one of the promissory notes he himself had written for formality's sake when he went out and ripped off an Azure Kingdom company.

"Why do you have those?!"

Masato's answer was simple. "We bought 'em."

"Y-you…what?"

"That's right. *As Elm Trading Company*, we went around to Berkutsk and all the other companies you owe money to and paid them for the rights to your debt."

"Y-you can't just go and do that…!"

"Sure we can. A credit is a creditor's asset—they can do whatever they want with 'em. Don't worry. We've got letters of intent to transfer obligations from them, too. Legally, we're all squared away."

To demonstrate, Masato flashed him the signed documents

detailing how Sergei's former creditors had transferred the rights to his dues over to Elm Trading Company.

"Heh… Y'know, it's funny. All of 'em sold us the rights for a song, and they thanked us while they signed the papers. After all, you're a pretty big deal in the Azure Kingdom. They can't turn you down when you ask for money, and they can't wring it out of you when payments are expected. I mean, you wanna talk about nonperforming loans? All these bad boys were over a year out of date. They were happy to get anything out of 'em. But that power of yours stops at Azure's borders. A foreign firm like Elm Trading, see, we don't have to put up with your bullshit. So it's time to pay the piper. With interest, that's seventy million celis of debt you're looking at."

"_____!"

In terms of gold, that was a mind-boggling sum of seventy thousand coins. Even if Sergei sold off every asset he owned, it wouldn't cover even half that amount.

Naturally, collecting on the debt had never been Masato's true goal. He merely wanted to gather up and inflate Sergei's bills so that the man would give him the floor. It was similar to becoming a major shareholder in a joint-stock company.

In the world of business, this was a reasonable, legitimate tool used all the time. Unfortunately, therein lay the problem.

"Why the hell should I have to pay money to the likes of you…?! That debt is void, all of it!" Sergei was not the sort of man who would just listen to logic. In the face of such overwhelming egotism, all those dues were little more than scraps of paper.

Masato's actions had been like trying to have a conversation with a baboon. They simply held no common ground.

Enraged, Sergei grabbed at the promissory notes to try to rip them up.

However, Masato was the Prodigy businessman who would wheel and deal his way through the fiercest gambling dens on Earth. He knew a way to make belligerent beasts listen to reason. All you had to do was show them that you held power over their very lives.

So what was it that enabled Sergei's rampant narcissism?

Masato saw through him like a window, and he used that knowledge to deal a decisive blow.

"If you can't pay, then I guess we'll just have to take these up with your king."

Sergei's face, which had been scarlet with fury, instantly went pale as a sheet. That one sentence had struck him right in the vitals. "Huh?! Wh-why get the king involved?! He has nothing to do with this!"

"He's got everything to do with it. You're one of Azure's cabinet ministers. So when you screw up too bad, sometimes your government has to come clean up your mess. And I gotta say, it isn't a great look having a high-ranking official massively in debt to a foreign company. Your king'll probably want to step in, if only to save face. Compared to Azure's national budget, what you owe is just a drop in the bucket. But chew on this..." Masato gave Sergei a cruel smile and a scornful laugh. "Wanna guess what he'll think of you afterward?"

The foundation of Sergei's egotism was the high status he held.

His role as minister of foreign affairs let him get away with all the things that he did. If the king ended up having to come to save him, though, his political life would be over. He'd be ruined. In other words, *that* was Sergei Pavlovich's weakness.

Taking full advantage of that vulnerability, Masato spoke words that even a belligerent baboon like Sergei would understand. "C'mon, Elch. Let's go pay the king a visit."

"W-wait! Wait, please!!!!" At that point, Sergei's attitude was a complete one-eighty from the aggressive stance he'd had earlier. "Please, I beg of you! Anything but that! Th-that would destroy me! I'm on my hands and knees here!"

"Then, are you gonna pay up?" Masato inquired.

"I, er, well, that's…"

"You can't, I know. We looked into your finances. You could sell off your furniture, your house…even your cute little granddaughter, and it wouldn't be enough. Sad to say, you're not leaving me a whole lot of options here. You won't pay the money, but you don't want me to go to the king, either. How do you think that's supposed to play, huh?"

"I—I…I'm sure we can work something out!"

Sergei bowed his head low as he begged for mercy.

Once he'd realized that he didn't hold the upper hand, his arrogance had vanished with surprising speed.

There was no shortage of people in the world who would dash themselves against the rocks to preserve their dignity. Masato mused that perhaps Sergei's utter lack of pride—or to put it more generously, his flexibility—was the talent that had allowed a man of his incompetence to rise as high in the world as he had. One way or another, though, seeing the Azure official prostrated brought Masato little joy. "Here's the deal. You meet my demands, and I might be willing to write off the debt."

Now Masato was finally getting to the true reason he'd come there.

"…Right now, your job is to shut up and listen. As you might guess, I'm here about the currency exchange."

"It pains me to say this, but if you want me to sell you our gold… I'm afraid I can't. It's the ownership rights, you see, I…"

"Handed 'em over to Freyjagard, right?"

"Wh—?! You knew about that already?"

"I took a detour down to Freyjagard before coming here and had a little chat with the nice Lakan lady. She told me all about it, how you were each leasing out gold from the others so none of you could sell it before the exchange date. Secret contracts aren't worth jack, but there's no need to keep it secret this time around. It's a little weird, sure, but I'm sure you could come up with some bullshit excuse why you all needed to lease gold from one another. And since it's on the level, that means it's legally binding. Not a bad plan… But don't worry. I'm not here for your gold."

"Y-you aren't? Even though the deadline is just two days away?"

"Yup. And if you let me talk, I might even be able to explain why."

"In that case…please, go ahead. The floor is yours."

Now that Sergei was finally ready to listen, Masato laid out everything to him. He detailed how the sudden spike in raw gold's price had sent the Republic of Elm into a crisis. He also revealed the all-or-nothing plan they were going to use to get out of it.

"W-wait, hold on a minute, have you lost your mind?! That's utterly preposterous… There's no way it will work…!"

The scheme sounded like little more than a bad joke. It was ridiculous enough to make anyone from this world break out into laughter.

Two days had passed since Masato and Elch's meeting with Sergei.

Now all the members who attended the trade conference were once more gathered in the Gustav domain's Port Town Laurier. The deadline was upon them. Elm was finally going to put their newly issued goss up for exchange. Freyjagard's representative, Rosenlink, was naturally in attendance.

"It's finally time, Duke Rosenlink!"

A horse-drawn carriage with the Freyjagard imperial crest emblazoned on its side leisurely made its way through Laurier.

Inside, one of the merchants accompanying Rosenlink spoke with an elated expression. "We haven't received a single report about the Elm government successfully acquiring any gold. It seems clear that they've failed to provide the promised currency."

"I should certainly think so." Rosenlink smiled knowingly. "Our efforts made sure of that."

Everything was proceeding in exact accordance with his plan. That angel had certainly talked big about needing to save some energy for the momentous day, but in the end, Elm had failed to accomplish anything.

"The Republic of Elm boasts of being a legitimate nation, but they failed to honor even the simplest of contracts and mint their currency," Rosenlink stated. "Surely, that will be enough to show the world how dangerous it is to allow such an immature country to introduce a new money into the marketplace freely. Monitoring from a more…established nation is essential to prevent things from descending into madness. Of course, such a role would no doubt demand compensation."

"So you're saying…we won't just cause the value of Elm's currency to fall, but we'll be able to observe their minting process and bleed them dry off the labor costs?"

"I must say, Lord Duke, your shrewdness sends shivers down my spine," said one of Rosenlink's adherents.

"But will Elm really allow us to meddle like that?" wondered another.

"If they refuse, all the better," Rosenlink replied to his fellow carriage passenger's concern. "That would allow us to brand them as malicious actors, harming economic stability across the continent and in our three nations. We could impose heavy sanctions against them… and nullify the peace treaty that spineless Blue Grandmaster signed."

"Ah, I see…!" exclaimed the one who'd asked the question.

"Truly, your brilliance knows no bounds," complimented a different underling.

"I should think not. My veins run rich with superior, well-pedigreed blood. For people, pedigree really is everything. How else would my family have held such distinguished titles across so many generations if not for the excellence of our lineage? If our nation weren't in the hands of that nobody of a Blue Grandmaster, we would never have had our land plundered by a band of peasants, and we similarly would never have signed that laughingstock of a nonaggression pact. I'm sure our nation's first kaiser, Emperor Gottfried, is rolling in his grave."

"You're absolutely right."

"If you highborn Bluebloods had been in charge, the empire would never have been bested by that common trash."

"Of course not. And as imperial nobles of the great Freyjagard Empire, we Bluebloods have a solemn duty to set our nation back on the path of righteousness in Emperor Gottfried's illustrious name. The task before us is simple. We have to oust the Four Grandmasters…and off that *idiot warmonger* who handed them our country's reins in the first place."

"""""……!"""""

The merchants all gawked at Rosenlink in wordless shock. It was a natural reaction. After all, he had just alluded to having the emperor killed. Such a statement was unforgivable, even for a prestigious aristocrat such as Rosenlink.

However, the merchants' silence didn't seem to faze Rosenlink in the slightest. "Once we've dealt with him, we can deliver our leader and the late emperor's nephew, Archduke Weltenbruger, to his rightful place at the throne, and he'll return the Freyjagard Empire to the way it should be. Doesn't that just sound wonderful?" As Rosenlink continued toying with the rose in his hand, he laid out the Bluebloods' actual plan.

They weren't just a group dedicated to opposing the Four Grandmasters, whose questionable origins hadn't stopped them from stealing the seats that imperial nobles had monopolized for generations. No, they were a radical organization seeking to overthrow the emperor who put them there and take Freyjagard for themselves. In a nation that revered its emperor as the untouchable apex of humanity, their way of thinking was in complete defiance of its laws.

The merchants went pale, though that only lasted for a moment. After a short silence, the oldest of the group steeled himself and spoke up. "...If I may be so bold, Emperor Lindworm's war-loving ways are a blight on our nation. The taxes we merchants have suffered to support his campaign are downright crippling."

After the first stone had been tossed, the other traders all voiced their support of the Bluebloods' cause one after another.

"That barbarian Lindworm stamped out his own family when he took the throne. By any reasonable metric, you Bluebloods are the true inheritors of the empire's will."

"If you ever need our help, we'd be happy to answer the call."

Rosenlink had expected nothing less. The nobles and wealthy merchants of Freyjagard had been closely linked for generations. If the aristocrats were a great tree, then the traders were like parasitic mistletoe sponging off of it. They didn't much care who filled the emperor's throne. Without the nobles, though, they'd never have been able to enjoy the stability they'd had up until then. And they understood as much quite well.

It was only a matter of course that they would side with the highborn over their tax-guzzling, warmongering emperor.

"I'll be counting on it." Rosenlink nodded in satisfaction. "But before we worry about the kaiser, we have those Elm pests to crush."

He opened the carriage door. Beyond the aperture was his destination: Laurier City Hall.

After alighting from the carriage, Rosenlink and his entourage made their way to the building's courtyard. The Elm, Azure, and Lakan Archipelago delegations were all waiting for them inside.

"Hello there, everyone! Ever so sorry for the wait," Rosenlink greeted them.

The dark-haired *byuma* Shenmei Li shot him a reproachful comment. "You certainly took your sweet time."

"If you insist on pointing fingers, blame Elm," Rosenlink shamelessly replied. "Their roads are in such poor shape that one of my carriage's wheels came off on the ride up here. It took a while to get it back on."

That was a barefaced lie. For someone of such elevated pedigree, being forced to wait on the riffraff would have been the height of humiliation. Out of consideration for that fact, Rosenlink had planned it out so that he would arrive at city hall well after the prescribed meeting time.

"Well, at least the seigniorage from today's currency exchange should give Elm a tidy little windfall. Maybe they'll have enough to finally maintain their high streets. As your neighbors, I must say, it's a little embarrassing."

They were big words, coming from a man who'd expended no small amount of effort obstructing that very exchange. Elch was as short-tempered as ever, and his eyebrows twitched. The first one to speak up, however, was Masato.

"I do apologize about that. Well-maintained roads are the backbone of a strong infrastructure, which is why we're planning on completely remodeling ours over the next year. I hope you'll forgive any of their shortcomings in the interim." After deftly handling Rosenlink's snide remark in a level, formal tone, he turned to the rest of the assembled group. "And thank you all for coming such a long way to be here. Today, we'll be conducting the goss currency exchange as agreed in the previous trade conference. Before that, though, I'd like to go back over a few details about the agreement signed in the preceding conference and the exchange rates detailed within. Allow me to read the relevant parts back—"

"Oh, enough of that nonsense," someone interrupted. Unsurprisingly, it was Rosenlink. With an expression that was the very image of boredom, he urged Masato to pick up the pace. "Come on, we all know what the contract says. And we're all busy people here. Let's just cut to the chase, shall we?"

From Rosenlink's perspective, it was plain as day that Elm hadn't been able to manufacture the coins. Playing along with Masato's long-winded introduction would be meaningless.

"It was a stroke of bad fortune that the price of gold rose so precipitously at the very moment you found yourselves in need of quite a lot of it. However, the Republic of Elm is a member of the international community whose independence was recognized by my own nation's Blue Grandmaster. I had the utmost confidence that you could overcome whatever difficulties were lying in the path of fulfilling your obligations as an autonomous state. So come on! Let's see this new currency of yours already!"

Even though Rosenlink had confessed just days before that he was the one behind Elm's inability to procure gold, he now feigned innocence and spat hollow statements about how much he trusted the young country. It was a calculated ploy to drive Elm into a corner once they failed to make good on their contract. Every last word that came out of the nobleman's mouth was steeped in malice.

Masato responded to that twisted man's demand—

"As you wish."

—with a concise, decisive acknowledgment. He turned to one of his men and told him to bring the money.

"Huh?"

Rosenlink's eyes went wide. Masato's unhesitant response threw him for a loop.

What's going on…? Why did the angel accept the demand so readily? Rosenlink was confident that Elm had failed to obtain the necessary metal and was unable to mint their coins. As such, they obviously couldn't carry out the exchange. They should have been trying to delay it until the bitter end.

Surprisingly, Elm agreed to go forward with it without question. And now, right before Rosenlink's eyes, they were wheeling a large, cloth-covered cart over. Given its heft, there was unquestionably something piled up under that sheet.

Could it be…? Did they figure out some way to get their hands on gold bullion…? Rosenlink immediately discarded that notion. It was impossible. Azure and Lakan didn't have the rights to their own gold anymore. Furthermore, Rosenlink hadn't gotten any reports about the previous metal being moved out of their storehouses, so he knew Elm definitely couldn't have gotten their gold from the other foreign states.

Besides that, the only way he could imagine them getting enough gold would be scooping up foreign currency from domestic Elm companies and melting it down for its raw materials.

Depending on how aggressive they were about it, getting enough gold that way wouldn't be impossible. However, Rosenlink's spies would have surely noticed something if Elm had tried to pull off an operation that elaborate. It was hard for Rosenlink to imagine his agents missing something like that. That being the case…

They're just backed into a corner and making a final, desperate ploy…!

There was certainly *something* piled atop that cart, but odds were that they'd taken the little bit of gold they scraped together and mixed it with all kinds of inferior metals to make coins that were gold in little more than name alone. That was Rosenlink's new theory. If he was right, then it posed no issue to him.

Rosenlink possessed enough foresight to bring along an Imperial Prime Baptist from the Imperial Mint who could check the gold's purity. Their magic made it possible to conduct the test right then and there.

The trap he concocted was perfect. There was no way for Elm to get out of it. No such escape route even existed. After going back over his scheme one last time, Rosenlink was more certain of that than ever. Much to his astonishment, though, his confidence was wholly misplaced.

For hidden beneath the sheet and atop the cart—

"Here you have it. The Republic of Elm's answer to gold and the rook—goss."

—was something that defied every expectation and shred of common sense in Rosenlink's mind.

"Huh…? Wh-what exactly are those supposed to be?!"

Masato had ripped off the sheet. When Rosenlink had seen what was stacked there, he was utterly dumbfounded. Then, a moment later, he'd let out a shocked yelp.

"They're goss. Isn't that obvious?" Masato replied.

Goss. The official Elm currency the delegates had examined during the trade conference.

What sat on the cart *couldn't possibly be the same money*. After all…

*   *   *

"Th-that's preposterous! Th-those are nothing more than *scraps of paper!*"

Stacks of paper had been set on the trolley instead of proper metallic coins. Each one had Akatsuki's face printed on it.

"You expect me to believe that's currency? Are you out of your mind?!" Rosenlink shrieked.

"I'm sorry, is there a problem?" Masato needled.

"Of course there is! Do those look like coins to you?!" the Freyjagard representative fumed.

"It's obvious that they aren't," Shenmei replied. "But is there some reason they should be?"

"WHAT?!"

As Rosenlink roared in indignation, Masato tilted his head to the side as if he was unable to understand why the other man was mad. "Good grief. Weren't you the one who said we didn't need to go back over the contract?"

With a sigh, Masato held out the contract that Rosenlink had so rudely stopped him from reading aloud.

"This here is the agreement you all signed at the trade conference. As you can see, all it says is 'one goss shall be traded to the Freyjagard Empire at a rate of one goss to one rook, to the Lakan Archipelago at a rate of one goss to one and one-third ira, and to the Azure Kingdom at a rate of one goss to one and one-quarter celis.' It doesn't make any mention whatsoever of precious metals or what form the currency must take. In other words…there's no reason why our money should have to be coins minted out of gold."

""""……?!?!"""""

Rosenlink and all the Freyjagard merchants accompanying him stared blankly at the Republic of Elm's absurd claim. What was the angel even talking about? It was so ridiculous that they weren't even sure what to make of it at first. However, their confusion only lasted a moment. Before long, a different emotion rose up inside them and overtook their anger and surprise.

"""..Heh. Heh. Ah-ha-ha-ha-ha!"""

Amusement and scorn came pouring from their mouths.

"Ah, so that's it! You weren't able to procure the gold bullion you needed to mint coins, so you decided to try to weasel your way out of the contract breach penalty with cheap sophistry! Ah-ha-ha-ha! What do you think of his jest, gentlemen?" invited Rosenlink.

"Good grief. There's a time and place for childish pranks!"

"Are you mocking us?!"

"If you looked up the definition of *shameless* in the dictionary, you'd find a picture of the Republic of Elm!"

The merchants followed Rosenlink's lead and mocked Elm in turn. The Lakan and Azure merchants' reactions were much the same. None of them considered Elm's paper money to be an acceptable currency in the slightest.

With the mood in the room serving as his tailwind, Rosenlink began pressuring Masato. "...Ah, that was a good laugh. You truly do have a unique sense of humor. I figured you might supplement your insufficient gold coins with silver or copper, but I never imagined you would sink so much lower than that. Clearly, I was giving your republic too much credit. I mean, introducing scraps into the marketplace as currency like a child? The minds of the uneducated are a terrifying sight to behold. You won't get away with just paying the breach of contract penalty now. It's clear that you need a more established nation overseeing your mint before you cause irreparable damage to our four nations' economies."

Rosenlink was poising himself to seize control of all of Elm's finances. The Freyjagard merchants nodded in agreement, as did the merchants from the other two countries.

But despite the headwind pushing against him, Masato spoke undaunted. "Oh, that won't be necessary."

"What?"

"We prepared the currency by the deadline, just like the agreement stipulated. Every goss is there and accounted for. With no fault on our end, I see little reason why we should have to pay the penalty, much less have some third party come to meddle with our mint," Masato boldly replied. He was adamant that they had done nothing wrong.

"...Come on, enough is enough," Rosenlink shot back. His shoulders bristled, and his voice was tinged with irritation. "You don't know when to give up, do you? That logic wouldn't even fool an infant. At first, your joke was funny, don't get me wrong, but it's run its course and then some. The international community will never accept these strips of paper as currency. If you persist in this absurd farce and refuse to admit fault, then we three entities—Freyjagard, Azure, and the Lakan Archipelago Alliance—will be forced to give you a proper spanking. Isn't that right, everyone?!" Rosenlink turned to the representatives from Lakan and Azure. Together, they could impose harsh sanctions on Elm.

At that moment, Rosenlink's expression was full to the brim with confidence. There wasn't a doubt in his mind that his victory was at hand. And why would there be? Elm had promised to trade them gold coins. The contract may not have specified anything about the currency's form or material, but the stunt Elm was pulling went beyond humoring.

Rosenlink wasn't going to let it stand, nor would the other countries. There was no reason for them to acquiesce. When one considered the situation from a rational viewpoint, it was an impossibility.

*　　*　　*

But that right there was Rosenlink's great mistake.

Logic. He himself had spoken of the nature of history's "truth," yet here he was clinging to something as flimsy as "logic." Diplomacy and negotiations were places where the tides of history shifted to accommodate man's greed. At present, they were performing the most warped act in the world. What value did something like reason have in a place like that?

If anything, the fact that Rosenlink was relying on rationale made Rosenlink the irrational one. After all, he was the one who'd pretended to be a company in order to buy up gold and hinder Elm's attempt to issue their new currency.

In a world bound by reason, such a thing could never happen, yet it had, successfully throwing Elm into dire peril. Logic wasn't something you let yourself be bound by. It was merely a tool you could use against others. Rosenlink knew that full well.

There was one other person there who did, too, however.

Rosenlink had failed to acknowledge that. Because he was so confident of his inherent superiority, there was something he was unable to realize until it was much too late.

There was one person present who was a greater picaro than he.

""………""

When Rosenlink turned to secure the other two countries' assistance, all he was met with was silence.

"…? What's wrong, you two? Why so quiet?"

Then Pavlovich gave him a very unexpected answer. "Speaking for the Azure Kingdom…we have no objections to this paper currency."

"WH-WHAT?! What the hell do you mean by that?!"

"E-exactly what I said. He's right. The agreement never specified gold coins, so…we see no grounds to accuse them of breach of contract."

"ExCUSE me?!?!" Despite himself, Rosenlink let out a hysterical cry.

Suddenly, Sergei averted his gaze a little. That tic was enough to tell Rosenlink what was going on.

Th-that rotten codger! He double-crossed me again…! How indecisive can that idiot get? Exasperated, Rosenlink turned and tried his luck with Shenmei. "Ms. Shenmei! Surely you see why—…?!" Unfortunately, when he looked her way, his eyes went wide with shock.

What Shenmei was doing was simply that unfathomable. Everyone had been offered drinks while they were waiting for Rosenlink to show up, and she had just taken one of Elm's paper bills and dunked it in her cup.

"Wh-what are you doing?" Rosenlink couldn't help but ask.

However, Shenmei offered no response. Instead, she just stared intently at the wet bill. Then she let out a sigh of admiration. "Whew… When you told me about this, I was certain you were just promising the impossible, but it's true—the ink doesn't bleed, and the paper doesn't tear, even when it's soaked in water. This durability…could it be that it's not paper at all, but some kind of fabric?"

"Bingo." Masato grinned. "That's a good eye you've got there. I'd expect nothing less from the merchant hailed as the pride of Lakan. As you guessed, that thousand-goss bill is made primarily from a combination of cotton and hemp. That's why it's sturdy enough to take a good bit of abuse without tearing."

"I doubted you at first, but…it looks like you came through."

"Oh, I have a rule about not lying to women. 'Specially not when they're so pretty."

"Heh…you got us good. Well, so be it. As promised, Lakan will side with you."

With the two of them carrying on the conversation without him, Rosenlink got fed up and angrily cut in. "Shenmei?! Think about what you're saying!"

"Hmm? It's true, though. Elm's currency really is impressive," she replied casually.

"This is preposterous! You call those flimsy scraps money?! There's a limit to how much a man will put up with, you know! When Elm showed us their goss at the trade conference, they were gold coins!"

"Did they?" Shenmei asked. "Sergei, do you remember that?"

"…I—I don't know…I can't seem to recall…"

"Quit joking around! You, from Elm! You said it yourself! How you based your coins on the empire's gold and rook, even down to their metal ratios! That's what you said, isn't it?!" Rosenlink was practically screaming.

Masato shot him *the most vicious smile imaginable.*

"I have no idea what you're talking about. I'm afraid you must be mistaken."

It was a response stolen word for word from Rosenlink's own mouth.

"Rrrrrrrrgh!!!!"

It was then that Rosenlink finally realized what was happening to him. In order to enable the ridiculous act of passing paper off as money, the young man before him had employed some sort of scheme to win over Lakan and Azure.

Rosenlink didn't know how he'd done it. What he did know, though—

"D-do you two understand what it is you're doing?! If you allow this, if you let them get away with not using gold, then its price will crash! The ingots we have will be no exception!"

—was that without the increased demand for gold, there would be nothing to prop up its inflated market price, and the three of them would all suffer tremendous losses.

"Stop this madness and think things over! It's not too late to—"

"Huh? But I thought you said that your governments didn't have anything to do with the gold shortage," Masato quipped.

"Shut up! This has nothing to do with you!" No longer interested in keeping up appearances, Rosenlink violently shouted Masato down.

"If you say so," Masato replied indifferently. "Well, I'm sure I have *no idea* what it is you're talking about, but...if this is about the unreasonable amounts of gold that Lakan and Azure had lying around *by sheer happenstance*, Elm already bought it all up." He then casually informed Rosenlink about how he made sure the other two countries' investments weren't going to be a problem.

"There's no way you could have done that," Rosenlink immediately shot back.

Each of the three countries had temporarily lent the rights to their gold over to the others. If they violated that agreement and sold the stuff, they would be subject to eye-popping penalties for breach of contract. It was an officially recognized international accord, so there was no way to get around it. In short, what Masato was claiming was impossible.

Surprisingly, Masato just gave Rosenlink's rebuttal a small nod. "Yeah, you're right. You know, it was the *weirdest thing*. When we went to try to buy their gold, we found out that for *no explicable reason*, both of 'em had their gold reserves all tied up until today, the day of the currency exchange."

"Exactly! That's why—"

"So instead, we settled for buying the rights to acquire their gold tomorrow at the price it was at the time." Rosenlink was a little slow on the uptake, so Masato had to spell everything out for him. "Nifty, how we can do business like that even when the gold's all locked up."

"Wh...wh...whaaaat?!?!"

Masato had agreed to buy the precious metal at a later date but at its current price. This is what was known as a futures contract.

That was the one chink in Rosenlink's armor. While his plan to exchange the rights to the gold was perfect for *keeping Elm from getting their hands on it before the deadline*, it was worthless for preventing the three involved countries from betraying one another. Rosenlink had failed to realize this. Clever though the man was, he was a noble and not a merchant. A system whereby you paid for something that didn't exist yet and picked it up later was foreign to him. That gap in his understanding was the opening through which Masato had stabbed.

Having taken control of the room, Masato tried to begin the exchange. "Now, let's get this show on the road, shall we? Like you said, sir, we're all busy people here."

Unfortunately...

"Rrgh... You won't make a fool of me, you cheap swindler! I refuse to sit here and play along with this farce! This trade is null and void! Come on, everyone, we're leaving!"

As Rosenlink shouted, he squared up his shoulders and turned back the way he came. His merchant posse frantically hurried along after him to question his actions.

"A-are you sure about this, Duke Rosenlink?!"

"We have a formal contract with them. Breaching it will incur a penalty!"

All concerns were met with Rosenlink's flat indignation, however.

"A fine?! They're the ones who changed the deal, aren't they?!

Why should we be the ones to pay the penalty?! If they dare make such a travesty of a demand, we'll just answer it with arms! Justice is on our side! Besides, nobody will acknowledge those pathetic slips as currency. The market will never accept it! Before long, they won't be worth the paper they're printed on! They're dreaming if they think they can get cold, hard Freyjagard gold for them!"

Then Rosenlink turned back toward the people in the courtyard.

"You'll regret this; mark my words! When your 'bills' become worthless, I'll show you true despair! And that goes for you two as well!! You'll pay for trying to make a laughingstock out of me!!"

After vowing revenge on Masato, Sergei, and Shenmei, Rosenlink left Laurier City Hall.

"Aah, there he goes. What a fool." After the Freyjagard delegation departed, Shenmei Li let out an exasperated sigh as she gazed at the closed door they went through. "Imagine throwing away your final chance of your own accord, just like that. I thought he was cleverer."

That statement came from Shenmei's knowledge about what was about to happen to the market. She had initially risen to prominence and made her name as a merchant, so her insight into the matter was keen. She knew precisely what the true nature of "money" was, and that was why she understood that paper money was about to turn the entire world's economy on its head.

For that reason, when Masato came to her and asked if she would help them if he could produce a paper currency that wouldn't bleed or tear when submerged in water, she had agreed to switch her allegiances from Freyjagard in a heartbeat.

Masato's other ally, Sergei of Azure, had been different. Just like Rosenlink, *he failed to understand what money really was*. Instead, he was still stuck under the assumption that gold coins were currency because of the metal they were minted out of.

"B-but at the end of the day, will your childish prank...er, rather, your paper money, really work out? Won't it become worthless when people refuse to use them?"

That was why, when they got to the point where Sergei had to exchange his gold coins for their printed sheets, he voiced the same concerns Rosenlink had.

Shenmei gave Sergei a confused look. "Hmm? If that's really how you feel, then why did you side with us?"

"That's, uh...well...that's none of your concern."

"Some manner of blackmail, then? You really need to learn to watch your back better."

"Rgh... I said it's none of your concern! The better question is: Why are *you* accepting the trade so readily? Aren't you worried?"

"Hmm." Shenmei gave Sergei's question a moment's thought. "Let me answer your question with one of my own, love. What makes you think the market won't accept this paper currency—these 'bills'?"

The question was designed to get Sergei to think about money's true nature.

"Why? They're just strips with ink on them. Why else?! They're durable, I'll give them that, but at the end of the day, paper is just paper. It's utterly worthless...!"

"Yes, but...gold and silver are just rocks, aren't they?"

"What?"

Sergei froze, his mouth hanging open in shock like a fool. Shenmei took a copper coin from her pocket and tossed it over to him. "Take this ten-ira coin, for example. The people of Lakan use them to do their daily shopping, but when someone uses one to buy a bag of rice, does the rice seller turn around and melt it down into pots and pans?"

"Well, no…"

"Oh? Then why would the shopkeeper give away delicious rice for a lump of metal they aren't even going to use?"

"Because they can use that copper coin to go and buy other things; that should go without saying."

"Then let's say they use it to buy some fish for dinner. Why does the fishmonger take it? It's not as though they need such material, either. It's useless to them."

"Obviously, it's so they can go buy something else with it! That's the difference between copper coins and copper ore. Everyone knows that!"

Sergei probably thought that the line of questioning was meant to mock him. Enraged, he hurled the coin back at Shenmei.

Shenmei deftly snatched it out of the air…then grinned. "And there you have it. That there is the crux of the matter."

"Huh?"

"The vast majority of people perceive this shiny disc as 'something that can be exchanged for other items.' Nobody cares about the metals it's made of. Ore, currency…they're two different things. And if that's the case, then *why does it need to be metal at all*?"

"Well, because— …Huh?" Sergei couldn't find the words to argue back. He wanted to come up with a reason why currency had to be made of precious materials, but he couldn't think of one. There was a simple explanation for that: No such argument existed.

"From the moment of birth, we were raised to believe that these chunks of metal had value, but when you stop and think about it, isn't it odd? I realized the same thing back in my merchant days. What was it about those rocks that granted them power over people's very lives?"

"T-true enough. Why *do* we take it for granted that coins have value?"

"I haven't the slightest. I'm sure there was a reason at some point, but I've never been one for getting hung up on the past. The one thing I am certain of, though, is currency's existence is wholly predicated on widespread acceptance of its value and a nation willing to spread that acceptance and support that system. But looking at it the other way, a monetary system that can fulfill those conditions doesn't necessarily have to be metal... Isn't that right, Masato dear?"

Masato replied in a casual tone. "You hit the nail on the head there, miss. Hell, you could take that same idea even further and say that as long as people acknowledge it has value, a currency doesn't even have to be physical objects. That said, I don't think this world is quite ready for that yet."

On Earth, a world whose culture had developed far beyond this one's, a formless type of currency called "points" was widely used and accepted. This was made possible thanks to two facts: First, that there was a system by which people could trade bills or points for goods, and second, people used that system. So long as you had users and a framework, literally anything could be treated as currency.

"Plus, the bill itself is proof of how unparalleled Elm's technology is. The material's one thing, but the 'relief printing' technique we use doesn't exist anywhere else. Once we get these babies out into circulation, people'll be scrambling over one another to get their hands on 'em. Some of 'em will try to buy our tech, some of 'em will try to learn it, but as long as they're doing business with the Republic of Elm, they're gonna need our currency. That'll be enough to get everyone in and out of Elm to see our bills as worth something, and at that point, they'll have no reason *not* to use em."

After hearing Shenmei's and Masato's explanations, Sergei nodded in understanding. "Okay, so I get it now that something doesn't have to be metal to be money." Even after acknowledging that, though, he still had doubts. "B-but...even if a country collapses, gold and silver still hold some value. But with paper currency, doesn't it become totally worthless?"

Sergei's two merchant counterparts reacted to his question with surprise.

"Oh, so you *do* have an eye for detail. Perhaps I misjudged you."

"What a funny coincidence, miss. I was just thinkin' the same thing."

"Rrr..." Sergei nearly blew his lid over Masato and Shenmei clearly making fun of him, but he managed to restrain himself. Rather than getting angry, he was more interested in hearing Masato's answer to his question.

Masato, impressed by the uncharacteristically intellectual display, complimented Sergei on his insight. "The fact that a metal's value can survive a country's destruction is definitely one of its strengths, yeah. And you're right, if the country that issued 'em falls, bills become worthless. That's one of the hard downsides to shake when you're dealing with paper money. But you only get half credit for just noticing the downside. Y'see, our money has big upsides from being made of paper, too."

"There's upsides...?"

"For one, it's way cheaper to make than metal coins, so you get way more seigniorage. For another, you don't have to worry about metal content varying year after year as you do with coins, so people are more confident that 'one goss' always means the same thing. And as for the big one...does the former merchant mademoiselle want to take a stab at it?"

Shenmei's reply was immediate. "Easy. Weight."

"What do you mean?" pressed Sergei.

"Merchants like me often have to deal with large sums, and the weight of the coinage involved is no laughing matter. It's simply not feasible to travel around with that many coins. There are security concerns, too. If you get attacked by bandits, coins weigh too much to easily flee with. You've got no choice but to leave them behind. Highwaymen know that, and it emboldens them."

"That does sound inconvenient...and dangerous."

"Doesn't it? That's why most merchants just use 'promissory notes.' For instance, if I were going from Lakan to Azure to buy some pelts from a company there, I wouldn't actually bring the gold along. Instead, I'd bring my money to a broker in Lakan and exchange it for a promissory note verifying how much I paid them. Then I'd take that across the sea with me and complete my trade with the company by giving them the note to prove I'd paid." That way, Shenmei wouldn't need to bring any coins along with her.

"But promissory notes have downsides just like paper money does," continued Shenmei. "To get one, you have to pay exorbitant taxes and commission. It's a basic rule of business—more middlemen, more pointless expenses. In terms of raw profit, taking the gold and silver all the way over is a better deal."

In that regard, bills had all the convenience of promissory notes with all the low overhead of coins. What Shenmei pointed out was the unvarnished truth. Initially, using paper as money sounded like a childish prank, but in fact, it was a groundbreaking invention that was going to change the course of history.

"The market will have no trouble accepting bills. And in fifty years...no, twenty. Twenty years from now, it will be paper money, not metal coins, that make up the world economy's backbone. You'll want to get your hands on Elm's printing techniques while the getting's still good," concluded Shenmei.

And sure enough...things played out exactly the way she and Masato described.

Having thrown off the Freyjagard Empire's oppressive yoke, the Republic of Elm minted a fresh currency as a symbol of their newly won freedom and dignity—goss.

It came in four denominations: one- and ten-goss coins made of copper, and hundred- and thousand-goss bills made of paper. Between its symbolic meaning and the absolute faith the Elm people had in the Seven Luminaries who issued it, goss spread across the republic with little incident. It quickly supplanted its gold and rook predecessors from the era of oppression.

Its advance didn't stop at Elm's borders, either. Between the wealthy foreign merchants who wanted access to Elm's unrivaled technology and the young, idealistic merchants who felt that Elm's stance on open trade free of exploitation was the wave of the future, goss rapidly exploded in popularity. That desirability brought a corresponding explosion in price. Rates that had started at one goss to one rook rose to one goss to one and two-thirds rook.

However, there was another reason for that spike beyond the massive demand for Elm's new money. Namely, the price of raw gold had cratered.

Rosenlink and the others had forced up the stuff's value to interfere with Elm's efforts to mint its new currency. Unfortunately for them, their plan had been for Elm's large purchase to prop up the inflated price. Elm was creating its money from wholly different materials, though, so the demand that Rosenlink was expecting never came to be.

Unable to withstand the pressure from all the gold Elm and Freyjagard were offloading, the bottom fell out. The market descended into pandemonium with people desperate to sell off their gold, and it started to affect the value of gold-based coinage. When that happened, the only countries with massive gold surpluses were Elm and Freyjagard.

Goss's excellent performance allowed Elm to offset their losses and ultimately turn a tidy profit, but Freyjagard's situation was best summarized as a catastrophe.

The empire was saddled with a tremendous amount of gold bullion that it couldn't get rid of for anything near the purchase price. What's more, Freyjagard had walked out on the goss exchange, denying the nation its chance to profit off its tremendous demand. No matter what sort of advantages they held in the international market beforehand, they now found themselves a few steps behind.

In the end, the four-nation trade conference went down as a historic defeat for the Freyjagard Empire. And whose fault was that? Nobody in the imperial government dared say it, but they all knew who shouldered the blame. The man himself undoubtedly felt the weight of that silent pressure.

With each day that passed in Drachen's Imperial Mint, Rosenlink's face grew paler, his body withered away, and his lack of combing caused his previously well-tended, nigh-feminine hair to grow more and more disheveled.

"U-um, milord…our exchange rate against the goss grew worse again today…"

"And what of it?!" Rosenlink roared at the mint employee who reported on market conditions. "That has nothing to do with us! Don't waste my time with reports on trivialities!"

"B-but, milord, if we don't come up with a plan, they're going to capture the entire share of the international market we maintained for so long!"

"If they grow fat and content, then all the better! That just means more meat for us to strip from their bones when we slay them! Am I wrong?!"

"………"

Rosenlink's tone was practically a threat. Between that and his dry, bloodshot eyes, his attendant realized something. None of the wisdom that man once possessed yet remained.

Rosenlink wasn't a fool. Or he hadn't been, at any rate. To some degree, he'd anticipated the tremendous demand there would be when Elm released their new currency. Unfortunately, he'd had one hangup—a single, fatal flaw.

He hadn't been able to disabuse himself of the notion that *money had to be forged of metal*. That had led to his crushing defeat, and the humiliation from that loss had caused damage to his soul that could never be repaired.

With Rosenlink looking like he was on the verge of burning away, another messenger rushed in. "Director, we have a problem! The Elm government is demanding three hundred million in reparations! And not in Freyjagard gold—in goss!"

Rosenlink rose from his chair, furious at the claim. He roared at his men, "Th-three hundred million…?! Just ignore it! They're the ones who pulled that bullshit stunt. Why are they trying to make us out to be the villains?! That's wrong, I tell you, wrong! I see no reason to play along with their nonsense!"

However, his men insisted that such a course of action wasn't possible. "This isn't a penalty for violating the currency exchange agreement, though! These are the remunerations Grandmaster Neuro promised Elm in the cease-fire pact!"

"Rrgh…!" Rosenlink let out a groan. That was an accord that the man entrusted by the emperor to manage the empire had affixed the Great Seal of State to. If nothing else, that meant it was something that Rosenlink didn't have the power to ignore on his own authority.

As a member of the Freyjagard Empire, Rosenlink had a duty to make sure those reparations got paid. The trouble was, between the empire's numerous wars, their development project in the New World, and most recently, their massive gold speculation losses,

Freyjagard's coffers were dry. Their ability to come up with that sum was nonexistent.

What to do, then? Rosenlink plucked hysterically at his hair as he thought.

"D-Director, shouldn't we just go tell the grandmasters that we screwed up and have them arrange some diplomatic assistance for us?"

"You want me to go make a fool of myself in front of those upstarts?! Me, an exalted, imperial noble?! Nonsense! Listen here and listen well—under no circumstances are you to breathe a word of our money shortages to them!"

"B-but we'll never be able to raise that much capital!"

"Wh-what should we do, Director?!"

"That's what I'm trying to figure out, dammit!!!!"

With his underlings begging him for instruction, Rosenlink slammed his fists down on his desk.

"Besides, what's your problem?! All of you just sitting there quietly, asking the same question day in and day out!! 'What do we do? What do we do?' Try figuring it out yourselves for a change, you useless apes!!!!" Rosenlink hurled his nearby pen holder at his underlings in a rage.

"L-Lord Duke..."

"...What? What's with that look?! You think *I'm* at fault here?! If that fucker Neuro hadn't agreed to pay those reparations, we wouldn't be in this mess!!"

"Y-you're absolutely right, milord! B-but...for generations, the Rosenlink family head has determined the empire's economic policy, and that's you, Duke Heinrich! If you don't lead us, then...we're lost...!"

"Rrrr!!!!"

Rosenlink's subordinates were demanding that he fulfill his

responsibilities. At that moment, the final thread holding Rosenlink together finally snapped.

"...Is that so," he muttered. Suddenly, he looked up. A twitchy smile was plastered across his pallid face. "Hee-hee... Fine. Very well. If it's a plan you want, then as director of the mint, it's a plan I'll damn well give you! You! Send word to the foundry chief at once! Tell him that we're minting an extra six hundred thousand ten-gold coins!"

"Y-you're going to increase the money supply?!"

"Exactly. Right now, one goss is worth about two rook! That means three hundred million goss is six hundred million rook! We have all that useless raw gold rotting away in our storehouses; time to put it to good use!"

"H-hold on just a minute!" With a face just as pale as Rosenlink's, one of his attending bureaucrats made an impassioned plea. "Please, Lord Duke, calm down and think this through rationally! The value of our currency is down as it is because of the gold crash. If we produce that much more out of nowhere, our exchange rate will grow even worse! We had to perform quantitative easing just last month to finance the New World Colonization Project. Think about the chaos that would ensue if we did it again...!"

"And what of it?" Rosenlink laughed scornfully at his subordinate's sound argument. "I don't see how that's my problem. Petty matters like that are for the common trash to worry about, not pure-blooded nobles like me."

"........."

"Those lowlifes probably thought they were driving me into a corner, but they were oh so very mistaken. It's time to teach them that their grubby hands can never reach the lofty, elevated heights that we Bluebloods live in!" By now, the light of reason had wholly vanished from Rosenlink's eyes. Now he was simply lashing out.

When things were good, the powerful were all too happy to boast about the tremendous obligations they shouldered. However…when the going got tough, they rarely rose to the occasion.

Their sole concern was only ever their own profits. Never once did they take responsibility for their actions. Whenever their failures brought about losses, it was always the powerless who bore ensuing burdens.

The mighty were able to escape unscathed by using the weak as shields. Then they feasted to their hearts' content while they waited for the heat to die down. That was no different here than it had been on Earth. It was a fundamental mechanic of skewed power dynamics.

And that was why—

"What are you waiting for?! Go deliver my order at once!"

—a certain someone had taken steps to prevent that from happening.

"Good heavens, what a sorry sight. You're doing exactly what *he* predicted you would, right down to the letter. This goes beyond aggravating—it's downright pathetic."

A voice dripping with contempt had cut through Rosenlink's raving. Rosenlink looked to see who it belonged to—

"B-Blue Grandmaster?!"

—and saw Neuro ul Levias standing at the room's entrance.

It had all started a few days ago when Tsukasa Mikogami of the Seven Luminaries asked Neuro for a meeting out of the blue and came down to the imperial capital with a minimal protective escort.

After thanking Neuro for honoring his abrupt request, Tsukasa got down to business. He explained to Neuro all the unfortunate incidents that had occurred between Elm and Freyjagard regarding Elm's new currency, as well as the fact that Freyjagard was on track to suffer catastrophic losses because of it all.

Then he laid out how the cratering price of gold and the exploding cost of goss were putting Rosenlink in a desperate position. Tsukasa wanted Neuro to stop him before he did anything reckless.

"So imagine my surprise when I come over to check up on things, and you're in this sorry state. Quite the deplorable show you're putting on."

Neuro shrugged in exasperation.

Upon realizing he was being mocked, Rosenlink's eyebrows rose. "All of this is because of those inane reparations you promised them! Do you have any idea the damage you've dealt to our great nation's reputation—the reputation we emperors and nobles have built up over generations?!"

"If we'd continued our war against Elm, ten million gold wouldn't have begun to cover our expenses. Considering that, I feel that the choice I made was the rational one. In any case, though, there's no need to perform such drastic, quantitative easing."

"Hmm...? What do you mean?" Rosenlink asked.

Neuro elaborated. At the emergency meeting, Tsukasa had offered to trade goss to Freyjagard at the originally agreed-upon rate, as well as to revisit the number of reparations to be paid out of consideration for the losses the empire suffered on their gold investment.

"He offered all that, of his own volition...?"

"That he did. The Republic of Elm espouses the values of equality for all. Tsukasa claimed that he didn't want to see the masses suffer, even in other countries. As such, there's no need to rush off and mint gold by the cartload. That's what I came here today to tell you."

After Neuro told Rosenlink about the concessions Tsukasa made,

Rosenlink went silent for a moment. Then he burst into an uncontrollable fit of laughter. "Ha...ha-ha! Ah-ha-ha-ha!"

"That's amusing to you?"

"How could it not be?! I had an inkling when I first heard the words *equality for all*, but goodness, what a sappy bunch! Ha-ha-ha, what a riot!"

Elm had abandoned their own advantage to help a foreign nation's people. To a man who held no such sympathy for those living in his homeland, the very notion seemed downright absurd.

"If you aren't willing to crush your foes, what business do you have running a country?!" Rosenlink spat.

"Oh, is that how you see it?" asked Neuro.

"Of course it is! How could it not be?! Only an utter fool would show mercy to his enemies. What, Grandmaster, don't tell me you disagree?"

Rosenlink sought assent from Neuro, but the reply he received wasn't quite what he was expecting.

"I do, actually." Neuro knew something that Rosenlink didn't. "In fact, I think it's an entirely reasonable concession to make.

"After all, we have a proud Blueblood of the glorious Freyjagard Empire here. The director of its very mint...

"...is ready and willing to atone for his mistake with his life."

Neuro knew that Tsukasa Mikogami wasn't as soft as Rosenlink assumed. Tsukasa was cold, sharp, and determined to make sure that the right people took responsibility.

"...Huh?"

"""L-Lord Grandmaster?!"""

Neuro calmly pointed his staff at Rosenlink.

The assembled bureaucrats stirred in shock, and Rosenlink's eyes went wide with disbelief. "Have you gone mad?! You would turn your staff on an ally—and a noble, no less?!"

As Rosenlink panicked over the sudden display of hostility, Neuro let out a long sigh. "…You still don't understand what's going on? You aren't the sharpest tool in the shed, are you? The fact of the matter is, all manners of sabotage and interference plagued this business about Elm's new currency. You being the ringleader behind those plots, Heinrich von Rosenlink, the empire was offered reconciliation for the meager price of your head."

That was the move Tsukasa had played. He had given up all the advantages Masato had won, but in exchange, he went to Neuro, the empire's greatest authority in the emperor's absence, and demanded that he make the right person pay the price for the empire's conspiracies and failure. After accepting Tsukasa's offer, Neuro had come to make good on his end of the bargain.

Neuro's staff glowed with a bluish-white light. The glow brimmed with malice as its hue intensified. Upon seeing that, Rosenlink collapsed backward with his face twitching. "You bastard, you sold out a priceless Imperial Duke to those lowlife peasants?!"

"I did indeed. What purpose did I have to refuse? The only reason we're in this mess is because of your needless meddling. Only reasonable that the man responsible take responsibility, right?"

"You think a mere upstart like you can get away with laying your hands on a purebred noble like me?! The Bluebloods keep order in this empire, and they won't stand for this!"

"Ha!" A snicker escaped Neuro's lips as he listened to Rosenlink's belligerent raving. "*You* want to talk about *order*? With the same tongue you used to plot the emperor's death and plan a coup d'état?"

"——?!"

"Your expression is telling me you're curious how I know. Please,

Rosey, you have to give me more credit than that. It's no secret that you Bluebloods resent us grandmasters for usurping your authority. And it's plain as day that you're cooking up schemes to take that power back for yourselves. Heavens, what a pathetic lot you are.

"You, your Blueblood friends, *and your naked Emperor Lindworm*. From our perspective, all you people in this world are primitives, barely better than chimps, yet you scramble all the same to rule over your puny little hills."

"Y-you're insulting the kaiser, too…?! Aren't you supposed to be his loyal retainer?!"

Neuro's words had rung with contempt for all of humanity, and that filled Rosenlink with confusion.

Neuro's scornful smile deepened as he replied. "As if. The one we serve is far superior—a veritable god, from the perspective of you apes. Soon my master will be released to descend upon this world *once more*. We need the Key Maiden for that, but…we have a good idea of where she is.

"With that out of the way, all that's left is to return those pesky Seven Heroes to their original world, and everything will fall into place. Unfortunately, an era of discord does us no good, I'm afraid. And any actors who refuse to stick to the script…need to be swiftly escorted off the stage."

With that, a beam of light shot from the tip of Neuro's staff toward Rosenlink's feet.

It was aimed at his shadow. When the light penetrated it, Rosenlink's shadow immediately began frothing, and a pack of black dogs burst forth from within it and sank their teeth into his limbs and throat.

"AAAAAAAAAAARGH!!!!"

After dragging the man onto the ground, they began eating him whole with their uneven, yellowed teeth.

Unpleasant crunching and cracking sounds filled the air. As the

dogs chewed Rosenlink up, they slowly dragged his body down into the shadow. Rosenlink flailed about to try to resist, but that didn't last long. Suddenly, the dog chomping down on his windpipe snapped his neck.

The screaming stopped, and Rosenlink's body vanished into the darkness. The only sign he had even fallen there was a mussed-up patch of carpet. Not even a drop of blood remained.

Rosenlink was dead at the hands of Neuro's magic. The grandmaster nodded in satisfaction at his tidy handiwork. The room wasn't the slightest bit soiled.

"Now, then," Neuro said, turning to the mint officials who were looking on in horror. "You heard all that, I suppose?"

The next moment, ebony hounds burst forth from their shadows as well.

Officially, the massacre at the Imperial Mint was passed off as Rosenlink committing suicide and a series of corresponding personnel revisions. When the Republic of Elm heard the news, they responded by offering their condolences about Rosenlink and making good on their promise.

In the end, the currency exchange went down between the two countries the way it had initially been supposed to, and the empire successfully paid their reparations. The value of gold finally bottomed out, too. From there, it began slowly creeping back up to its original price.

With that, the Republic of Elm finally closed the book on their biggest ordeal since the nation's founding. They had successfully issued their money.

"And you all lived happily ever after, eh?"

After summing up the whole sequence of events from start to finish, Lakan Archipelago Alliance vice chief, Shenmei Li, spoke once more to Masato as he sat across from her.

"To be honest, I'm a little surprised... Given the expression you were wearing back when you came and visited me in our Freyjagard embassy, I was worried that just killing the duke wouldn't be enough to quell your rage. You looked ready to destroy the whole empire. It was a scary sight to behold."

Masato took a sip from his white Lakan-made clay teacup, then gave her a pained smile. "Well, I've got a pretty good handle on what kind of person I am. I just made sure to talk to the right guy to confirm it wouldn't come to that; that's all."

Back then, Masato knew that the rage burning inside him was beyond his ability to stop. And given his methods, his revenge was liable to have adverse effects on innocent people's lives. That was why Masato had made sure to show Tsukasa how dangerous he was so Tsukasa would start to take measures of his own.

All the powerful cared about were their profits. They dodged consequences at every turn. Masato knew that that was something Tsukasa refused to abide. That much had been true since Tsukasa's days shrewdly exercising his talents as Japan's prime minister.

As Tsukasa had worked to revitalize Japan's flagging finances and public order, he'd had another project that he'd treated with just as much importance. It was a communal website that listed which bills each member of the Diet supported, which ones they opposed, and what promises they'd made to the people. It was laid out so intuitively that anyone could flip through it with ease. Thanks to that site, information that had previously only been accessible to political enthusiasts became approachable for everyone.

In this way, nobody—Tsukasa included—could escape their responsibilities.

That was the kind of person Tsukasa was. Understanding that, Masato had been confident that Tsukasa would find some way to go after Rosenlink that wouldn't let him use the empire's people as shields. Sure enough, Tsukasa had done precisely that, blocking off Rosenlink's flight at every turn.

"It sounds like your friend has a good head on his shoulders."

"Yeah, I'm lucky to have him." Masato nodded at Shenmei's praise. "We owe some of it to you, too. For dumping Goldilocks and shackin' up with me, I mean."

Masato put down his teacup.

"Given your mercantile track record, I was pretty sure you'd see how useful paper money is, but I never imagined you'd get on board with my plan that easily. A little birdie told me that you and the duke were pretty hot and heavy with each other."

Masato was pretty sure of that intel. It had come from the most reliable source, Shinobu Sarutobi. She was currently deep in the empire under the guise of being an exchange student. Because of that, Masato had considered the possibility that Shenmei would turn him down for personal reasons. In practice, though, Shenmei had chosen Masato and the profit he represented so quickly that it was almost anticlimactic.

"Oh, I didn't do anything worth thanking me for," she replied. "I just weighed the profits you two represented against each other and switched ships when Rosenlink's side came up lacking."

"What, so it was never about love in the first place?"

"Please. A woman's love doesn't come cheap."

"As a guy, I can't say I love hearin' that."

"What, you think there's something wrong with a woman using her feminine charm to get ahead in the world?"

"Oh, not at all. Hell, I prefer a lady who's got a little bite to her."

"You've got a smooth tongue, for an angel."

"What're you talking about? You hear stories about angels comin' down to chase a little tail all the time. Course, those stories tend to end with God getting pissed and sending down floods, mind you."

"Goodness me. Wouldn't want that happening, now, would we?" Shenmei chuckled elegantly at Masato's banter.

Honestly, Masato felt a little let down. After the dust finished settling, Shenmei had called for him personally. When he came, he was expecting her to shake him down for compensation for her betrayal. However, it didn't seem like she was planning on demanding a reward. But if that was the case...

"...So if it's not my gratitude you're after, then why'd you call for me?" Masato inquired.

Shenmei took another sip of her imported Lakan tea, then licked her lips. "Oh, I'm not here to talk about money or politics. There was just this one niggling question I had for you that I couldn't get off my mind."

She narrowed her eyes, then asked her question so bluntly it was downright disrespectful.

"So how long are you planning on playing along with this 'equality for all' bullshit?"

"_____!"

"I don't know what you really are. You could be an angel, a devil, a regular old human; I haven't the faintest. But there's one thing I do know—you're a damn fine merchant. And no merchant worth their salt would ever buy into that nonsense. Why, trying to get more than others is basic mercantile sense.

"That's why we run all over creation, why we buy and sell, why we build connections, and why we remake the world's rules into forms that better suit us. We sweat and *bleed* to get a leg up on the competition. And sometimes it even costs us our lives. But the reason we keep living that dangerous lifestyle is that we want to have more than others. Why would people like us ever go along with a system where everyone is the same?"

Shenmei had a point.

People were born different from one another. They had different sexes, races, and talents. That was natural. In a sense, people were *only equal in their inequality.*

"Assets, wealth, power... People know greed because there are things they don't have. And that's why they work—so they can obtain them. That's what gives life its *meaning.* Any world where that isn't true, where people are made equal, is a world I don't want to live in... And you're the same way."

It was impossible for someone without that sort of fight to be successful in the world of business.

"I'm sure you've realized it by now. There's no place for you in this country. And there's nothing you can do here. You do know that, don't you?" Shenmei's question was piercing, and given her tone, she was sure of her assessment.

Masato gave her a shrug and a wry smile. "I could say no, but it looks like you wouldn't believe me if I did."

"Not even a little. The only place tigers try to get along with bunnies is in children's stories."

"Heh. I could name a couple of people here who aren't exactly cute enough to be called bunnies... But hey, let's say I agreed with you. What then?"

Shenmei gave Masato a broad grin. "Look, I'm not trying to give you ideas, but..." She extended her hand toward him.

"...You should come with me. Together, we'll buy up the whole world."

Masato could tell that this was the real reason Shenmei had sought an audience with him. To put it bluntly, she wanted to make him her pawn. Of course, Masato wasn't going to accept. He had no reason to.

After all, he was going to leave this world behind before long. Attaining fame and status here was of little interest to him. Accepting Shenmei's invitation would be meaningless.

…And yet…

No place for me here, huh?

Masato didn't give his refusal immediately. Shenmei's questioning had touched on a truth he knew. The whole situation involving Elm's new currency had proven it to him. He wasn't cut out to help lead a democracy.

The reason for that was simple—Masato was a full-fledged one-man army. His style was to drag everyone else along with his overwhelming talent and charisma. If anything, a monarchy like Freyjagard suited him far better. Understanding this aspect of himself, Masato had intentionally hung back during this most recent escapade.

Doing so, however, had left him with fierce regrets. Masato wished he had gone in from the get-go. He cursed himself for not doing it all himself. If he had, no one would've gotten hurt, and nobody would've died. Knowing that ate at him.

Masato's logic seemed considerate at first, but in reality, it was the height of self-righteousness. Someone who was eventually going to leave this world and could not take responsibility for its populace's future had no right to rob the people of an opportunity to grow.

And like, I get that, but…

To his own chagrin, Masato had no confidence that he'd be able to sit back and watch if a situation like the currency crisis ever reared its head again. At that point, he was nothing but a hindrance to the Republic of Elm. It was just as Shenmei said—there was nothing for him to do there.

But if that's the case, what I can do…what I should do is…

"………"

Masato gazed down at his reflection in the dark-brown tea, then let out a murmur. "Y'know, back in my world, there's this idea called a universal basic income."

"What's this, now?"

"I just wanna get your thoughts on something. Thing is, we don't really know each other yet. Before I can decide whether I wanna team up with you or give you the cold shoulder, I wanna see for myself just what kind of merchant Shenmei Li is."

"…Well, I'm afraid I haven't heard of this universe thing."

"Universal basic income is a system where the government provides each of its citizens just enough money to get by, no strings attached."

"So basically, people don't have to work to survive?"

"Yup… What's your take on that?"

"My take? Well, for one, how in the world does such a system support itself? Where does the money come from?"

"A reasonable question. The government takes it from deep-pocketed folks like you and me and divvies it out among the population. That way, they're able to give everyone enough for them to get by even without working, so that nobody has to live in poverty. The idea is to make a world where nobody ever has to starve."

After listening to his explanation, Shenmei's expression contorted in unconcealed revulsion. "…That's out of the question. Why should we have to give over our hard-earned cash to a bunch of strangers? If I heard anyone trying to enact that horseshit, I'd crush them by any means necessary."

Masato gave Shenmei's determined answer a nod. He felt the exact same way. While he wouldn't go so far as to call the idea horseshit, it certainly wasn't compatible with the way people like Shenmei and him lived their lives. The two sides were mutually exclusive. And because they couldn't coexist, one of them would have to get stamped out. There was no future where such polar opposites could live together in harmony.

"Figures. Y'know, unlike a certain buddy of mine and me, you and I might actually make a good team."

"Wonderful! Then—"

"But I'm still gonna have to pass on your offer."

"!"

"You said we could buy 'the world,' but...for now, it's a product that ain't worth my time." Masato gulped down the last bit of tea in his white clay cup, then stood. It was his way of showing that there was nothing left to discuss.

Even after being shot down, Shenmei smiled all the same. She had gotten a nibble; she could feel it. "Fair enough. You said 'for now,' so I'll just wait until that changes. Patience is an invaluable skill for any good merchant to have."

⚜ Run-In with a Ghost ⚜

After successfully forging a peace treaty with the Freyjagard Empire and issuing—albeit not without some setbacks—their new currency, goss, the Republic of Elm obtained a solid foothold on its continent.

However, that had all been accomplished off the backs of Tsukasa and the other Prodigies. That was no good. As it was, Elm was no true democracy.

A democratic state was supposed to be managed in accordance with the will and the pride of the people who lived in it. For that to happen, a system to make the nation's actions reflect its people's wants needed to be established. That was what Tsukasa had been ceaselessly preparing for since Elm's founding.

It was time for an election.

The republic needed to be split up into regions, and each one had to elect a representative. Those representatives would then come together into a national assembly and make decisions on behalf of the country.

Thanks to the cease-fire pact, Elm had secured peace for the time being. The country's new currency and open markets had also been gifted a period of growth. That just left the government. If there was ever a time to create a national assembly, now was the time to do it.

As such, Tsukasa prepared a stage to declare that the Republic of Elm would soon be holding its first elections. The announcement was to take place in the central plaza of the country's capital, Dulleskoff.

There, a special stage had been prepared so that Tsukasa could give his address in front of all the city's people. Plus, his voice and visage were being broadcast all across Elm so the entire nation could hear the news.

One month from the day of the announcement, the people of this world would be taking over for the Seven Luminaries and leading the country themselves. Once that happened, the Republic of Elm would truly be a democratic nation.

Or rather, that was how it was supposed to go.

"Pray, forgive this sudden visit."

As Tsukasa stood atop the stage, he found himself interrupted right as he was about to announce the elections. Something *leaped over* the crowd and landed directly before the others and him.

It was the girl and the white wolf who had saved the Prodigies in their hour of need, as well as a dark-haired woman with ears that looked just like Lyrule's.

As screams rose from the Dulleskoff crowd, the woman gracefully alighted from the wolf.

Then, with a wise smile…she spoke.

"I am Empress Kaguya of the Yamato Empire. As ye Seven Luminaries and your Republic of Elm *promote the doctrine of equality for all*, I hath come seeking salvation for my country, now oppressed by the wicked Freyjagard Empire. If ye would remain true to your convictions, then might you find it in your hearts to aid us?"

In the blink of an eye, her words marked the end of the Prodigies' peaceful days, and a storm descended on the continent once more.

AFTERWORD

Thank you all for buying and reading Volume 4.

You know, the nickname for this series is Choyoyu, which translates roughly to *Prodigiously Easy*, but writing it as of late has been anything *but* easy, dammit! I'm Riku Misora, the guy who's enough of a dork to stick a bad one-liner like that in his book.

I'm writing this afterword in September, and while it's nice that the humid summer is finally over, and it's starting to cool down, the rain is really getting out of control.

I live in an ancient, wood house, so every time the wind picks up, the whole place creaks and rattles. It's murder on my heart.

I hope the weather and temperature settle down a bit by the time this book comes out in October...

This time around, the story picked up with the Republic of Elm being properly founded after winning its independence. The tale shifted from being about a rebellion in a single country to an international scope with many moving parts and actors.

There was Neuro, from Freyjagard, as well as Shenmei, from

Lakan. And at the very end, we got a glimpse of Empress Kaguya from the defunct land of Yamato.

How will Elm fare as a democracy in an international world where seemingly everyone is a villain with ideologies, schemes, and ulterior motives? And what will Ringo and Lyrule do, now that the battle lines between them are drawn? I hope you'll join me for the next volume, where we begin the brand-new Yamato Empire story arc.

Finally, I'd like to take this space to thank all the people who help make this series possible.

Thank you to my editor, Kohara. To my illustrator, Sacraneco. To my artist for the manga adaptation, Kotaro Yamada.

And to all you readers who stuck with the series for this long. Because of you, Choyoyu reached four volumes and successfully entered a new story arc. Thank you all from the bottom of my heart.

I hope I can count on your support again when Volume 5 comes out.

On that note, I hope we meet again then.